‖‖ ‖ ‖‖‖‖‖‖‖‖ ‖‖ ‖ ‖‖‖‖‖‖‖‖‖‖‖ ‖‖‖ ‖‖ ‖‖

⟅ **W9-BDR-495**

Ket turned to the man nearest her, a heavy-set, tattooed biker-type, and said, "Gentlemen, please. Let us take care of our friend."

The biker put a hand on Ket's shoulder. "That's where you're wrong, Blondie. *We'll* take care of your friend. And maybe you too."

Frank and Bobby turned to each other. "Uh-oh," they said in unison.

Without rising from her barstool, Ket turned to the biker and smiled slightly. In an action too quick for the eye to capture, she placed her hand under his chin and pushed.

The biker flew across the room, flipped over a table, and struck the rear wall under the dartboard.

Another biker took a swing at Ket, who caught the fist in her much smaller hand and floored her assailant with a head butt.

"Kathy!" Frank called. "Let's get—"

"Sit down!" The order came in a voice that hadn't issued from her since Thradon, a low, powerful tone that cut through all of the noise in the bar.

The general had spoken.

"Have you noticed something interesting about our script girl?" Frank asked Bobby. "Because I have."

"And what might that be?" Bobby replied.

"She doesn't fight like a girl," Frank replied, raising his beer as a hapless Ket-fighter slid along the bar past him.

"What do you think?" Frank asked Bobby, who had been staring openmouthed throughout the proceedings.

He stared at his friend with a bewildered face. "I think I'm in love," Bobby said.

Bobby's Girl

J. D. AUSTIN

ACE BOOKS, NEW YORK

If you purchased this book without a cover, you should be aware that this book is stolen property. It was reported as "unsold and destroyed" to the publisher, and neither the author nor the publisher has received any payment for this "stripped book."

This is a work of fiction. Names, characters, places, and incidents either are the product of the author's imagination or are used fictitiously, and any resemblance to actual persons, living or dead, business establishments, events, or locales is entirely coincidental.

BOBBY'S GIRL

An Ace Book / published by arrangement with
the author

PRINTING HISTORY
Ace mass-market edition / April 2001

All rights reserved.
Copyright © 2001 by Joshua Dann
Cover art by Walter Velez

This book, or parts thereof, may not be reproduced in any form without permission.
For information address: The Berkley Publishing Group, a division of Penguin Putnam Inc.,
375 Hudson Street, New York, New York 10014.

The Penguin Putnam Inc. World Wide Web site address is
http://www.penguinputnam.com

Check out the ACE Science Fiction & Fantasy newsletter
and much more on the Internet at Club PPI!

ISBN: 0-441-00823-2

ACE®
Ace Books are published by The Berkley Publishing Group,
a division of Penguin Putnam Inc.,
375 Hudson Street, New York, New York 10014.
ACE and the "A" design
are trademarks belonging to Penguin Putnam Inc.

PRINTED IN THE UNITED STATES OF AMERICA

10 9 8 7 6 5 4 3 2 1

Thradon
TWO YEARS AGO

Prologue

FROM THE DESK OF THE PREMIER OF DALYI

MOST SECRET

Eyes only
General Ket Mhulhar
Her Excellency, the High Marshal of Defense

Ket,

All is lost.

Our nation is finished, and as we've always known, as Dalyi goes, so goes Thradon. Our forces can only hold for a few more days. A few more days until the sunless, senseless dawn of a new dark age.

Sorry. I was a poet, once, as you may recall. What I lacked in talent I made up for in intensity. That's all I think about now, those days, when we were both young and immortal and . . . forgive me. But you see, Ket, I'm going to terminate as soon as I've finished this communiqué. You can't blame me for stalling just a little.

You must survive. That is my final order to you as your Premier. What fortune for us all that this disaster caught you in your home city of Kasma Dor instead of the capital. General Hederes has made special preparations for your escape, rescue, exile—whatever you want to call it. Follow his instructions to the letter. Someday, you must return to pick up the mantle of leadership. I know that your instincts are to join the fight, and I'm sure that you, better than anyone, could stage a brave resistance. But it would be futile, and without you, there'd be no hope left.

Go. Leave me in peace, with the knowledge that you have made it to safety. Grant me this, in the last moments of my life. I don't want to die as a troubled and defeated premier of a nation soon to be devoid of freedom and beauty.

I want to die as the fiery young student I once was. The fighter, quick to anger, quick to cool, quick to laugh, quick to love. Especially you. Why the hell did we ever have to grow up? And why did I ever let you go?

El.

A tear plopped onto the page. Ket looked up quickly to see if anyone had noticed. They all had, but they were tactful men and women. They knew that the late Premier and the High Marshal had been lovers as young students and had always remained loyal friends.

"Premier," General Hederes began tentatively.

"I am *not* the premier," Ket declared.

"With respect, ma'am, technically, you are. The vice-premier and the minister of state are dead, which makes you the—"

"All *right,* General, let's not belabor the point. Give me a sitrep. Has the government fallen?" Ket had just returned from an international policy meeting in the nation of Truska and had been out of touch.

"The capital has fallen. The rebels have—"

"Sha'n Res has fallen?"

"Yes. The capital is in enemy hands and the government is . . ." Hederes could not finish.

"General? Give it to me straight."

"They've killed everyone, ma'am. Even low-level bureaucrats. Premier . . . Marshal . . ."

"General. Call me Ket. We're a little past formalities at this point."

"Understood. We have your escape prepared. If you'll follow me?"

Ket made a face of wry disbelief. "Escape? I'm not going anywhere. The Resistance movement starts here."

"But, Your Excellency—"

"I hate that! Don't *ever* call me that again. If I'm really the premier, that's my first executive order. From now on, no one calls me 'Your Excellency.'"

"Ma'am, we have our orders from the premier as well. And those orders are to get you to safety."

"Hederes, this is getting tiresome. Now, let's get down to business. How much do we still contr—"

"Leave us," Hederes sternly ordered the rest of the surviving ministers and generals. There were a few moments of shuffling and scraping of chairs, but the room soon emptied, leaving the two of them alone.

"That was rude," Ket remarked.

"You're making this harder for everyone than it has to be," Hederes admonished her.

"Am I?"

Hederes stood over her desk, wagging his long, bony finger angrily. "I've looked up to you ever since my plebe year at Tira Gen. You've always set the right example and I've always followed you. But now . . . I'm ashamed."

His words stung her. For a moment he was no longer the commanding general of the Dalyi Defense Forces, her successor, and one of the most highly respected military men on the planet—he was suddenly transformed into the frightened young plebe at Tira Gen who her fellow upperclassmen had been sure would be the first to drop out. But she had seen it, even then, beyond the fear, beyond the frailty. The kid had backbone, and she saw it first, long before events proved her more than right.

Events that made him the most highly decorated soldier in the history of Dalyi—next to her, of course.

"Nev," she said, "oh, Nev, what would you have me do? Run away when my country needs me most? Could you?"

"I would follow my orders," he replied stiffly.

She laughed humorlessly. "We both know that's a damn lie," she said. "How often have we both disobeyed orders that we knew in our hearts were wrong? How often have you disobeyed *my* orders?"

"This is different," he said stubbornly. "The stakes are higher. And your orders come straight from the premier."

"Oh, come on, Nev. The Ebereans may defeat us, but they'll never be able to hold on to their conquest. Don't give me that look, you know damned well that's true. Once we get organized and start fighting back, they're finished!"

"You don't know that. We've never been defeated and occupied before. Anyway, the premier—"

"I do know that. And as for the premier, he's—he *was* a politician, not a soldier."

"That's right, and he was our politician. He was elected by the people and you weren't."

"Nev, if I go away, who commands the Resistance?"

"I do."

She nodded. "Very well. Then tell me this: What're your objectives?"

He smiled for the first time. "Why don't you tell me?"

She counted them off on her fingers: "To disrupt enemy communications; to undermine enemy morale; to force the ruling government into unpopular decisions that eventually deprive the population of freedom and sec—"

"If I may," Hederes interjected. "You're missing the obvious."

"I am?"

"Yes, Your Exc—I mean, Premier. It's far simpler than that. Everything you've mentioned is the means, not the end."

"And what is . . . the end?"

He locked his eyes with her own. "*To keep hope alive,*" he whispered.

• • •

Colonel Holak Ven paced nervously in the waiting area outside the operating theatre.

"They're going to screw it up, I just know it," he muttered.

"Why don't you sit down," Nev Hederes said irritably. "You're making me as jumpy as you are."

"Well, I'm sorry, General. There's a lot on the line here. Damn it! I wish they'd have let me in there!"

"Oh, good idea, Holak. That's just where a mellow guy like you belongs—getting in everyone's way in an operating room. Whose bright idea was it to make you an astronaut, anyway? A bundle of nerves like you in a spacecraft!"

Colonel Ven smiled. "It was my charm and good looks," he replied, and Hederes had to admit, Holak Ven did have looks and charm to burn when he wasn't on edge. Ven was the prime pilot of Dalyi's space program and had logged years worth of voyages. His fame among his countrymen bordered on reverential, but his outspokenness had stalled him on the promotion ladder. He should have made general years before and now never would.

"Do you think we can get her out in time?" Ven asked suddenly.

Hederes grunted. The situation did not look promising. The rebel forces were now a mere day away from Kasma Dor, and entire regiments were already surrendering.

"They'll be in range for air strikes in six hours," Hederes figured, "and artillery range in twelve."

"Then those idiots better hurry up," Ven remarked.

But it was another nerve-wracking, maddeningly slow-passing hour before the surgery doors whooshed open and the chief surgeon emerged, pulling off his sterile helmet.

Colonel Ven leapt to his feet. "Well?"

"She's fine. Resting comfortably. Are you going to tell her?"

"Tell her what?"

Hederes cleared his throat explosively. The doctor winced.

"Oh," he said, his face betraying a monumental goof up.

"What aren't you telling me?" Ven demanded. "Or her?"

"Look, you're the expert on that planet," Hederes whispered gruffly, pulling Ven aside. "Why should you be so surprised?"

Ven stood his ground. "Are you going to tell me?"

Hederes threw up his hands and nodded to the chief surgeon.

"It's the surgery," the doctor began.

"Well, what about it, for God's sake?"

"It's . . . it's irreversible."

"What!" Ven shouted.

"Oh, come on, Holak," Hederes argued. "You know about that . . . that *place* she's going to. You know what the people look like. They're . . . smaller . . . than we are. There's just . . . less of them. We had to turn her into one of them, didn't we?"

"Great!" Ven said miserably. "What happens when she comes back? She'll look like *them*."

"We'll just have to live with it," Hederes said. "Keeping her safe, keeping her *alive*, that was the premier's final order. I don't like it anymore than you do."

"That's not all," the surgeon began tentatively.

"Oh, good," Ven replied with fake jollity. "Another venue heard from."

"I had to do it," the doctor said. He pointed an accusing finger at Ven. "You're the expert on this planet. You said they weren't ready for us. I had no choice."

"No choice?"

"Our new premier . . . well, it was never any secret. She always had a long . . . romantic . . . streak."

"So?"

The surgeon threw himself into a chair, exhausted. "Well, she'll be there a long, long time. A counterrevolution takes decades. What if she—well, falls in love?"

"With one of *them*?"

"It's possible," Hederes nodded. "I'd say, even probable. Holak, we've known Her Excellency since academy days at Tira Gen. She always took special pleasure in . . . pleasure."

"So, what are you saying, Doc," Colonel Ven demanded.

"I had to consider all contingencies, Colonel. What if she falls in love, takes a mate, and has a child? How would she explain a Thradonian issue? How would she live the quiet, safe, and obscure life that is supposed to protect her *then*?"

"What did you do?" Ven growled, ready to slug the doctor.

"I had to alter her genetic codes! Make them match theirs. I don't feel real good about it, okay? But what else was I supposed to do?"

Ven stalked over to the window and stared out at the capital city. Kasma Dor, the jewel of Dalyi! Sha'n Res might have been the capital, but it was dull, charmless, and bureaucratic, a paper mill of a city that closed down as soon as the government finished its work for the day. His own Kasma Dor, that was the real Dalyi! The center of the arts, trade, and fashion. "It Happens Here First." That was the city's motto. And it was *his* city, the place of his birth, his childhood, his riotous adolescent and student years. It was Ket Mhulhar's as well, and that was why they had always been friends—even at the academy. Their cockiness and urban sophistication had drawn them together, the two big-city kids, anomalies in the military, whose career ranks were largely populated by rubes from the country. They had often been lovers, albeit briefly, because the last place Ket ever belonged was in a cage. But they had always been friends. Ket's lovers always stayed her friends.

He peered out at the gleaming skyline and almost wept. The proud city of Kasma Dor, which had never, in its entire eight thousand–year history, ever been conquered, occupied, or even touched by war. The prize of Dalyi. It would be declared an open city, of course. No one could bear the thought of Dalyi's oldest yet most modern city smoldering in ashes. And so, soon, the city would no longer be his. Or Ket's.

His life was over. Oh, he'd last a little while, pull a few hit-and-run raids, the usual guerilla things. But they'd get him in sooner or later. Probably sooner. They were probably toting up the price on his head at this very moment. Save Ket—keep her alive—that was the important thing now.

He turned away from the window. "All right, Doctor. Let's go admire your handiwork."

The sheets were drawn back and the premier, still asleep, lay naked on the recovery table.

"You fool!" Ven shouted at the doctor.

The doctor fought an urge to throw up his hands and protect his face.

"You idiot! You jerk! Look at her, you moron!"

The doctor was one of the most respected surgeons in Kasma Dor. He had enjoyed a long and distinguished career, filled with honors and accolades. He was even a general in the reserves, one of the highest-ranking medical officers in the Defense Force. And now this . . . *flyboy* . . . was calling him stupid. If this was the way his life was going, the enemy was welcome to him.

"I did the best I could, within obvious limits, Colonel. What's the problem?"

"Look at what you did to her! Then you tell me!"

Hederes put a hand on Ven's shoulder. "You're being unreasonable, Holak."

"What did I do to her?" the doctor demanded. "She's not deformed—I went by *your* specifications. If I made her too ugly, I'm sorry! How am I supposed to know what they consider goodloo—"

"You didn't make her too ugly," Ven argued. "I could've lived with that! *You made her too pretty!*"

"I what!" the doctor shouted back.

"Look at this. The hair! The face! It's perfect. Everything in proportion. The body! Look at those bumps! They go nuts for bumps like that!"

"For those?" Hederes wondered, pointing to them. "Whatever for?"

Ven ignored him. "Look at those legs! Terran males go to sleep hoping they'll *dream* about someone who looks like this! Oh, you really screwed the pooch, *Doctor*."

"Well, I'm sorry, Colonel—"

"What is *wrong* with you? Don't you realize that now . . . she'll never be left alone! The men'll be all over her! Women will hate her! Everyone will *remember* her!"

"Colonel, you've observed this planet for years. You've even been there. I haven't. You're being unfair!"

"All right, enough!" Hederes barked. "If the premier is beautiful—by their standards—then that's the way it is. There's no more time. Doctor, get her prepped for the voyage."

"Yes, General."

Hederes turned to Ven. "Holak, we've got to get her launched."

"Nev? What have we done?"

"We've obeyed our orders and saved her life. Now—"

"Don't you want to wake her first? Say good-bye? Come on, Nev, she's been our pal since—"

"No," Hederes said sharply. He shrugged and gave Ven a quick apologetic grin. "Look, Holak, we've got lots of good-byes ahead of us. Not one of them will be easy. So let's spare ourselves this hardest one of all, all right?"

"I suppose you're right. Damn! I wish—"

"That's an end to it, Colonel. May I remind you, we have more pressing business at hand? Such as, starting a revolution? So that maybe, just maybe, when the time comes, the concept of *freedom* won't be entirely dead? You know, Holak, *freedom*? The only word in our language that means the same thing backwards and forwards? *Ven? Nev?*"

Ven slapped Hederes on the shoulder. "You know, Nev, back when you were just a whiny little plebe, Ket and I should've stuck you in a laundry sack somewhere."

"You *did* stick me in a laundry sack," Nev reminded him, still not able to look back and laugh entirely at the memory.

"Yeah, but we should've kept you there. I warned her, but she wouldn't listen. And so it happened. We created a monster."

The launching site was at Cresvo Denor, a small island to the east of the city. Hederes had already sent a delegation to the enemy to discuss terms of surrender. There was really nothing to negotiate; all was lost, and the delegation's real job was to buy a little more time.

For the last four hundred years, since the beginning of the space program, Cresvo Denor had been its headquarters. Cresvo Denor was almost a scaled-down replica of Kasma Dor, with smaller versions of its gleaming spires, needle-topped domes, and even the same swooping, pneumatic monorail girding its perimeter. It was a city in itself, a booming and vibrant company town with a vast housing complex and its own shops, theatres, and schools. All of which were deserted now, as the workers and their children had been evacuated to Kasma Dor and its suburbs.

In fact, there were only three people left on the entire island, and one of them wasn't even conscious.

The spacecraft was the latest of the Juma Series, a teardrop-shaped craft meant for a crew of ten. Hopefully, the supplies it carried might last the trip.

"Is there enough fuel in this thing?" Hederes asked distastefully. His only fear, that of flying, was legendary throughout the service. He had been quite happy as a foot soldier, thank you. Leave the air to psychopaths like Ven.

"No way," Ven replied. "Not a chance. There's a prototype I've hidden, that could—easily. But we'll need that to bring her back."

"Well, then, how do you expect—"

"I've laid in all the navigational settings. Each solar system has a sun, right?"

"That's why they call it a 'solar' system, Holak," Hederes replied.

"Right. The sun has a powerful gravitational pull. So does each planet. The way we've done it in the past is, we cut power and use those gravitational fields to pull us through the galaxy."

Hederes's jaw dropped. "Do you mean to tell me," he began slowly, in extreme disbelief, "that she's going to career through space from one planet's gravitational field to the next, *like a drunk bouncing down the walls of a narrow hallway?*"

Ven shrugged. "Well, it's not that simple, but, basically, yes."

"And this lunacy is actually expected to work?"

"Nev, it does work. I've done it, what, half a dozen times. And I'm here to talk about it."

"I still don't believe it."

"Well, whether you believe it or not, it's her only chance. General, I suggest we get her launched. I've set the charges and this whole island is going to blow in about forty-five minutes."

Ven had planned for the destruction of Cresvo Denor since the revolution had begun. There was no way that he was going to allow the rebels to assume Dalyi's planetary franchise on space travel. And that would serve another purpose as well—no one would be able to go after Ket. *If* all went as planned.

"Can we say good-bye to her?"

"I think we should."

They climbed the short gangway into the blunt end of the teardrop. Ket was strapped into a fold-down compartment. Nev Hederes looked at the strange figure that had once been, and he supposed, still was the person he most admired. He pushed the unfamiliar golden . . . hair . . . Ven had called it, from her forehead.

"I can say it now," he whispered to her. "I've always loved you." He kissed her eyes softly.

Hederes stood up and surveyed the ship. "Good thing there's room for ten people," he said. "She'll need it."

"It'll get smaller," Ven said. "It soon does. But she'll have a lot to do."

"Such as?"

"First, she has to learn the language."

"Of the planet?"

"Nev, what planet has only one language? No, of the nation we're sending her to. Then, like a child, she has to learn their ways from the ground up. Understand their collective consciousness. I wanted to give her every possible advantage, so I chose the country that is the most like ours. The richest, strongest, most relaxed—their version of Dalyi. It's a young country, but it's the best they've got."

"A young country? How young?"

"About two hundred years. It's called—"

"Two hundred years!" Hederes cried in disbelief. "That's not a country . . . it's a *sperm!*"

"Believe me, it'll do. I've been there. And to tell you the truth, I kind of like it. And there's something else."

Hederes didn't want to know, but he asked anyway. "What else?"

"It's their atmosphere. They haven't mastered it yet, but we have. Once she gets there, she'll find that she's quite . . . formidable."

"Formidable? What does that mean?"

Ven's answer was cut off by a shriek from overhead. "Spy probes," he mused. "Nev, we've got to get her out of here and blow the place." He paused. "Can I have a minute with her?"

"Very well." He turned and went down the gangway.

Ven knelt next to Ket. He allowed himself a rueful chuckle.

"You know, Ket," he began tenderly, "after all these years, there's still no one else I'd rather end the day with. I figured, now that it's what, seventy years since Tira Gen and we're both still available. If all this hadn't happened—or even if it had—I was going to ask you to become mates. You probably would've said no, but, then again, maybe you'd've thought, it might be fun. I mean, come on, Ket, who knows you better than I? Who ever will? And who knows me better than you? We might've even had some great kids.

"You'll find someone where you're going, Ket. I just . . . I have that feeling that even if we both live through this, that I've lost you forever. You'll be there awhile, and eventually someone's going to start looking good to you . . . like in a bar after six hours and twice as many drinks. Just make sure he's worthy of you. Do that for me."

Then Holak Ven did something extraordinary. He gave Ket the Five-Point Kiss—which in Dalyi tradition sealed the ceremonial rite of mates.

"I'll die calling your name, Ket. I hope you hear me."

The preset launch sequence reached its crescendo and the ship vanished. Hederes had seen launches before and still couldn't believe how fast the ship went from the ground into space. One moment, it was squatting serenely on the launch site, and the next instant, it was gone. A pebble at the top of the sky.

"Let's hit it, Nev," Holak Ven said. "This place is archives in less than ten minutes."

"I'm curious, Holak. Where is she going to live?"

"I told you, a planet called—"

Hederes cut him off. "I don't mean the planet. I don't even mean the country. I mean, *where* will she live? A city? An exurb? What will she do? How will she fill her days? How will she fit in?"

Ven laughed and put his arm around his friend's shoulder. "That's the beauty of it! Where she's going, she won't have to fit in!"

"I don't understand," Hederes replied.

"Neither do I. But from what I know about that planet, there was really just one place for her to go. She actually *will* fit right in."

"She will? What kind of place is this?"

"A city. A strange, wonderful city. Perfect for a woman from outer space. It's called 'Los Angeles.' "

Earth
PRESENT DAY

1

DESERT HOT SPRINGS, CALIFORNIA

Sy and Shirley Albertson lived for golf. Both were seventy-five extraordinarily fit years of age—so vigorous that they played tennis just to stay in shape for golf.

They played a minimum of eighteen holes a day, weather permitting, sometimes more, never less. They ate healthy meals, exercised religiously, slept fast, and rose early so as to not lose even an hour of sunlight on the links. They were a tanned and handsome couple who had worked hard, built a life, and raised a family. Now they were enjoying the fruits of their considerable labor and freely indulging themselves in their greatest passion.

Their standing deal—beginning thirty-eight years before, the day that they had each picked up a club for the first time— was that the loser bought dinner. Tonight, as had happened more than half the time for the last four decades, Sy had paid for the meal. Shirley could not compete with his booming drives off the tee, but he was equally helpless in the face of her gifted putting and fairway placement skills.

Today they had shot a particularly satisfying round at PGA

West, some twenty miles south of their home in Rancho Mirage. They had been paired up with a couple of "kids," that is to say, two men in their forties, and it had been a sheer pleasure to beat the pants off them. The only thing they enjoyed more than beating each other was to wipe the patronizing grins off the faces of smug young twerps by trouncing them soundly. When that happened, they would treat themselves to a special victory dinner of prime rib—a medium-rare departure from their more healthy diet staples of grilled chicken or fish.

They cruised homeward in their Corvette, feeling warm and at peace with each other and the world at large. The awesomely powerful convertible purred happily northward on Highway 111 in the gathering twilight. Not for Sy and Shirley what they privately referred to as "old-coot-mobiles," the ponderously luxurious, heavy touring cars so often favored by well-heeled lugubrious drivers of their generation. Sy and Shirley hadn't busted their backs for forty-five years to stop having fun now. Their reflexes were very much intact and both had undergone corrective eye surgery. They were better drivers now than they had been ten years before.

Now, at the close of another full and satisfying day, they could look forward to a quick swim, a soak in the Jacuzzi, and some light reading before bed. An agreeable life, thought Sy Albertson, and boy, do we ever deserve it. Through forty-odd years of fifteen-hour workdays, quickly devoured meals, and little exercise, they had raised and educated three children and kept seventy-five people gainfully employed in the furniture business they had built from nothing and which had made them prosperous enough for the life they now led. The store had been sold to their employees on generous terms, and now the only deadline they had to meet was tee-time.

The overweight, haggard couple had slowly metamorphosed into a pair of trim athletes who glowed with health and a newly rediscovered zest for life. And living in the desert certainly helped. There was something about the hot, dry climate, the unfailingly blue sky and the jagged, serene mountains that seemed to generate an eternal youth—a Shangri-la that radiated invisible yet palpable waves of health.

"Sy! Stop the car!"

He obligingly slammed on the brakes; why waste time asking what for? The tires shrieked, leaving a long, double track of skid marks.

"Now you can tell me why I stopped, Sweetie," he said.

"You didn't see her?"

"You got better eyesight than I do. I'm only twenty-twenty—you're twenty-ten. I might miss something once in a while."

She nudged him. "Old fud." It was said with a trace of wryness, as Sy was far more vigorous now—in *all* ways—than he had been fifteen years before. He had even thrown away his Viagra prescription. "Back up," she commanded.

"Yes, Miss Daisy." He threw his right elbow over his seatback and looked carefully behind him as he backed up. "This gives me the creeps," he said. They were on an empty stretch of highway that had been long since earmarked for—guess what—another retirement community. But no construction had started yet, and this hunk of desert scrub was as barren as it had been a hundred years ago.

"Oh, don't be such a—look!" she said. "Look! It's a girl, staggering around. Was she in an accident, do you think?"

"Maybe she needs help," Sy offered. "You have the cell phone?"

"Right here. Hurry up, Sy, she doesn't look good."

Sy accelerated and backed the car to where the girl seemed to be swaying on her feet. She seemed not to notice the vehicle as it screeched to a halt in front of her.

Shirley was out of the car first. She approached the girl cautiously. "Honey? Are you all right?"

When Shirley became confident that the forlorn girl posed no threat, she went in closer. The girl was badly bruised about the face and arms, but Shirley could tell that she was unusually pretty.

"Miss, are you feeling okay? Do you need some help?"

"Look at those bruises, Shirl! You think maybe her husband knocked her around?"

"Not her husband—no ring," Shirley replied. "But she needs help. We'd better get her to the hospital."

A look of fear crossed the girl's face. "N-n-no! N-n-no hos-pi-hosp—no!"

"Foreigner," Sy declared. "Doesn't want to go the hospital . . . no green card, maybe?"

"Sy! Who the hell cares! She needs help!"

"Okay, okay, let's get her in the car."

"You're such a pretty girl," Shirley scolded gently. "You don't need a creep who doesn't appreciate you."

The blonde girl looked at her uncomprehendingly.

"Can we fit her in the back?" Sy wondered.

"I'll get in the back. I'll manage it somehow. Pick up her suitcase and her purse."

"What's your name, Miss?" asked Sy.

For an answer, the girl swayed on her feet and collapsed into his arms.

"Well, what do you know, Sy," Shirley remarked. "You still have an effect on women!"

When Sy and Shirley had decided to retire to Rancho Mirage, it was with the somewhat morbid assumption that wherever they chose to live would be the last house they'd ever own. Therefore, they believed, it should be something special, and indeed it was. Located in a gated luxury development off Frank Sinatra Drive, the house overlooked the seventh hole of a championship golf course. It was large, bright and airy, a four-bedroom dream home finished in varying shades of white, with a huge kitchen, a multimedia-equipped family room, and a pool and Jacuzzi built into the stone deck. It was the kind of house an active couple could enjoy by themselves, but one where they could also comfortably entertain legions of grandchildren.

It was their long overdue payoff for a lifetime of unrelenting hard work and sacrifice, and they loved every square foot of it.

They half-walked, half-carried the semiconscious girl into the room used by their married children, the one furnished with a queen-sized bed. They removed her shoes, put her on the bed, and covered her with a soft cotton throw-blanket.

Sy put the kettle on for tea, while Shirley searched the girl's purse for a clue to her identity.

"I don't know quite how to put this, Shirl," Sy began as he tore open a package of herbal teabags, "but with those bruises—in the middle of the desert, yet—you think maybe the guy . . . you think we're talking trailer-trash, here?"

Shirley dismissed it at once. "Her teeth were too good. And did you see the shape she was in? That girl works out! And her nails . . . she's from money, Sy. The hair? A hundred and fifty bucks easily, for those highlights." She let out a small cry of triumph and extracted a wallet from the purse.

"Okaaay, here we go! It's an Ohio driver's license. 'Miller, Kathy, 821 Derry Circle, Indian Hill.' Indian Hill? Where's that near? Cleveland? Columbus?"

"Cincinnati," Sy replied decisively. "You were right. That's a good neighborhood. She's well-off. How old is she?"

"It says 5/20/68. She's thirty-two, Sy. Let's see—Master-Card—gold; Visa—gold; American Express—*platinum.* Very nice. A lovely girl like that. She'd be a good catch for some lucky fella. Smart as a whip, too, I'll bet."

"Not too smart to stay away from trailer-trash who beats her," Sy commented, pouring boiling water into two mugs.

"Oh, Sy! We're not even sure that's what happened." She thumbed a laminated ID card from its slot in the wallet. "Employee ID card, General Electric Aircraft Engine Group, Evendale, Ohio. Kathy Miller, Systems Engineering Management. I told you; a whip, this girl."

"Then what's she doing here?" Sy asked her.

"I don't know," Shirley replied.

Sy shrugged. He knew his Shirl; if anybody could find out, she could.

Ket Mhulhar tossed and sweated and was assaulted by vivid dreams in which she relived the ship's terrifying entry sequence. As the ship penetrated the earth's atmosphere, it began to burn up. In her dream, she didn't make it into the escape pod and the heat began to sear her skin. She woke up screaming.

A light flicked on. She was in a strange, strange room, in a big . . . bed, she guessed, with all kinds of—

"Kathy? Kathy? Are you all right?"

Who were these . . . strange . . . creatures? What were they saying? What kind of gibberish were they speaking?

"Kathy? Kathy?"

Kathy? What the hell was Kathy? What was happening to her?

"Has Kasma Dor fallen?" she asked, her voice creaking. "Does General Hederes yet live?"

"Sy, what's she saying?"

"Do I work for the UN as an interpreter?" he shot back. "I don't even know what language that is!"

"Holak Ven . . . the Five-Point Kiss! Oh, Holak! I remember! Why did you never tell me?"

"I don't know what she's saying," Sy began, "but I'd say she's upset."

"Thank you," his wife replied, "go and sign up at CNN, you can make profound observations like that."

"Oh, Dalyi! I should have saved you! My beautiful country!" Ket wailed.

One of the strange creatures—she could somehow tell it was a woman—sat next to her on the bed and took her in her arms.

"There, Sweetie, it's all right," the woman soothed. "Let it all out. It's okay. Your Aunt Shirley and Uncle Sy are here. Sy! Get her some tea!"

"Yeah, okay, right away!" he said, hurrying out of the room.

Kathy felt the woman stroking her forehead. It was a strangely comforting feeling, the kind she remembered from her . . . mother? These aliens were like her *parents*?

"You don't have to talk now, Sweetie," Shirley told her. "Shhh, it's okay . . . rest."

Sy bustled in with a mug of tea. "I nuked it so I could get it to her faster," Sy explained. "The cup'll be hot."

Ket couldn't understand a word, but there was no mistaking the comfort from the woman who held her, and the deep concern of the woman's mate, who had brought in a cup of something for her to drink.

This place will do, she thought, drifting back to sleep. She felt it, as surely as she felt the tears on her cheek. She could sense it filling her being, and it came straight from these two aliens.

It was the same in this place as it was on Thradon. It was love.

Shirley and Sy sat up all night keeping an eye on her. Shirley constantly monitored her pulse and felt her head for signs of fever. She seemed all right, at least physically. It would be a long night, but Shirley and Sy didn't mind. It almost brought them back to a time when their children were young.

Some things are universal, Ket remembered Holak's voice saying, the voice that had been her tutor throughout the two-year voyage. Her new body, when she first saw it in the mirror of the ship's tiny washroom, had caused her to fall to her knees and wail for the better part of an hour. Then her deeply ingrained sense of duty kicked in and she ordered herself to forget it and get on with the job at hand. Ket always obeyed her own orders. She was that strong.

"Some things are universal, Ket," he had said, in English— all prerecorded communications and instructional programs were in English, to teach her to even think in that language and speak it like a native.

Those universal things? Love. Sexual attraction. Warmth. Wit. Ambition. Vanity. Honor. Sacrifice. The possibility of a supreme being and an afterlife. Parents. Children. Mates— they called it "marriage" on Earth.

"What'd she say?" asked Sy, who was dozing off in a chair.

"She said 'marriage,' I think," Shirley replied. "Or something like it—marr-i-edge, it sounded like."

"Why would she say that?" Sy wondered. "You think she

maybe left someone at the altar? The dirtbag who beat her up?"

"I don't know. But at least she's talking English now."

"Terrans place a high premium on laughter," Holak had lectured, "especially Americans, those of the nation of which you are now a part. We pay our comedians well in Dalyi; in America, the good ones can achieve wealth almost beyond measure."

"Beyond measure," Ket murmured.

"The miltary is not a popular career for most Americans," Holak had instructed. "And for some strange reason, they are only beginning to shed the conviction that women do not belong in combat. Your government post, which in your new home would be called 'secretary of defense,' would have been out of your reach as a woman on Earth—much less your previous job, the one now held by Nev Hederes."

"That's stupid! I'm the best soldier there ever was!"

"Did you hear *that*!" Shirley gasped. "A soldier?"

"She's in shape for it. We're not that far from Twentynine Palms—maybe she's on reserve duty or something."

"Who saved the day at Ugon?" Ket demanded, though she knew Holak couldn't hear her. "Who cut the Eberean supply line at the siege of Hilva? Who took a single battalion and held out against two full divisions at Truska? What kind of planet *is* this?"

Sy stood up. Shirley jumped off the bed.

"Did you hear *that*, Sy?"

"She talking about *planets* now? Oo-gon? Troo-ska?"

"Maybe she's an ecology nut," Sy offered lamely. "You know how they're always, 'the planet' this, 'the planet' that."

"I . . . don't think so, Sy."

"I've been in the army for seventy-four years," Ket mumbled in her sleep, "I've never heard of such a thing. What if I have a daughter someday? What do I tell her?"

"I thought she was . . . thirty-two," Sy croaked after a long pause.

"She's in the army seventy-four years, and she talks about having a daughter? Sy? Should we . . . call someone?"

"No," he replied decisively. Sy could agonize over trivial things forever, but his judgment was quick and flawless when it came to major decisions. "Anyway, who would we call? The police? The Air Force? The FBI? NASA? Based on what? A pretty blonde who talks in her sleep?"

"There's something strange about her, Sy. You know it and I know it."

He took her hand. "Shirl. What we've got is a nice girl who is in trouble. Let's not jump to any conclusions, or make any rushes to judgment. Why don't we just let her sleep. Maybe she'll talk to us in the morning."

A powerful ray of sunlight streamed through the window. As the sun moved higher across the sky, the ray worked its way across Ket's pillow until it bathed her face in warmth and light. She awoke immediately.

Seventy-five years of soldiering kicked in, and her first impulse was to reach for a weapon. Finding none, she panicked slightly until it all came back to her. The escape pod, the hard landing, the pod burying itself five thousand feet below the earth's surface.

The parent-like aliens and their incredible kindness.

Ket stood up and stretched, then made her way into the kitchen. The two were sitting at the kitchen table eating breakfast. A place was set for her.

Acts of kindness in Dalyi went neither unnoticed nor were they fussed over. The two stood up when she entered the room. She went to the woman, gave her the Dalyinese Embrace of Thanks, a brief but tight and firm hug. After the embrace, no further expression of gratitude was considered necessary. She followed suit with the male.

If Sy and Shirley were unfamiliar with the gesture, they were still able to appreciate its gravity. They accepted their respective embraces solemnly.

With formalities gotten out of the way, the couple introduced themselves. The woman pointed to herself. "Shirley," she said, mouthing it exaggeratedly. "Shirlee."

The man did the same. "Sy," he said a bit too loudly. "I'm Sy."

"Sy!" the woman snapped. "She's foreign, not deaf."

"No, it's all . . . right," Ket replied carefully. "I can understand you now."

"Oh, that's wonderful," Shirley said. "We have so much we want to ask you! Kathy—that's your name, isn't it?"

Ket nodded; last night, in shock after the landing, her English had momentarily deserted her, even her Earth name. "Yes," she replied. "I am Kathy."

"Let her eat, Shirl," Sy urged. He turned to Ket. "Listen, we only drink decaf coffee, when we have it at all. I figured a young girl like you wanted the real stuff, so I went out early and picked up some French roast."

Ket had no idea what he was talking about, but knew that once again, the couple had gone out of their way for her, a complete stranger. What an amazing planet! "Thank . . . you," she said.

"Do you take sugar? Half-and-half?"

Ket looked at both of them blankly. The woman called Shirley gave her an understanding smile. "You've never had coffee before, have you?"

"N-no, I haven't," Ket replied.

"Scrambled Egg-Beaters?" Sy asked her. "Toast with apricot marmalade?"

Ket shook her head.

Shirley cocked her head to one side. "Where you come from, do people . . . eat?"

Ket nodded.

"Then it shouldn't be a problem," Shirley said, jumping up. She went over to the stove and spooned out a healthy portion of eggs onto a plate. Then she poured out a cup of coffee and added sugar substitute and a vanilla-flavored nondairy creamer.

"Here," Shirley said, setting the plate and coffee in front of Ket. "Try this."

Having been a soldier for most of her life, Ket took little

interest in food. Food was merely fuel; a soldier ate what was rationed and liked it. Still, the scrambled eggs, as they were called, had a pleasant taste, and the coffee was . . . *zafra*!

"Zafra!" Ket cried in delight.

"That's what you call it . . . where you're from?" Shirley asked.

"Yes!" It tasted the same, almost exactly the same. Perhaps even . . . better?

Shirley sat down next to Ket. "Listen, Kathy. I want you to know that your . . . secret, whatever it is, is safe with us. You can stay here as long as you like. You don't have to tell us anything."

Ket didn't understand what was happening to her; it was probably caused by this Terran constitution they had given her. But she felt hot tears after the woman called Shirley spoke to her.

"You are so kind," she said. "Why do you treat a stranger thus?" That didn't sound right, Ket cautioned herself. Too formal. "Like this?"

"We're not strangers now, are we?" Shirley replied.

Ket didn't know what to say to that, so she didn't say anything. She looked around the room, her gaze lighting on two preservations—they called them *photographs,* she recalled from her instruction—of whom she guessed were Sy and Shirley many, many years ago. The photographs were not life-colored, but in varying shades of grey. Both wore similar clothing, almost exact clothing, perhaps, *uniforms*?

Kate turned back to Sy and Shirley. "Soldiers?" she asked.

"Many moons ago," Shirley said.

"Back in W-W-Two," Sy added.

Soldiers! That was why they acted as they did! That was why they didn't think twice about sharing their bounty with another! They were soldiers, like her!

"What were your regiments?" she asked them.

"Oh, I was a WAC," Shirley replied. "Signal Corps, worked at the Pentagon. Sy was in the Air Corps, waist gunner on a B-17. He got a Purple Heart for the Schweinfurt raid."

"She's a kid," Sy told Shirley. "She wouldn't know from World War Two."

But she did. Holak Ven had seen to it. He had wanted her to know that Terrans were as capable of great brutality as they were of great kindness. This world war—the *second* of its kind—had not just caused the deaths of millions of soldiers, but noncombatants, as well. Ket had fought in many battles, but always against soldiers—and only soldiers. In her army, the killing of a civilian was considered a disgrace.

"Were you a general?" she asked Sy.

"No," he replied, laughing. "I was a kid! I was just a buck sergeant, and I only got that high because I was air crew."

Shirley looked at her knowingly. "You were a general, though, weren't you, dear? I'm sorry, but you did talk in your sleep. And, let's face it, honey—you do have sort of an air of command about you."

"It's all right," Ket said. "You're such good people. I won't keep it from you."

"You don't have to say a word. But—where do you really come from, anyway, dear?"

When Sy and Shirley first retired, one of the many plans they had made was to play at least one round of golf on each of the six habitable continents of the world. Antarctica was out, of course, but Sy still harbored a secret wish to someday at least knock a ball off a tee down there, like the astronauts had done on the moon.

Still, they had already achieved their wish. They had golfed in Australia and on the British Isles—Sy was still smarting over having double-bogeyed the seventeenth, the infamous Road Hole, at St. Andrews. They had played in Spain and Morocco, in New Zealand, Venezula, Brazil, Japan, and Hong Kong.

They had kept meticulous video records of their travels, but they knew better than to subject anyone else to viewing them. However, to their great surprise, their guest proved a rapt audience. Not for the golf, of course, but for the unconscious lesson in geography those videos provided.

Ket could not understand why she trusted these people so implicitly and after such a brief acquaintance. Yet, she knew, because she somehow *felt,* that they were worthy of her trust. It went beyond instinct, and it went beyond knowledge of Thradonian—check that—human nature. It was much more clear, somehow more vivid. It was as though she now had a power to look into their very souls.

When she had time, she'd have to figure that out.

In any event, it was figured out for her almost immediately.

Her new friends had insisted that she unpack her suitcase and her belongings; she was welcome to the guest room for as long she needed it. Struck again by their kindness, she went to her room and started to unpack. She stopped at once, realizing that she hadn't the slightest idea of how to go about it. She opened the closet and saw a few articles on hangers and tried her best to imitate it. It was a sloppy job at first, but she gradually got better at it.

It was when her suitcase was empty that she saw the video-cassette on the bottom. That was what Sy and Shirley had called it when they showed her those pictures on their video player. But that wasn't the only thing that shocked her.

For Ket's New Friends was written in a spidery hand on the cover. She recognized Holak Ven's writing, unsure as it was in a foreign—*very* foreign—language.

"Colonel," she said aloud, "I demand a report . . . *now.*"

Shirley Albertson poked her head into the room. "Something the matter, Kathy?"

"I think," she began haltingly, "I think it's time to use your viewscreen again."

2

"Greetings from my heart, my newest friends. I am Astronaut-Colonel Holak Ven of the Dalyi Defense Force Military Air Arm."

Ven was standing in front of a blank white wall. He was wearing his full dress uniform, minus headcover. His decorations reached from his shoulder to his waist.

He was still the most handsome officer in the entire service, thought Ket.

"He looks like those guys on *Star Trek!*" Sy blurted. "The whosis . . . they were bad guys with T. J. Hooker and then they became good guys with the Englishman from *I, Claudius* . . ."

"The Klingons?" Shirley countered. "No he doesn't."

"Well, he doesn't have that crap on his forehead, and he's bald, but—"

"And he doesn't have bad-guy eyebrows or a beard, and he's like a light gold color, and he has almost no nose, and *Sy*—you don't know what the hell you're talking about."

"I stand corrected," Sy backed off, throwing up his hands.

"Is he a friend of yours?" Shirley asked Ket.

Ket nodded.

Shirley also nodded, immediately understanding how close a friend he was.

"Is that how you look?" she asked.

"I suppose . . . to you . . . I would look something like that."

"I'll bet you're stunning," Shirley said, and Ket felt that she meant it. Because Ket had been considered one of the most beautiful women in the government.

"Friends," Ven continued after Shirley pushed the pause button, "I give you my deepest thanks for taking Ket into your hearts."

"Where'd he learn English?" Shirley wondered. "He has almost no accent at all."

"I do not know if Ket—or, Kathy, as I'm sure you are calling her—has told you, but our planet is called Thradon. It is far, far from your delightful world—so far, so many . . . miles, I believe is your measurement, that to borrow a joke from your world, you probably can't count that high . . . even with your shoes off."

Sy and Shirley smiled at the small joke.

"Ket's journey has taken her two of your years. If you are watching this now, then she is safe and I am greatly relieved."

"Why, he's a charmer!" Shirley cried. This completely alien . . . alien . . . was actually, well, sexy! Obviously, a lady killer—even the seemingly unreadable, flat features betrayed a devilish charm. "I can see why he was special to you, Kathy."

Kathy nodded, somehow unsurprised that Holak's considerable attraction had crossed even the wide barrier of space and species.

"I am sure you have many questions," Ven continued, "and I will answer them as best I can. First, you are no doubt wondering if this is a hoax. I know I would. Sightings of extraterrestrials and what you refer to as UFOs, are still in the province of conjecture on your world. I cannot prove otherwise . . . but, be assured that it is not a hoax. The only proof will come later . . . many years from now. Someone will come for her. He or she will be either a friend, whose mission will be to bring her home; or an enemy, whose mission will be to hunt her down."

Sy and Shirley's head snapped in Ket's direction. Ket felt a strange, violent sensation in her stomach. These people had suddenly become afraid.

"Therefore," Holak continued, "I beg you now, consider the risk you have assumed. I will not be offended, nor think less of you, nor will Ket, if you ask her to leave at this moment. Ket will manage. Her 'credit cards,' I believe they are called, are no good, which should not surprise you. The employee identification card came from a company name I saw on one of your orbiting satellites. They are merely for identification purposes. But she does have $5,000 in your American currency. That should see her through for a little while. So I implore you: Stop this viewscreen now and think hard."

Sy hit the pause button on the remote. He looked at his wife and the beginnings of a small grin crossed each of their faces. They got up as one and crossed to the sofa, sitting next to Ket and taking her hands.

"Depend on us, Kathy," Shirley said.

The violent sensation still roiled Ket's stomach, but now it was overshadowed by a sense of determination and almost . . . fun?

"Turn it back on, Sy," Shirley ordered.

Sy touched the the play button and Holak Ven's image unfroze instantly.

"If you are still watching, then you have made a great sacrifice and I honor you. You have the eternal gratitude of our nation. And when we reemerge as the free leaders of a freedom-loving world, your names will be added to the monument in the Valley of Honor."

Ket now sensed a chill from her two protectors. Not a chill of fear, but one of profound emotion. She knew at that moment that fate had smiled upon her when these two were chosen as her safe harbor.

"You're probably wondering," Holak continued, "I know I would be, where in the hell does an alien get a VCR and five thousand dollars?" He leaned into the camera and whispered. "I was a very bad boy," he said conspiratorially.

Shirley laughed and switched off the viewscreen. "Kathy," she said becoming serious, "why were you sent here? What happened to your country?"

"We were defeated by our blood enemy," she replied simply. "Not in battle, but in . . . other ways."

Sy looked at her solemnly. "Kathy," he said, "like you, I fought in a war. I saw young men die, even in my arms once or twice. I've felt the pain of a wound. And I've killed. But unlike you, I'm not a soldier. I never was. Our country, our very way of life, was in danger, so I did what I had to do, and when it was over, and we won, I felt I had earned the right to come home and live a good life. That's what *my* country is about. We hate to fight, but when we must, we do it to win so that as many of us as possible can go home."

Shirley glanced at her husband. It was more than he'd said in one go for years. She nodded at him to continue.

"Well, Kathy," Sy continued, "it seems like that time may be here again. If someone comes after you, it'll put this country, and maybe this world, in danger. Now, we'll do our part, but you have to help us help you. So please, Kathy, tell us about your planet. And tell us about your enemies."

"Could I have some more of your cof-fee?" Ket asked.

Shirley smiled, breaking the tension. "What did you call it? Zafra? One cup of hot zafra, coming up."

3

The long war against Eberes, like so many conflicts, was one pro-tracted grudge match. A grudge held against Dalyi, and Ket added, with good reason, if one takes an honest look at history.

Dalyi's first advantage, like that of any world power, was that of geography. Thradon had significant landmasses and fifty-eight percent of its surface was water. Dalyi covered an entire continent, a continent rich in farmland and natural resources. Its climate ranged from temperate to subtropical, with moderate rainfall.

"Wait a minute," Shirley interrupted. "Your planet is like our planet? I always thought of other planets as being, I don't know, kind of orange, sandy, bleak places..." She shrugged. "Too many movies, I guess."

Ket smiled sadly. "I'm a soldier, not a scientist, but it seems logical, doesn't it? Planets that support life would have to be the same, or almost the same, wouldn't they? We look different, but we need the same things to survive, don't we?"

"How many other planets are there?" Sy asked. "That have people, I mean."

"This is the only one that we know of," Ket replied. "But

that doesn't mean there aren't others. We just haven't found them yet."

"Okay," Sy said. "About your war. This country—Eberes? What happened?"

What had happened read like a textbook of Western civilization. Dalyi, rich, powerful, blessed with natural resources and technologically far advanced, had colonized a backward nation called Eberes. While the colonization had not been particularly brutal, it had been humiliatingly condescending. The sahibs of Dalyi had created an expatriate ruling class that disenfranchised even the highest-ranking Ebereans. Dalyinese technology made possible the plunder of Eberes's own natural wealth, which had been previously unexploited by its poor natives.

"Where have I heard this before?" Shirley asked rhetorically.

"This has happened on your planet?"

"Just about everywhere," Sy replied. "What finally happened?"

The Ebereans began to progress, at first, unwillingly against a swelling tide of Dalyinese influence, and then, of their own accord. But the assimilation was deceptive; while Ebereans fully accepted Dalyinese technology, they deeply resented the invasion of Dalyinese culture. This smoldering resentment soon ignited into full-blown hatred, and sixty years before, Eberes revolted.

The first hostile act was an attack on the Colonial Government House in the Eberean capital of Hilva, which took place while the ruling body was in session. Every Dalyinese official in residence was brutally murdered, an act that was recorded on the House archives for all Thradon to witness. The attack was known from then on as the Massacre of Hilva.

Dalyi's response was swift and decisive. Three full armies were immediately dispatched to Eberes, a strike force that included Lieutenants Ket Mhulhar and Nev Hederes and Air Lieutenant Holak Ven. All three would distinguish themselves in a long, bloody war of attrition.

"The army hated that war," Ket told Sy and Shirley. "It never should have happened. Nev and Holak and I never talk about it. It always makes us feel a little sick."

"Why, Kathy?" Shirley asked. "I mean, of course war itself is an abomination, but what was it about that particular war?"

"I think I know," Sy remarked. "The army felt that the politicians should have taken the hint. It was time to leave. Tell me if I'm right, Kathy."

Ket nodded sadly, again impressed by Sy's unusually cogent grasp of politics. "They hated us," Ket said. "They truly despised us with the kind of hatred that never goes away. In Dalyi, we're not accustomed to that kind of hatred."

The degree of this abhorrence became shockingly evident in the aftermath of the Dalyinese counterattack. Ket earned her first Bravery Cluster in the Hilva invasion, which went off almost exactly according to its precise and complex plan. Hilva was taken in three days. The victorious army began its occupation of the capital after defeating the remnants of the Eberean rebel force, who made a final stand that amounted to little more than mass suicide.

"The army killed them all?" Shirley asked in revulsion.

"They wouldn't surrender," Ket replied, the difficult memory still vivid. "They fought with unimaginably savage bravery."

The Dalyinese army was victorous but dispirited. They were soldiers, not murderers, and therefore did not celebrate their victory. All they wanted was to go home and forget the entire grisly business.

"But you guys weren't going anywhere," Sy noted. "Even though you can't occupy a country if the people don't want you there. It might take years, decades even, but they'll kick you out eventually. Am I right?"

"Exactly," Ket said. "Sy . . . forgive me, but if you're a furniture salesman, how do you know all this?"

"Too many countries on Earth have learned it the hard way," Sy replied.

The Dalyinese army established martial law over a strangely compliant population. The army expected resistance and acts of terrorism, but none were forthcoming. Even though the Eberean force had been destroyed, the army couldn't believe the grimly determined Eberean people would do nothing.

The army was discontented and felt dishonored. The government attempted to boost morale with field promotions and medals; both Ket and Holak won early appointments as captains. But this generosity went largely unappreciated. A petition circulated within its ranks, one that threatened a mass resignation if the government didn't face facts and pull out of Eberes. Every soldier in the occupation force signed.

However, the petition was never sent to Dalyi.

It was a routine reconnaissance flight by a young pilot named Holak Ven that changed everything.

"Your boyfriend," Shirley murmured.

"Excuse me?"

"Please," Sy remarked.

"Please what?" Shirley asked.

"I was talking to Kathy. If you're supposed to be from Cincinnati, you don't say 'excuse me.' People from Cincinnati say 'please.'"

"I really don't care, Sy, but you might as well tell us why," said Shirley.

"I'm not sure, but I would guess that it's a German thing. Cincy is a German town, see, and Germans say '*bitte*,' which means please, the same way we'd say 'excuse me.'"

"Thank you, Sy. I'm sure we'll all sleep better knowing that. As I was saying, Kathy, before we were so rudely interrupted, the flyboy, he was your . . . what did the kids use to call it? Ah, your *squeeze*."

Kathy laughed in spite of the darkness that she felt within whenever she thought of the Eberean Conflict. "I'm sorry," she said. "I was given some instruction in your vernacular, but . . . *squeeze*?"

"It's a kid thing," Shirley replied. "Anyway, go on."

Squeeze, thought Ket. It does work. She and Holak had, after all, squeezed each other quite often and with a great deal of enjoyment.

"Holak was flying a routine mission over the . . . the *skrev*— the . . . what is it? The direction," she added. "I forgot the English word. The . . . top of your Earth would be which way?"

"North," Shirley and Sy said together.

"North," she nodded. "Holak was covering the north—" She made a V with her hands, the left pointing to twelve o'clock and the right to two o'clock.

"West," said Shirley.

"East," said Sy.

"Do you mean as we look at it, or as you look at it?" Shirley asked.

"Uh, as I look at it," Ket replied.

"East," Sy triumphed.

"Hmm. *Denor* is east," Ket told herself. So many words in this language!

Holak Ven's assigned patrol grid was the security zone to the northeast of Hilva. He had flown the same search pattern for weeks on end, since the end of the war, and was now bored out of his skull. Like every soldier and airman in the occupying force, he was homesick and unhappy. Even the third delta on his shoulder, the one that proclaimed him a captain, failed to stir him in the slightest. He thought of little else but home, until his ADF indicator shrieked in his ear.

Although he was still very young, and Hilva was only his first action, Holak was well trained and had excellent instincts. The atmospheric displacement finder sounded with a high-pitched whistle that hurt his ears—but only for a moment. Holak, therefore, did the smart thing, which was nothing. The well-hidden Eberean antifighter pulse gun crews had been tracking him for weeks and had become familiar with his search pattern and his flying habits. Had he suddenly jinked his aircraft, or dived or increased his speed—or shown any sign whatever that he had picked up the signal from the momentarily off-line deceiver array, the guns would have erupted and turned his fighter into a dust particle instantly.

His heart pounding in his ears, Holak nevertheless affected a bored listless patrol, appearing on the Eberean command screens as he had for weeks, a junior pilot assigned a tedious reconnaissance in a nothing sector. The Eberean corporal who had tracked him for weeks even congratulated himself and breathed a sigh of relief as Holak made a wide lazy turn at the usual coordinates and headed for home.

The flight back to base was torture for Holak as he desperately fought the urge to rocket home at top speed. He rightly suspected that Eberean sensors were recording his every move from takeoff to landing, so he made his final approach as deliberate as possible. Because Ven was by nature impulsive and short on patience, this was the hardest part of the patrol.

Taking no chances on landing, instead of reporting to the intelligence officer as usual, he went straight to the base commander's office. The air general commanding ordered the flight recorders pulled from Ven's aircraft, and after hearing the telltale shriek, lost no time in getting both himself and Ven to the quarters of the theatre commander.

The Dalyinese might have been rotten colonizers, but they were nonpareil as soldiers. The theatre commander, an ancient who had never lost his edge as a field general, knew immediately that the very presence of a deceiver array could only mean the concealment of a great force. Tactically, the old general couldn't understand what the hidden Eberean force was waiting for; the Dalyinese way was to attack and counterattack, never retreat and always press home any advantage.

But the Ebereans, a long-suffering and fatalistic people, knew that time was not their enemy. Time was an investment commodity meant to be lovingly shepherded for coming generations. If things didn't work out in their own lifetimes, well, that was the way it went. Inevitable changes would benefit succeeding generations, if not their own. Historians would later make the finding that Ebereans took any defeat, no matter how total, as a temporary setback. They *always* had a backup plan.

Failure to read this inherent trait of the Eberean character would result in short-term tactical success for the Dalyinese, to be followed by long-term strategic disaster.

Two divisions had been sent as reconnaissance-in-force to probe the Eberean lines. At the spearhead of this advance was a company commanded by Ket Mhulhar, which included a platoon headed by newly commissioned Second Lieutenant Nev Hederes.

They found that the Ebereans had fallen back to the mountains commanding the Plains of Ugon, a strong defensive position, because rings of artillery perched atop the mountain could easily repel any attack from the ground or the air. Any massive offensive would be brutally and decisively repelled.

Therefore, the key to success was to figuratively spike the guns atop the mountain.

Like any army throughout time or space, the Dalyinese Occupation Force was awash in bureaucracy and politics. Each general lobbied for the adoption of his or her own plan. The supply line would have to be shortened; from Hilva to Ugon was a long way for an army that was in a hostile country to begin with. How could they be sure that once committed to an attack on Ugon, their weakened backside in Hilva proper wouldn't be exposed and targeted? The wrangling went on for weeks.

Captain Ket Mhulhar had finally had enough. She was tired of Eberes, sick of the whole occupation, and missed her then lover, the future premier, Elar Kro, a law student in Kasma Dor, whose passionate love letters also included equally passionate harangues against Dalyi's colonization of Eberes. All she wanted was to go home, and so did her company. "Let's get it over with" became the company's impatient motto.

She talked it over in secret meetings with other junior officers she trusted and finally decided to risk her career. If her plan failed, perhaps, even if it worked, she would be cashiered and tried for mutiny. But Ket's loyalty was to her troops, and she owed them the chance they so desperately wanted. If her life wound up forfeit, so be it. There were worse things for which to die.

Operation Srho, optimistically named for the mountain lake resort so popular with furloughed troops, was sound, despite the haste in which it was put together. It was simple, which was why it worked. A massive airborne assault group would capture the artillery emplacements and capture the huge pulse guns, clearing the way for ground forces to attack. The ground force would be small and outnumbered at first. But the ground contingent would signal the main body that Ebereans were attacking in force, and reinforcements would be brought up immediately. The Ebereans, caught between their own artillery atop the mountains and the entire Dalyinese Army at the bottom, would have nowhere to go.

The only concern Ket had was that she, as a mere and very junior captain, would be heading a force of inexperienced officers. In fact, because the intricate airborne assault required every veteran she had, plus artillery specialists, the ground units would be headed by her most junior officer, Nev Hederes.

While Dalyinese generals back in Hilva still argued and postured and wrote memos, an airborne assault force led by Ket Mhulhar headed north to Ugon. At precisely the time called for in the battle plan, the team donned their single-use jump-packs—small thrusters that enabled them to control their descent—and thus began the execution of Operation Srho, which would become an elegant addition to the textbooks at the military academy.

The Ebereans learned a tragic lesson about themselves on that night; they learned that their strength was in neither defensive nor offensive warfare. If you fight an army vastly more powerful than your own, you must fight it on your terms, not theirs. A static line with fixed emplacements is useless if it is breached. The lesson for the Ebereans would be cruel and costly, but it would be well learned.

The Dalyinese assault team had set their weapons to fire non-lethal rounds, sacrificing range for silence. The surprised gun crews were therefore the most fortunate of the hapless defenders, as the pneumatic pulses rendered them temporarily helpless and winded or unconscious, but largely unhurt. The hill was captured in complete silence, and when it was secured, Ket called in the second wave of airborne invaders, artillery experts to man the guns and infantry serving as military police to manage the prisoners.

The artillerymen resighted the guns onto the Eberean Army below them. When that task was done, Ket sent out the soon-to-be-legendary signal "the casino is open," a reference to the resort's major visitor attraction. That was Nev Hederes's cue to launch his attack.

Although Ket had always been sure that the frail young officer's appearance belied his true strength, she was somewhat concerned because this was his first major command. But she needn't have worried. The assault commenced immediately and in good order. Nev had placed his units in such a way as to maximize their firepower, creating the illusion of a much larger body of troops. He also signalled HQ exactly on schedule, be-

fore the landing of the second airborne wave. The main body
was on its way as Nev commenced his attack.

High atop the mountain, the captured communications appa-
ratus sparked to life. The order came from down the hill, by a
commander who had no way of knowing that his guns were in
enemy hands. "We are under attack, fire-fire-fire!"

The reply by the wide-eyed commications sergeant manning
the array, was most unmilitary: "Under fire? No kiddin'."

"Under attack, dammit, fire-fire-fire!"

"Fire?" replied the sergeant. "No-o-oo problem!"

Ket gave the order, and a salvo of hellacious and destructive
fire ripped through the troops below them. The Eberean general
in charge, no fool, immediately deduced that the guns had been
captured and wasted little time rallying his men. With nowhere
else to go, the Ebereans poured down the mountain straight for
Nev Hederes's ground force.

High atop the mountain, her captured artillery pouring deadly
fire into the enemy's fleeing rear, Ket closed her eyes and prayed
that the untried Nev Hederes would not let her down.

The Ebereans attacked Nev's smaller force, inflicting fierce
damage. But Nev regrouped and counterattacked. The counterattack was hard-fought and bloody, at times hand-to-hand. Finally, he received confirmation that the Dalyinese main body
was arriving.

"Okay, Nev!" Ket shouted into her communication pin, "Now!
Now! Now!"

In an instant, Nev Hederes gave the order to his troops: "Fall
back! Disengage and fall back!"

The Eberean general smelled victory. Although his big guns
had been captured, the ground battle had turned into a rout, with
the enemy fleeing before him. He therefore did what any sea-
soned professional would do; he pressed home the attack, intent
on destroying the retreating opposing force.

What the Eberean general didn't know, however, but would
soon find out, was that Nev Hederes's troops weren't the main
body of the opposing force, and secondly, their retreat was strategic and in fact, critical to the success of Operation Srho.

For as Nev's troops fell back, they linked up with the ad-
vancing main body from Hilva. The old general, who had de-

cided to command this particular action himself, was somewhat surprised to meet the officer in charge of the spearhead and find him to be a second lieutenant mere months out of the academy at Tira Gen. But he listened carefully to Nev's report, which he accepted like a long-awaited gift. The Ebereans had walked, or rather charged, into the final phase of Ket's trap, rushing headlong for the Dalyinese main body.

Suddenly, the Eberean general, instead of mopping up the tattered remnants of an army less than half the size of his own, was now committed to an attack against a fresh and well-equipped force that outnumbered him five-to-one.

What followed was a lesson in classic textbook battle tactics. Nev Hederes's units, now augmented by a larger force from Hilva, turned and faced the attackers, who had no choice but to press home their attack, as retreat would put them back into range of Ket's mountaintop artillery. The rest of the Dalyinese Army moved up on each flank and poured murderous fire into both sides of the Eberean Army, which went further into the trap with each step forward. Finally, with his army decimated, the Eberean commander struck his colors.

"My God, Kathy," Sy said after a long silence, "that was *brilliant.*"

"My dear," said Shirley, "you are nothing short of a military genius. And what leadership! That Nev Hederes! He must be a general by now. Tell me he is."

"He's the supreme general of Dalyi—or, he was."

Shirley gasped and put a hand to her cheek. "He's not . . . he's still—"

"I don't know," Ket said softly. "He was leading the Resistance, at least, when I left."

Shirley patted her comfortingly. "That man is too brave, and too intelligent," Shirley said. "I'm sure he's fine." She looked at Sy. "Can you imagine a second lieutenant handling that kind of responsibility, so young?"

"I can't imagine a second lieutenant tying his own shoes," Sy replied from experience. "But Kathy, let me understand this. A group of junior, *very* junior, officers take it upon themselves to plan and execute an entire battle operation. All right, it worked, but still, how did you get away with it?"

Ket slipped into a brief reverie. When she returned, she said, "Holak Ven visited your planet, four or five times that I know of. He loves your country, and he especially loved your language. 'Such wonderful phrases,' he always said. There was one thing he said, after a voyage. 'It doesn't translate real well, but the Americans have a saying. "'If it works, you're a hero, if not, you're a bum.'"'"

Ket, Nev Hederes, Holak Ven—who had been forward air controller throughout the battle—and every officer who had participated in Operation Srho's planning and execution had been arrested and confined to quarters pending court-martial proceedings for mutiny.

That lasted about six and a half minutes, or the time it took for the ancient general to gather his staff and shout, "What are we, crazy?" The army closed ranks and reported to the government that Operation Srho was a general staff project from start to finish. "Intelligence reports, Your Excellency," the old general lied smoothly to the premier, "indicated that the hidden Eberean Army was about to attack, so we, uh, cooked up this little plan in the short time we had. Brilliantly executed by these young officers, really smart little squirts who even helped in the overall planning. I don't know what they're teaching at Tira Gen these days, Your Excellency, but they certainly should keep it up."

There were promotions and medals for all concerned, but that wasn't the real triumph of Operation Srho. The army circulated another petition, signed by every trooper from the old general to the lowliest private, again threatening mass resignation if peace was not concluded with Eberes and total troop withdrawal begun. This time, the petition *was* sent to the government, as well as mysteriously leaked to the press. The army, now in high public esteem after their great victory, had the support of the people, and the government, in danger of toppling, initiated the pullout from Eberes.

•　　•　　•

"And so," Shirley said, "you won the war and went home."

Ket shook her head. "We won a *battle*," she replied. "The war . . . we lost."

The government in Dalyi fell anyway. The voters had had enough of foreign wars and maintaining colonies that drained the treasury instead of enriching it. The opposition party, which saw an opening through which an entire army could be force-marched, immediately called for a vote of censure or confidence. The ruling party was summarily dimissed by the voters, sweeping in the opposition, which included a young lawyer named Elar Kro, who was elected to a seat in Dalyi's governing assembly.

The first order of business for the new government was to establish relations with their former colony; a giant reconstruction loan to Eberes was underwritten with the full approval of the electorate. Dalyi and Eberes began to trade as equals, and Dalyinese engineers and technicians flocked to Eberes to help restore the infrastructure and modernize the rest of the country. Nor was the peaceful mass-exodus merely one-sided. Eberean children were sent to Dalyi to be educated, and Eberean cultural studies were introduced in the schools. Eberean students returned home to help rebuild their fast-developing nation.

Eberes rapidly came into its own, developing a close rapport with its former mother country. Travel between the two countries was reestablished and widened. Ebereans began settling in Dalyi, marrying Dalyinese, and even serving in the army and running for public office. It seemed the two nations had almost melded.

That was what the Dalyinese told themselves, anyway.

What the Dalyinese had failed to realize, however, was that for the Ebereans, the end of the armed conflict did not mean peace was at hand. For Eberes, the war had merely entered a new phase. For although they knew they had borne horrific losses in battle, the ultimate victory would be theirs. It would just take a long, long time.

In any event, it took just short of sixty years.

When the Dalyinese won the war, they went home and tried to put it behind them. But for the Ebereans, even as they charged down Mount Ugon and into Nev Hederes's troops, they knew that win or lose, this part of the war was just a phase. Had they won and chased the Dalyinese back to their transports and home, that would have been fine. But victory in the field was never really expected. Besides, it was not the Eberean way.

The Eberean way was far more subtle. Although Ebereans were strong and disciplined as individuals, they had never been good soldiers. Their philosophy belittled armed conflict, strength versus strength, as idiocy, and a criminal waste of Thradonian life just for a victory that was fleeting at best. For the Ebereans, the best way to win was to pretend to have lost. Awake the compassion in their former enemy, lull him into a sense of trust, wait until just the right time, and then total victory was theirs for the taking.

Had the Ebereans been boxers on Earth, they would have been masters of the rope-a-dope.

Unbeknownst to the Dalyinese, the Eberean Central Authority had never surrendered. In fact, it was not widely known that there even was a Central Authority. But there was, and now in its prime element, the Central Authority executed its new phase of the war flawlessly.

The new secret battle cry of the emerging young nation became "every man a mission." At infancy, children of mixed nationality were implanted with microscopic detectors; the Central Authority could then track the loyalties of every Dalyinese-Eberean child from an early age. By the time a child reached the formative and most impressionable years, it could be easily determined whether or not he or she was a candidate to join the fight. Those deemed unwilling or unfit would be dealt with later.

Ebereans living in Dalyi became writers, artists, and celebrities. They became Dalyinese citizens with careers in business, the military, and in the government. They became teachers, doctors, attorneys, police officers, and merchants. In every walk of life was an Eberean with a mission.

While this was occurring, the Dalyinese were helping the Ebereans rebuild their army. They even fought as allies, forty years after the Battle of the Plains of Ugon, in a brief war against Truska, a smaller, normally peaceful and progressive nation that had been taken over by a strongman. In Ket Mhulhar's first action as commanding general, the allies toppled the dictator and restored democracy within a week. This strengthened the ties between the two nations, and to the Dalyinese, at least, put their past emnity even further behind them.

After sixty years, the secret Central Authority concluded that the giant's sleep was deep enough. Ebereans by now controlled ten percent of all Dalyinese life. The timing would never be better.

The Eberean government arranged for its army to hold a joint exercise with its Dalyinese brothers-in-arms. Of course, unbeknownst to the Dalyinese, their allies would be using real ammunition. When reports came in of the first "tragic misunderstanding," as early news bulletins called it, the Ebereans in civilian life sprung into action. Communications were suddenly disrupted. Police officers were imprisoned by their own commanders. Business leaders were murdered by their own subordinates. In some cases, husbands killed their wives and wives killed their husbands. There was even an instance where an Eberean-born stand-up comic opened fire on his audience. "I *really* killed tonight," he remarked later. "That's what they get for being a tough room."

In the confusion that followed, the frightened nation turned to its government for help. The party that had negotiated peace and harmony with Eberes was still in power and was now headed by Elar Kro, who himself had an Eberean wife. The Ruling Chambers became a bloodbath as representatives coldly assassinated colleagues they had worked with for decades. Elar Kro's own wife was stopped from killing him only because of quick action by the premier's bodyguards.

The lion's share of victims were in the military. Entire divisions were marched into ambush by turncoat commanders. Ships of the naval fleet fired on each other. And the air force bombed its own bases.

The chaos was total.

The only thing that saved Ket Mhulhar, Nev Hederes, and other senior members of the cabinet and the military was a little-known emergency plan called *Dupran,* named for one of the founders of Dalyi. Only the most senior members of the government and the military were in on Dupran, and many of them had been serving since before Ebereans reached senior positions. The plan, which was never expected to be employed, was a scenario for an emergency government in the event of a coup or an invasion. It called for all senior members to find their way to Kasma Dor on the soonest available transport. From there, the besieged government would consolidate, assess damage, and plan for the future, if there was one left.

It was a fortunate accident of history that no Eberean knew of the existence of Dupran. Without it, the defeat would have been total, and the counterrevolution could never have begun.

And Ket Mhulhar could never have been sent to Earth.

Sy, Shirley, and Ket were silent for quite awhile after Ket had finished. For Ket, it was the first time since arriving on Earth that she was able to think of what was really happening in her country two years after total defeat. How many millions were dead? What was the country like these days, with a vengeful and repressive regime in charge? What of her friends, her family, her colleagues? She didn't want to think about it.

"Why did they have to kill everybody?" Shirley wondered, a catch in her voice. These Dalyinese, Kathy's people, had become her people now, as well.

"Because it makes sense," Sy replied. "Oh, I'm sorry, Kathy, that was tactless of me."

"No, I understand."

"Think about it," Sy told his wife. "Not from your point of view, but as an Eberean. You've grown up for the last sixty years as a programmed secret weapon. You've been able to keep this a secret, too. Then you win the final victory. Are you going to trust the people you've beaten? Will you let them grow up nurturing a secret plan against you?"

"It's horrible." Shirley closed her eyes and shook her head. "What beastly people!"

"So many were my friends," Ket said. "It was unimaginable. And now it's—"

A key in the front door lock startled Ket, and she involuntarily went to her waist for the weapon that wasn't there.

Both Sy's and Shirley's faces lit up as a tall, dark-haired

young man burst into the room. He was dressed all in black, in a pair of motorcycle jeans, boots, and a leather jacket. His face was lit by a pair of startlingly blue eyes and shadowed by a fashionable day's growth of beard.

Ket sized him up quickly. No human was attractive to her, at least not yet. But there was something in the boy's smile that made her think of Holak Ven, and the way that even Shirley could tell that he was "a charmer," as she had called it.

"Bobby!" Sy and Shirley both jumped up.

"Hey, Ma, Pop, you're not gonna believe what hap—" he stopped as he saw Ket. He gave her a brief, assessing look, taking in her long blonde hair, slim figure, and smooth skin.

He glanced at the ceiling. "Thank you, God," he said.

4

Even on her own planet, before her surgical alteration, Ket had
been an unusually attractive woman, all the more so because of
the power she had come to radiate. She was used to the attention she received, comfortable with her looks, and enjoyed the
advantages her beauty gave her. But here on Earth, meeting this
son of her two protectors, she felt as though she was being un-
dressed, slowly and with great relish. It made her slightly uncomfortable, a feeling she hadn't experienced in many, many
years.

"Who is this?" Bobby wanted to know, turning his Holak
Ven-ish smile on Ket.

"Bobby," Shirley cautioned him. She slapped his hand lightly.
"This is our friend, Kathy Miller. She is not one of your bimbos, so behave!"

Bobby affected a surprised outrage. "Bimbos? *Moi*?"

"Yes. *Vous*. Kathy, this is our son Bobby. He's really a very
sweet boy, even though that may seem a little hard to believe
right now."

But Ket had no trouble sizing him up. This strange . . . gift . . .
that the earth had given her seemed to be signalling to her. He
was a good sort. There was a commitment to honor and a se-

rious integrity deep beneath the seemingly benign surface. She had nothing to fear from him, her odd new feelings told her . . . except that he obviously wanted to have sex with her. And that prospect, she discovered with surprise, was not *totally* unappealing.

Bobby kissed his mother and father and said, somewhat softly, "I love you guys." He turned to her. "Miss Miller, it's a pleasure to meet you. Now, if you'll excuse me, I'll be right back. I had a hell of a long drive, on top of a Seven-Eleven Big Gulp."

"Bobby!" Shirley warned.

"What'd I say?" Bobby asked. "See you in a minute."

"That's our youngest boy," Sy said after Bobby left the room. His pride was apparent. "He's a film director."

"His films . . ." Shirley said with bewilderment. "A fellow dresses in a black suit and a hat and black sunglasses, like it's 1963, gets out of a 1957 Plymouth, takes out a 1999 handgun, and goes into a 1958-looking diner and shoots people. Ugh! Blood all over the place! For *this* he wins at Cannes."

Ket was horrified. "He what?"

"Kathy, it's *movies*," Sy said. He glanced at her sideways. "Do you have movies—films—cinema—on your planet?"

"Oh. Oh! Movies!" Ket recalled from her long tutorial on board the spacecraft. "No, no, we don't. I can't imagine why not. But it just never happened on our planet. We have what you'd call . . . theatre. And comedians. And something like your . . ." Lost for words, she pointed to the entertainment center.

"Television?"

"Yes, but it's only for communications from the government."

Bobby returned. "Anyway . . . Kathy, where ya from?"

"Please?" Kathy said, turning to Sy, who nodded.

"Oh!" Bobby replied. "Cincinnati! What brings you out here?"

"Kathy's had to make a few . . . life changes," Shirley said smoothly.

"I'm all for life changes," Bobby said. "Where do you know my folks from?"

"Remember Sid Miller, the one who supplied us with the blonde-wood coffee tables? The ones from Sweden?"

"Not at all, Ma."

"Oh, sure you do. Sy, wasn't that one of our perennial big sellers? Young couples, the ones just starting out, they couldn't snap'em up fast enough. Inexpensive, but well made. Anyway, this is Sid's . . . niece."

Bobby turned to Ket. "Well, Sid's niece, I'm delighted you're here. What do you do?"

"Kathy's in aerospace technology," Sy jumped in. "Worked at GE for years."

"But I'm making a change," Ket attempted bravely.

"Bobby," Shirley began, coming to Ket's rescue, "what were you about to tell us, when you came in? You said we wouldn't believe what happened."

"Oh, oh yeah. Remember Jenny, my script supervisor?"

"That sweet girl? The one who did virtually *all* your donkey-work? How come you never—"

"Ma, you don't fool with your script girl. She's too important. None of the stuff that happens on the set ever works out, and it's always a mess eventually."

"In other words," Sy said, "she wasn't your type."

"Yeah, well, don't feel too sorry for her. I start shooting on Monday, and she's gone."

"Gone?" Shirley looked at her son accusingly. "What did you do to her?"

"Ma, you know me better than that. No, she's eloped!"

"She ran off and got married," Shirley said for Ket's benefit. "Who to?"

"It'll be all over the news any minute. Bryce Kilduff! Can you believe it?"

"Bryce Kilduff? The movie star?"

"No, Bryce Kilduff, the drywall salesman. Of course, the movie star! I mean, I knew she had a new boyfriend over the last few months—Jesus, she was mooning all over the place, but I never would have believed—anyway, what the hell do I do now? I start production in two days, and my script girl's in Maui making cow eyes with her new husband over mai tais at the bar of the Grand Wailea!"

"I have a wonderful idea!" Shirley exclaimed.

"Wait a minute," rejoined Sy.

"No, it's perfect! Kathy, you need a job. Bobby, you need a script supervisor."

Bobby threw up his hands. "Mom! Pop's right. Wait a minute. Kathy, nothing personal, but have you ever worked in the film business?"

"No, I—"

"Bobby, what is it, rocket science? She holds the script, and you say, 'okay, where was I,' and she looks at the script and says, 'the first gunman says don't move or I'll blow your effing head off.' Oh, boy, son, what a challenge. Kathy was a systems manager at GE Aircraft Engines, for God's sake. I think she can handle it."

"But it's not just that, Mom," Bobby argued. "Look, you know my movies have low budgets. Everybody has to double up! I mean, Jenny was my right arm! Look, Kathy, like I said, nothing personal, and by the way, I'd love to take you to dinner sometime, but—"

"Bobby," Shirley snapped. "Kathy's a bright girl. Give her a chance, at least."

"All right. Okay, Mom. I'll give her a chance. Kathy, do you think you can help manage production? Coordinate the movements of large groups of people and equipment?"

Sy and Shirley looked at each other and started to laugh, and even Ket, seeing the irony of such a question, joined in.

"I think Kathy can . . . do that," Shirley said finally. "She's got . . . some experience in that . . . arena . . ." Shirley could barely finish the sentence before breaking out into renewed laughter.

"I'm glad you think it's funny, Mom. I'm the one in deep—okay." He turned to Ket, who could now sense that all the fun, and all the sexual desire, was no longer evident. He was serious now, a man with a mission. "All right, Kathy. My folks think you're okay, so we'll take it from there." He glanced at his watch and stood up. "Let's go."

"Bobby! Wait a minute!" Shirley cried.

"Mom, we've got to get back. I want her to read the script. Check that, I want her to *learn* the script. Then I gotta teach her the job. I don't have any time left. I want her ready to go on Monday morning."

"But where'll she stay? What abou—"

"She can stay at my place. Mom, this is *business*. I've got plenty of room, we can go for days without even bumping into each other. And I promise I'll be about as sexually threatening as a neutered grey cat."

"Why don't we ask Kathy what she thinks?" Sy said.

Ket was apprehensive about leaving the warm cocoon of Sy and Shirley's protection. But there was something about Bobby, and this whole film business, that intrigued her. In her time she had braved pulse guns and blazer mines. She had won bar fights against multiple assailants armed with triple-bladed *Goula* knives. She didn't think this . . . film business . . . would be anything to worry about.

"It sounds like a new world," Kathy said.

Shirley put her hands on Ket's shoulders. "Are you sure you're ready?"

"No," Ket smiled sadly. "But I should go." She looked into Shirley's kindly eyes. "*Oonah*," she said, giving Shirley a tight hug.

"What does that mean?" Shirley asked.

Ket whispered so that only Shirley could hear. "Godmother," she said.

"You think it's too soon?" Sy asked as Bobby's forest green Porsche Turbo pulled away.

"Absolutely," Shirley said. "But I think Kathy needs to do something. The girl was a *general,* after all. And as young and beautiful as she looks, we forget, she's no kid. She's *our age.* Older, maybe."

"God, you're right! I did forget. Still, you think she'll be able to handle the movie business? All the loonies involved? Not to mention the fact that she's never even *seen* a movie."

Shirley turned to face her husband. "Sy, when she was younger than Bobby, she virtually commanded a whole army and won a war! I think she can handle Hollywood."

Sy laughed. "I guess you're right. But I wonder; can Hollywood handle *her*?"

Ket had faced terrifying gunfire, bloody hand-to-hand combat, and survived brutal political infighting to rise to the top of her profession. None of that, however, did anything to prepare her for a drive with Bobby Albertson in his new Porsche Turbo. The sensation was not unlike the helplessness she had felt when the escape pod began its fall to Earth.

Interstate 10 near Palm Springs is bleak and barren, with the mountains to the south and acres of wind turbine farms on the north. The speed limit is seventy miles an hour, in theory. Actually, the discrepancy between vehicle velocities makes for a rather exciting ride—which is fortunate, because there is a great deal of monotony to be broken. There are slow, heavy trucks that trundle along at fifty-five miles an hour, recreational vehicles going sixty, and always, it seems, some wide load that barely moves at all.

So, bored drivers like Bobby Albertson made things a bit more exciting by going one hundred and darting around the slower traffic.

"Do you always . . . drive like this?" a terrified Ket asked.

"Whenever I can get away with it," Bobby replied, downshifting when he couldn't get around an old pickup festooned with yard rakes. He found an opening and zoomed around it, downshifting again when he saw a large, solid-looking sedan up ahead.

"Spoilsport," Bobby murmured, as the words *Highway Patrol* came into focus on the sedan's trunk. Bobby slowed quickly to an acceptable speed. The cops usually gave you a break if you went only five, and sometimes ten miles over the limit on this appallingly boring stretch of road, but only if there was no traffic, and more importantly, if you weren't driving a Porsche. Bobby had learned the hard way that when you drove a Porsche, all bets were off. It was the car the Highway Patrol simply loved to ticket. He slowed even more, down to sixty-five, settling in behind a Lincoln Town Car on cruise control.

He reached behind him as he drove, pulling a bound script from the backseat. He handed it over to Ket.

"Well," he said, "this would be a great time to find out all about you, 'all that David Copperfield kind of crap,' to quote Holden Caulfield, but I'd rather you used the time to read this. Okay?"

Ket nodded and opened the script. Reading English wasn't a problem, because Holak's tutorial had prescribed several hours of reading per day, but she was unprepared for the script format. Because she knew nothing of cameras, and even less of camera angles, the shooting script looked completely foreign to her. But Bobby seemed to understand that.

"Never read a script before, huh?" he said. "Don't worry about it. Just read the stage directions—see there where it says, 'Elwood walks into the bar, stops, and looks around with contempt.' That's the stage direction. And then, of course, the dialog—see, the character's name and then the skinnier paragraphs underneath. Ever seen one of my movies?"

"No, I haven't. I'm sorry."

"That's okay. They're not for everybody."

"Did you write this?"

"I always direct my own stuff. Works out better that way. Go ahead, read it. Maybe, when we get to my place, we'll put one of my films in the VCR and you can see for yourself."

"I'd like that. I think."

To her surprise, Ket became so engrossed in the script that she forgot to look out the window and take in some of this new world. As Shirley had warned her, the script was full of violence and the script had many, many of the words that Shirley had told her were considered vulgar, but the story and the characters kept her riveted. Ket had been a voracious reader and as a general rated a good box at the theatre and went often, but she was keenly interested in seeing what these . . . movies . . . were like. But she also worried. If this was how Terrans entertained themselves, what kind of people were they?

• • •

All of the city of Los Angeles seemed like Thradon five hundred years before, right out of the history books. Everything seemed slapped together, crumbly old houses not far from tall glass structures. There seemed to be no plan for how the city was laid out, no rhyme or reason or sensible use of space. The place was filthy, as though every other building needed a new coat of paint. And the noise! Everything was so loud! The personal vehicles, the air transports! How did people stand this place?

"This is Los Angeles?" she asked Bobby.

He chuckled. "It's sort of a dump, in some places, and the traffic is of course murder, and it seems like the whole place went up in six months. Everybody who lives here says they hate it. But you'll see. It grows on you. Nothing like home, huh?"

"Not . . . not one bit," Ket replied.

"Yeah, that's L.A. But there's something . . . I guess it's because this is a movie town and I'm in the movie biz. And the town is finally getting old enough to have a sense of its own history. I feel . . . connected here. I can't imagine ever living anywhere else."

Bobby lived in a tall building overlooking the ocean in Santa Monica. Kathy felt a strange sensation of relief when he pulled into the building's underground garage. There was something about this structure that reminded her of her own quarters, an apartment in Kasma Dor's fashionable Grevas district overlooking the Dalyinese Ocean. She had always dreamed of such a place, and was overjoyed when, having achieved early promotion to general, she could finally afford it.

The elevator to the ninth floor was a little frightening the first time around—Dalyinese risers utilized solid cushions of air and therefore did not offer the perilous sensation of being suspended high in space.

"Ninth floor," Bobby announced, "ladies undergarments, purses, gloves and accessories, watch your step, please." He said it with a grin, so Ket guessed that he was joking. She offered a small smile.

It was a homey, comfortable quarters, with lots of wood tables and leather chairs, a man's apartment.

"There're three bedrooms," Bobby told her. "Yours is along here. You've got your own bathroom. I've got a maid comes in twice a week, and she also does the laundry and the shopping."

The room Bobby showed her was small but seemed pleasant, and Ket was glad that it had an ocean view. There was a large bed, a writing desk, and an entertainment console.

"I like this place," Ket said.

"Yeah, it's great. Cost me a fortune, and if there's another earthquake, I'm screwed blue, but I love it, and I'll probably be here forever. I can't understand Mom and Pop with their desert thing. I hate the damned desert. Give me the ocean any old day. But I wish they lived closer."

"I want to thank you," Ket began. "Your . . . Mom and Pop . . . have been very kind to me, and it's good of you to give me a place to live."

Bobby shrugged. "You can stay as long as you like. But you've got a lot of hard work ahead. I'll pay you well for it, but you'll earn it."

"I've always worked hard," Ket retorted.

"I don't doubt it." Bobby looked around the guest room. "Well, this is your room now. I won't enter again without your permission. The third bedroom has workout stuff in it. You look like someone who does a lot of exercise, so use it whenever you want. There's a health club downstairs, but it's always crowded and a pain in the ass. And with your looks, you'd have jerks hitting on you every twelve seconds. Oh, help yourself to anything in the fridge. Do you want to talk about the script now?"

"If you don't mind," she began, "I'd like to see one of your movies on the view—the VCR," she remembered quickly. "But I'd like to read that script first. Do you have a script and a movie of yours?"

"What a question," Bobby replied.

Ket, now more at ease with the shooting-script format, breezed through the script of *Valley Kingpin,* Bobby's first hit. The film had been an independent effort that had been snapped up by a big studio for distribution and ensured his place as a rising young director of note.

Reading the script, Ket was puzzled. The script she had read in the car had almost the same atmosphere, but it was well written and the characters made it memorable. But this, an earlier effort by the same writer, was inexplicable. It was filled with . . . vulgarities—that *effing* word Shirley had warned her about— was all over the script, in almost every line, it seemed. The characters were brutal and violent, even the frequent sex seemed to be more about anger than love or pleasure. There was almost as much blood in this story as there had been at the Battle of Ugon.

It was so awful, she thought, that it was almost embarrassing. If this were a play in a theatre in Kasma Dor, the audience would stand up and walk out. But how could she tell Bobby that his script was an excrescence?

Reluctantly, she placed the video into the cassette player, as she had seen Sy do so many times, and turned it on.

And there the magic began.

She found to her amazement that she had actually memorized the script without realizing it. She recognized every contemptible line as the actors spoke them.

But she was not prepared for the sorcery that actors, timing, good camera work, and the right location could perform on the written word. His words, which seemed the utterances of imbecilic cretins on paper, suddenly had meaning and context when issued from the mouths of these somehow believable characters on the screen. The action, which on paper seemed wanton and gratuitous, suddenly had logic and purpose.

It was brilliant. And to think, for all the technological and social superiority of her own planet, movies did not exist!

Because Thradonians lived so long, they often had two separate careers, each spanning about eighty or so years. After they succeeded in one career, they would start over in another. Those who remained in the same profession for life, like the old general commanding in the Hilva conflict, were called *ancients*. However, they were few and far between.

But Ket had reached the very pinnacle of a soldier's career. She could go no higher than high marshal of defense, and she couldn't stay there for the rest of her life. Even if she returned and assumed the office of premier, she couldn't hold that job forever; nor would she want to. So, for the last ten years, she had been considering other options for the second half of her life. There was teaching, perhaps at Tira Gen or the University of Kasma Dor. There was business, but buying and selling had never really appealed to her. Perhaps the law, but that was her last choice. There was really nothing left that excited her.

Until now. Imagine, bringing a whole new concept of entertainment to Thradon, a new form of the theatre! Thradonians would go mad for it! Yes. She'd return someday, help complete the counterrevolution, restore normalcy to Dalyi. And then— movies! There would be a whole new art form on Thradon, and she would be its pioneer!

She jumped up and ran into the living room, where Bobby was going over the script.

"Movies," she said breathlessly. "I have to see more movies! Do you have any?"

5

What kind of a body had that fool of a doctor given her, Ket wondered in silent outrage. And what kind of planet was this? *Everyone* wanted to sleep with her! How, if that was all they thought about, how did they ever get anything done?

Bobby had taken her around the set, a bar in a rundown part of town, and introduced her to the cast and crew. "This is Tom Courtland, our star." She recognized him from the film she had seen the night before and imagined that he was what Terrans would consider exceptionally handsome.

"Hi, Kathy, glad to be working with you," he said pleasantly and with what seemed to be a sincere smile. But all Ket could feel was a picture of herself in his head, a graphic scene of her naked and writhing with pleasure.

She would come to know that scene well, for it would replay with every introduction to every male and some of the females on the set. After about the tenth introduction, she took Bobby aside.

"Is there any way for me to speak with your mother," she asked. "There's something I might have left—"

"Sure," Bobby said, "but make it quick." He took the cell

phone from his hip and punched in a speed-dialed number. "Just hit end when you're done."

She thought she heard a voice coming from the little whatever-it-was, but she had no idea how to use it. Fortunately, someone else on the set was using a similar instrument and she copied him.

"Shirley?" she said. "Oonah?"

"Kathy, darling? Is that you? Is everything all right?"

Ket walked away from the set so as not to be overheard. "Oonah? Yes, everything is fine. No, Bobby is acting properly. It's just that . . ." She quickly explained her experiences of the morning so far.

"Well, *of course* they all want to sleep with you, dear," Shirley replied. "I don't know if you're aware of it, but you are a very, *very* beautiful woman. It comes with the territory."

"What territory?"

"Just a phrase, dear. Listen, I know it's upsetting, but you can't change the way people think. Is there any way you could, well, *control* that power of yours? Maybe, try and see around it?"

It hadn't occurred to Ket that she even could control her new power. "I don't know," she replied. "Perhaps."

"Think of it as a military exercise, Kathy. Use military discipline. Who's better at that than you?"

The hum of noise on the set reached an urgent level, and Ket knew she should return to Bobby's side, which was where she would belong for the rest of the shooting schedule.

"You're right, Oonah, I should have thought of it in those terms. I guess I'm still a little disoriented."

"Of course you are. Kathy, darling, when you think of you, you think of this proud, accomplished, and brave warrior general, who has spent seventy years fighting for her country. But that's not what any of us see. All we see is this extremely pretty girl, not much over thirty, certainly not looking it, who has beautiful hair and looks terrific in tight jeans. Kathy, you're *in disguise.*"

"I know," Ket replied. "I should have seen that myself. Thank you, Oonah."

"My dear," Shirley said. "I majored in sociology. I'm very

good at pointing out the obvious. Now, you'd better go. I can't
believe Bobby would allow anyone to take this long a break
during filming. Go on, and break a leg."

"What?" Why would Oonah, of all people, say such thing to
her? To Ket's surprise, she heard Shirley giggle on the other end
of the line.

"Kathy, it means good luck. Show biz people are very su-
perstitious and . . . go to work, hon. We'll talk later."

Ket pushed the end button as Bobby had instructed and
crossed back to the set proper. Bobby was talking with a man
wearing a dark suit and sunglasses. As she approached, the man
turned and removed the sunglasses. Kathy immediately recognized him as the actor who had played a soft-spoken, brutally
mechanical assassin in Bobby's first film.

"Kathy," Bobby said, "this is Frank Cosimo, who I'm sure
scared the hell out of you in *Valley Kingpin*. Frank, this is my
new script gir-supervisor, Kathy Miller."

Frank Cosimo was older than most of the cast and crew. He
was a good-looking man in a rugged way, only of medium height
but agile and obviously strong. He reminded Kathy of her own
army's sergeant-majors.

He stuck out a rough, dry hand for her to shake. "It's nice
to meet you, Kathy. I know we'll get along fine." He stopped
for a moment, looking at her searchingly. "Have I met you before?" he asked her.

"I don't think so," Kathy replied, but she smiled inwardly.
She was positive that this man had been a soldier, and that he had
somehow seen through her disguise. She found herself liking him
already, and was further pleased to discover that he wasn't imag-
ining her naked. All she could feel from him was respect.

"Say, Kath," Bobby said, "we're almost set up. Could you
run and tell Vicki we're almost ready?"

Kathy nodded and went outside the bar, where many trucks
and other vehicles, called trailers, were parked along the street.
There were also a couple of blue-uniformed men astride shiny
white two-wheeled vehicles of some sort; Bobby had told her
that they were police officers, assigned to traffic control and security.

She made her way down the shabby block toward the trailer

assigned to the female star of the picture, Victoria St. Louis. Bobby had told her that stars of the picture rated, and demanded, and always got trailers during shooting. Ket felt that giving one person expensive and luxurious quarters was criminally extravagant, but Bobby explained that stars spent more time waiting on the set than actually working, and they had to be kept comfortable and undisturbed so that they could maintain their concentration. The cost of a trailer rental, Bobby had said, was far less than shooting many additional takes of a scene because an actor was discontented. Ket thought that was ridiculous, coming from a sacrifice-oriented profession where prima donnas were largely shunned.

Nevertheless, she was looking forward to meeting Victoria St. Louis, whose performance in Bobby's first film had so moved her. Anyone capable of generating that much concern from a total stranger must be an extraordinary person, Ket believed.

She rapped firmly on the trailer door. It was opened immediately by an older man with a shock of white hair. Unlike everyone else she had met on the set, he was impeccably dressed in a grey suit. He was so well put together that in another setting, Ket would have taken him for a general in mufti.

But the man smiled when he saw her, and Ket had to quickly dismiss the nude picture of herself from her mind.

"I am Kathy Miller," she said formally. "Bobby asked me to inform Victoria St. Louis that she is needed on the set."

"Well, it's nice to meet you, Kathy Miller," he greeted her. "I'm John Rochford, Miss St. Louis's agent. Tell Bobby that she'll—"

"Who's that?" an angry young woman's voice demanded. "Who the hell is that?"

"The new script girl, Vicki. She's—"

Victoria St. Louis came to the door and glared at Ket. Ket could not recall feeling such hatred since the Hilva Occupation. And oddly enough, for just a moment, there was even a stronger sensation: Fear.

"Miss St. Louis," she began, but was interrupted.

"Who are you to talk to me?" The dark-haired, dark-eyed actress shouted at Ket. "You tell Bobby my hair looks like shit, my makeup blows, and this dress makes my ass look like Tweedledum! Now piss off, you blonde bitch!" And with that, she slammed the door in Ket's face.

Ket stood frozen in shock. No one, not a single soul in all of Dalyi would have dared speak to her that way. And secondly, what had she done to arouse such ire from someone she didn't even know?

She reported the incident to Bobby, who, surprisingly, shrugged. "Figures," he said. "Happens first day of every shooting. Don't take it personally. Come on, we'll sort this out right now."

Bobby strode out purposefully toward Victoria St. Louis's trailer. He knocked on the door, hard.

It was immediately opened by John Rochford, who saw Bobby and threw up his hands in a placating gesture. "Now, Bobby, you know how she is the first day."

"I don't care," Bobby replied. "I don't have the time, or the money for this." He took his cell phone off his hip and dialed a number. "Yeah, Bobby Albertson," he said into the phone. "Is he in? Okay, I'll wait, but not too long. Look John, I got Winona Ryder's agent on the phone right now. We'll shoot around Vic today and tomorrow, and then Win'll be able to step in."

"Bobby, you're not really talk—"

"Hi," Bobby said into the phone. "Look, Win's between pix right now, isn't she? Great!" He covered the phone with his hand. "Tell Vic she's fired," he told John, and began walking away.

"I'll get her," John said in resignation. "She'll be on the set in thirty seconds."

"Gotta go," Bobby said into the phone. "Tell Win I've got something for her a little down the road." He disconnected. "You tell your client," he said, pointing his finger like a gun, "that there's room for just one Alpha personality on my set, and that's *me*. You got that, John?"

"All right," John replied.

"And get her off that stupid trendy-assed diet. It's turning her into a lunatic. Come on, Kath, we've got work to do."

As they stepped back into the bar, Kathy turned to Bobby feeling a new sense of respect. "Who did you really have on the phone?" she asked him.

Bobby nodded approvingly. "Very good! Mom said you were bright."

"Thank you. So, who was it?"

He spread his hands. "Dad! Who else?"

The film business, if this first day was any indication, was much like the army, Ket decided. Most of the time and energy was spent in preparation and setting up. The time spent actually shooting the picture, like the duration of an actual battle compared to training, was brief in comparison.

And yet, those brief moments were golden. Ket had to admit, somewhat grudgingly, that despite her dislike for Victoria St. Louis, the actress was nothing short of brilliant when the cameras rolled. The spoiled and frightened young girl was able to project every possible emotion convincingly, and Ket guessed that was why she was worth the trouble she caused.

Ket herself felt her excitement mount when the stage-hand clapped the scene marker, and Bobby shouted *roll it!* and the soundman called *speed!* and Bobby yelled *action!* And then it would all begin. Ket would divide her viewing of the scene between what was happening on the set and the picture on the viewscreen recording the action. There, Frank Cosimo once again became a scary killer, Tom Courtland a slick drug dealer, and Victoria St. Louis at turns, a waif, a vixen, and a stone killer.

The whole business had Ket completely enraptured. And that was the beauty of Thradonian life. It was long enough for one to experience the thrill of discovery twice in a lifetime.

Through it all, Bobby Albertson remained in complete control. She noted that everyone on the set seemed dedicated and involved, and yet Bobby also kept the set relaxed and friendly. It reminded her of the divisions under her command; she could always tell a crack outfit by the cheerful efficiency with which the troops worked, a sure sign of an excellent commanding officer.

Ket got into a conversation with the makeup artist, a red-haired girl name Bonnie, who told her flatly that Bobby was one of the few young directors in the business who wasn't a conceited megalomaniac pain in the ass who ran his set like freakin' Alcatraz.

"He treats everyone like a human being," she told Ket. "But he doesn't go for any temperamental crap, not from anyone."

Ket replied that she had noticed that for herself this morning, with his handling of Victoria St. Louis.

"Oh, Vic's harmless," Bonnie said. "She's a little nuts, but hey, she's an *actress*. I mean, hell-o-o. What do you expect? Plus since she's been going out with Chuck—"

"Chuck?" asked Ket.

"Du-uh! Chuck Hansen, the guy who won the Oscar two years ago. Earth to Kathy! Hell-o-o? Anyway, he's like, the handsomest guy on the face of the earth, and every girl in the world wants to jump his bones, his muscles that is, and so she's like all scared he's gonna dump her for someone prettier, so she lost all this weight because she thinks he wants her skinny, and like no one can stand it, but she thinks it makes her look hot, so she's like on this diet from this like swami guy, this macrobiotic crap grown in, like, horse manure, and it's messing up her head, so she's a bitch."

Finding Bonnie to be a valuable font of information, Ket asked her how long she had known Bobby.

"Oh, like forever. We went to Taft High in Woodland Hills together. He was always like really sweet, but sort of a geek until he got out of the navy. I mean, you could tell he'd grow up to be cute, but by then I was already married."

"Bobby was in the navy?" Ket asked in surprise.

"Ee-yeah? Hell-o? What *planet* have you been on? It's like a famous story, been on *E* everytime he opens a new movie. He and Tom Courtland and Frank Cosimo were all in the Gulf War together."

"Bobby fought in a war?" Ket asked, shocked.

"I thought everybody knew that. Yeah, Bobby was gonna go to UCLA Film School right out of high school, but he took one look at his classmates and saw that none of them knew dick except sabotaging someone else's project, so he figured it would be a waste of his parents' money to go until he'd seen some of the world, so he like joined the navy. That was when we graduated, in '87. So like he's on this ship in the Gulf when Desert

Storm breaks out, and he meets Tom, who's from Iowa or something, and Frank who's a regular navy guy, a petty chief or whatever. And they have this job blasting off missiles at Baghdad a thousand miles away. And so after they kick Saddam in the anus, they all think they're gonna go home but they get orders to stay in the Gulf another six months. So like everybody on the ship is really pissed off and morale like sucks, so Bobby decides to put on a play. And it turns out that Tom always wanted to be an actor and was only in the navy so he could go to drama school on the GI Bill, and he gets really jazzed about it. So Bobby gets ahold of this script for this like all-guy play, 'cause on the ship is all guys—"

"Wait," Ket interrupted. "The navy is just *men*?"

"Hell-o, it's the *navy*. No women on ships in combat. Or, back then, anyway. Or at least, not his ship. So Bobby gets ahold of this play that was a monster hit like thirty years ago on Broadway, called *That Championship Season,* written by the guy from *The Exorcist,* about these four guys who won the state basketball championship and their coach who have a reunion every year. And they're all like self-deluding assholes and it's really good drama. So like, they're looking for a guy to play the coach, and since everybody is afraid of Big Frank and respects him, they think he's the obvious choice. So they're scared to ask him, but they do, and *surprise!* He's seen the play years before and would love to do it. So instead of putting it on like a play, they videotape it, just an hour or so a day because they're still on war alert and that's all the free time they have. And then, when it's all done, they show it on the ship's video and everybody freaks. They even send it out to like other ships in the Gulf, and everybody digs it. I mean, you could tell those guys were all good even back then."

"Am I interrupting anything?" Tom Courtland asked.

"Not while you're this cute," Bonnie replied.

"You're the ones who're cute. How do you like your first day, Kathy?"

"I like it very much," Kathy said. "It's new and it's different and—I think I'm going to enjoy it here."

"That's great! You're a welcome addition."

"Oh, get me a *shovel*," Bonnie groaned in mock disgust. "See, Kathy, that's what you get for being hot."

"You're hot, too," Tom argued.

"Yeah, but I'm married-hot. Anyways, I was telling Kathy about what like heroes you and Frank and Bobby are."

"Oh, please! I needed the money for acting school. If I'd known I'd actually be in a war . . ."

"How did the three of you get together after the . . . Gulf . . . for *Valley Kingpin*," Ket asked him.

"Bonnie, could you touch me up?" Tom asked, easing himself into the makeup chair.

"Will you give me that autographed photo for my mom?" Bonnie asked.

"Hell, I'd give your mom a grandchild, if only you'd leave that husband of yours."

"Oh, yeah, I've had this uncontrollable urge to be a one-night stand for some big star," Bonnie replied, patting down his face with foundation.

"Anyway, Kathy," Tom said through a contorted face, "Bobby's enlistment was up soon after we made the video. So he went back to film school. He never planned on graduating, just staying until he had learned all the technical skills of directing and producing. See, by that time, indie films were really starting to hit, and Bobby was getting antsy. He wrote most of *Kingpin* while still on the ship. So, he quits film school after three or four semesters and starts shopping *Kingpin* around to all the studios.

"Naturally, the studios mostly blew him off. Some were impressed by the script but wanted to take it away from him. Well, Bobby wouldn't have that. Finally, he's right in the middle of getting kissed off by the green-light guy at one of the big studios, when he stands up right in the middle of it and says, 'You know what? Forget it. I don't need you. Thanks for your time but I'll make it myself.' The green-light guy says, half-a-million? From where? And Bobby says, don't worry, I'll get it. The guy looks at Bobby and sees he's really serious. So he gives Bobby his card and says, 'Okay. Bring me the answer print and we'll talk again.'

"Now, Bobby has no idea where the hell he's gonna get a

half-mill from. He starts applying for all these credit cards, thinking he'll run them all up and if the film hits, no problem. If not—well, that's not an option. But his parents, who are just about to retire, see all these credit cards coming to him in the mail and totally freak. They ask what the story is, and he tells them. The next morning, his parents go to the bank, take a big mortgage out on the house—which had been paid off years before—and hand him a check for $378,000, which was all they could get. And they do this, mind you, without his having asked or them saying a word about it."

"Sy and Shirley did that?" Ket exclaimed.

"Okay, you know them, so you shouldn't be surprised."

Ket smiled at the thought of them. "I'm not," she said.

"Well, at first," Tom continued, "Bobby doesn't want to take it. But Sy and Shirley work on him for a week. Finally he says, okay, but you have to take points. If the movie hits, you'll be rich. They tell him not to worry about it, just try and pay them back if he can. Unbeknownst to Bobby, they put off their retirement indefinitely, just in case the whole thing flopped. When he found that out much later, he went nuts, but by then it was too late. Anyway, he still needed another hundred grand, give or take. But that was easy. I was just getting out of the navy. Big Frank was going to retire anyway, and he'd gotten word that Bobby wanted him to play the assassin. So Big Frank cashed in his pension and gave it to him."

"And don't forget," Bonnie joined in, "that you gave him all your money for acting school."

"Ah, that was nothing compared to what Sy and Shirley and Big Frank gave up."

"It was all you had in the world," Bonnie said.

"I had my looks," Tom protested. "Anyway, we shot the movie on a shoestring. We all pitched in, helping move stuff, driving the trucks, setting up, we even bought our own costumes. Bonnie here worked for free."

"Oh, stop!" Bonnie chided him. "You're making me sound like Mother Teresa. I knew it would pay off. Anyway, it was fun!"

Bonnie finished Tom's makeup job. "It *was* fun," Tom agreed, getting up. "It was also scary, because everything was riding on the outcome, but that just made it more exciting. And it made us work twice as hard. Sometimes we'd work for a week without even going home, slept on the set. It was wonderful." He looked at her and grinned. "But now is better. I should go run my lines. Nice talking with you, Kathy. Bonnie."

"He's got a stiffy for you, Kathy," Bonnie said as Tom walked away. "I've seen him operate hundreds of times."

"He's . . . very . . . attractive," Ket replied, somehow able to get the gist of Bonnie's meaning, "but I've found it can be awkward, getting involved with a colleague."

"God, you sound just like Bobby! He goes out with like a million girls, but never someone on one of his pictures. I mean, Tom is a sweetie-pie, but let's face it, he'd diddle an alligator if he was sure it was female and somebody drained the swamp. But not Bobby. Jenny, the girl who you just replaced, she had like a mondo loin-ache for Bobby forever. But Bobby won't even consider it, he thinks it's totally unprofessional. Even Victoria St. Louis had a thing for him once. That's what I like about Bobby, though, he always keeps his word. In this town, that means something. Where'd you get those highlights?"

"Please?" The subject change momentarily confused Ket.

"Your hair. Did you get it done around here somewhere?"

"Uh, no, around . . . home."

"Well, you look totally hot." Bonnie dropped her voice to a whisper. "We'd better get back to work. Looks like they're ready to go again."

"Oh, you're right. I'd better go. But thanks for the conversation."

"Oh, I've got a big mouth. Or that's what they tell me. Personally, I just don't see it."

At home that evening Ket was surprised to find that the long day had tired her out as much as a three-day war game. She made straight for her bed the second she and Bobby walked into the apartment. She was in the dream-state between sleep and wakefulness when she heard a tap on her bedroom door.

"May I come in?" Bobby asked.

"It's your house," Ket replied.

"Yes, but it's your room. I just wanted to know if you were hungry. I was thinking of ordering a pizza."

Pete-za, Ket thought, that sounds interesting. Not an English word, she was sure of that. "I couldn't eat a thing," she said. "I just need some rest."

"Well, you earned it," Bobby said kindly. "I can't think of a single thing you did wrong today."

Ket shrugged. "As your mother said, it's not rocket science."

"Well, everyone seemed to like you, and I'm happy about that."

"Everyone except Victoria St. Louis."

"She hates everyone who's prettier than she is. Like I said, don't take it personally. If she ran into you on the street, she'd shriek with joy and kiss you on both cheeks. May I sit down for a moment?"

Ket nodded and Bobby sat at the edge of her bed. "Look, I've got to talk to you about something. When Jenny eloped, I thought the whole thing was a lark, Bryce Kilduff would tire of her, and she'd be back soon. It turns out, I was being both unfair and unkind. Bryce Kilduff really does love her, and she's moving to England with him. She called me today and told me. I'm glad because she's really happy, for the first time since I've known her. And she deserves it.

"But that leaves me without a script girl. Now, Mom told me that you were an engineer, a corporate bigshot. Why the hell would you want to be just a gofer for me?"

Ket yawned. "Please? A go-fer?"

"You know, doing what you do now, no real glory or anything like that."

"I'm part of the team," Ket replied. "The job gets done, that's the important thing."

Bobby chuckled. "Were you ever in the military? What you just said, it reminds me of the navy."

"As a matter of fact, I was in the army."

"You were? Well, all right!" He looked at her, puzzled. "Why would you want to be a grunt?"

Ket nodded to herself, aware that *grunt* was probably a pejorative term for soldier. Apparently, army/navy rivalry was not restricted to just her native part of the universe.

"My father was a soldier," she said truthfully. "Anyway, like you and Tom, the military paid for my education."

"Oh, you know about that, huh? Well, anyway. Here's the thing: I'd like you to work for me permanently. I know you're probably ridiculously overqualified, but I have a good feeling about you. Don't decide now. We'll be done with filming in nine weeks, and then another three months of postproduction. Tell me then."

Ket sat up in bed and looked penetratingly at Bobby. "I'll tell you now. I accept your offer."

"Are you sure?"

"Yes. I said I was making a life change, and this seems the proper direction for me to take. But under these conditions—"

"Conditions? What conditions?"

"I'll continue as script supervisor—let's call it the way you really see it, script *girl*—for the duration of this film. I'll do all the—donkey work?—you need. But in exchange, I want to learn everything you know."

"*Everything* I know?"

"Everything about the film business. I'm not a writer like you, or a director, but I want to know everything else. I finished at the top of my class at Tir—at school, and I'm a quick learner."

"I see," Bobby replied. "Is that all?"

"No. It's not all. I was watching everything that went on today. I went over the shot list, the budget, all of the books you had on the set."

"And what did you find?" Bobby asked. He had no idea who this extraordinarily businesslike person before him could be.

"Bobby, you write, you direct, and you produce. The first two, you obviously do better than anyone. The people on the set all seem to love you and respect you. But as a producer, you leave a great deal to be desired."

"Oh, I do, do I?" Bobby made a sincere, almost-successful effort to keep his voice neutral.

"Yes. Because there are so many minor details on the set with which you should not have to waste your time. I noticed that today. Too many delays! And as you told me, delays cost money. Bobby, it's as if you're a . . . general. You have a battle to win. But you can't be concerned with some little piece of equipment, or a thread out of place on some soldier's uniform. You have a staff for all that."

"So, what would you do?"

"I would handle those things. Right now, as a script girl, I don't have the authority. That's fine. I'll see to those things as best I can without it. *For the course of this picture.* Because after that, if I prove that I'm capable, I want to be your producer as well."

"Jesus! You don't want much, do you?"

"You're the one who said I was overqualified to be a script girl. Well, you were right. No general is worth a damn without a good chief of staff, and that's what I want to be. You told me that a producer is given a certain amount of money with which to make a picture, is that correct? And if the picture is completed without spending all of it, you get to keep it, correct?"

Bobby looked away from her. "Correct. Never happens, though. With Clint Eastwood, maybe, but that's about it."

"It will happen this time, Bobby. I promise you that. And from now on."

Bobby sat silent for a long time. To her amazement, Ket could read nothing of his senses. What was it about him that cloaked his feelings and made them opaque?

"You know, Kathy," he said after a long while, "if you go back on the set and start throwing your weight around, people will think we're sleeping together."

"We *are* sleeping together," Ket replied. "Just not in the same room."

"Yeah, okay, ha-ha, that's funny, but it's my integrity you're fooling with. I don't sleep with women on my pictures. It's unprofessional, and if I compromise on that, I lose respect, and deservedly so."

"Well, then I'll . . . uh . . . d—date someone else. No sex, however. I'm through with *that* for awhile."

"Why does that bother me," Bobby murmured, almost inaudibly.

Why does that bother *me*, Ket asked herself. And why *doesn't* it bother me that not once today did I ever think of Holak Ven, Nev Hederes, or my beloved Dalyi?

Thradon

TWENTY MONTHS AGO

6

FREE CITIZENS OF DALYI!

Do not lose heart! Freedom is at hand! The evil that has spread throughout our land cannot survive. Their victory is but fleeting, for although they have made this nation a prison, they cannot imprison the Dalyinese spirit! Therefore, love your brothers and sisters and do not hate your enemies. Instead, look upon them with pity, for their day is almost gone and ours is coming.

Long live Freedom! Long live Dalyi!

> *Ket Mhulhar, Premier*
> *Nev Hederes, Commander,*
> *Revolutionary Forces*

Celin Kwa crumpled the leaflet and tossed it away. "Paper," he mused. "How quaint." The Eberean military governor of Dalyi turned to his chief of staff. "How many of these did you find?"

"They were all over the city this morning," replied Pasa Henz. "They must have gone up during the night." She picked up the crumpled sheet. "What I want to know is, where'd they get the paper? No one's used paper for twelve hundred years."

"From a tree, I would imagine," Kwa replied testily.

"Should I launch spy probes?" Henz asked. "See if there are any forests that have been—"

"Useless, since many homes are without heat after we raided the solar banks, and I'm sure the nearby forests are denuded by now. No, don't waste your time. That's not the problem, anyway."

"Sir?"

"Look at the signatures, Henz. Whose names appear on this document?"

"Why, Ket Mhulhar, sir, the premier-in-exile, and the senior general, Hederes."

"Yes. Of course. And why am I not convinced?"

"Convinced of what, sir?"

"Have you studied her file? Do you know anything about the premier at all?"

"I commanded a battalion under her at Truska," Henz said. "She was quite capable."

"Capable, yes. But that wasn't the word I was looking for. No, what I was thinking was that she's . . . absent."

"Absent? As in, not here? But she's in hiding, sir."

"Is she? I thought you knew her, General."

"I do, sir. I did."

"Bring up the Mhulhar file," the governor ordered. In an instant, an entire wall was covered with all vital information concerning Ket Mhulhar. "Four months, General Henz! Four months since our glorious victory. And how much resistance activity has there been?"

"A trickle, Excellency. Some communications disrupted, some food and weapons hijacked. Minor inconveniences."

"To be expected," the governor affirmed. "And who led these incursions?"

"In all probability, sir, intelligence believes the chief perpetrator to be Colonel Holak Ven."

"Ven!" the governor snorted. "A fool! A mere flyboy! Of course it was Ven. That's all he's good for. Leading useless cavalry charges."

"He's very brave, Excellency."

"Yes, and handsome, too, isn't he, General?"

The General stood her ground. "Yes, Excellency, women do find him attractive. That's in his file, as well."

"Do *you* find him attractive, General?"

Henz paused before responding. "Yes, Excellency, I do. But that doesn't mean I won't hunt him down."

"Very good, General. Now, because you're too obtuse to get my point, I'll spell it out for you. There has been little revolutionary activity because the Revolution has not yet given itself an identity. There has been no rallying point for the rebels, and there should be. But Ket Mhulhar has been conspicuously absent since Dalyi fell. All we have are a few minor and ineffective raids, courtesy of Colonel Ven, and this impassioned tract which is the obvious brainchild of General Hederes. What is missing is a leader with the exceptional qualities of both men, and that is Ket Mhulhar. She is a tactical genius, a charismatic leader, and a warrior nonpareil. And her footprint is nowhere to be found in any of these puny efforts. Why? What is she waiting for? Well, Henz, I want to know where she is. If we stop her, we stop the Revolution for good and all."

"How, sir?"

"Triple the price on the head of Holak Ven. He is the most vulnerable and high-profile of the the rebel leaders. Offer with it safe passage out of the country. That should get one of his own people to turn him in."

Henz shook her head. "No Dalyinese would dare do that, sir."

"Cut all Dalyinese power rations in half," the governor ordered. "And delay all food shipments into the city for a month. Let's see just how much the Dalyinese people love him when they're cold and starving. This is critical, Henz. As soon as the Resistance begins in earnest, we might as well pack up and go home. I said as much to the Central Authority the moment we raised our flag over this building."

Henz was stunned. "I don't understand, sir. I thought our victory was total."

Kwa laughed sardonically. "We are a small, poor country occupying a big rich country. We can only rule through terror, and those who survive soon become accustomed to it. You can get used to anything, Henz. We've proven that."

"But, sir, we've destroyed their army—"

"Have we? We killed their senior generals, most of them. Very well. There are still millions of veteran soldiers out there. When they become united, when they are supplied with weapons from hidden caches, when they once again reassume their vaunted Dalyinese military discipline, they'll defeat us in short order."

"Sir!" Henz was mortified.

"Henz, there's a reason why Dalyi has never lost a war. And that reason is that they are so well trained that any corporal could command a regiment if he had to. Remember Ket Mhulhar at Mount Ugon? I certainly do; I was wounded in the first wave that attacked down the mountain. And their navy; there are still four invincible ships of the line somewhere in the world, waiting for orders to sail against us. No, we cannot possibly hope to ever really win. Do I shatter your illusions, Henz?"

"No, sir," she replied miserably. Of course he had shattered her illusions—shattered them beyond repair.

"Henz, you're a soldier. Your decorations speak most eloquently of your bravery. Do you really belong here?"

"Sir, it's for my country—"

"Do you know what it means to occupy a nation, Henz? Do you really see yourself rounding up innocent civilians, murdering thirty of them because some wild-eyed revolutionary threw a grenade at a personnel transport?"

"Absolutely not, sir!" she was horrified. "Do you?"

"I'll be honest, Henz, because I respect you as a soldier. I have been . . . merciful, up to this point, but I'm not sure why. Is it because I find it so distasteful? Or is it merely because I know in my heart there will be a day of reckoning?"

"Sir? Why then, why are we here?"

"Because we're led by fools—those who believe that being right guarantees a total and permanent victory. And bigger fools we for following their orders."

"I don't know what to say, sir."

"Welcome to the real world, Henz. Glory is delicious, victory even more so, but real life always intrudes. Get used to it."

• • •

"This is a stupid plan, Holak," Nev Hederes argued.

"Oh, it's completely asinine, Nev. It's also suicidal." Holak Ven adjusted his body armor and checked the action on his pulsor.

"If they catch you, they'll make you talk. You know they will. And if you talk, we're all dead. And so is the Resistance."

"It won't matter if I talk. You'll be gone from here long before they can launch a search-and-destroy team. Just remember to blow the grid."

"Holak. You're the most wanted man in Dalyi. We can't risk you."

"I'm the only one who knows the comm-codes. It has to be me."

In the four months since the Ebereans seized power, Nev, Holak, and the rest of the Revolutionary Council had lived as the fugitives they were, rarely staying in one place for more than a week at a time. This peripatetic existence had not been good for the Revolution. They had thus far been unable to coordinate with other Resistance cells throughout the country, and the Revolution had therefore stalled. Despite a few guerilla raids by Holak Ven and a few others, the Revolution, as the Eberean commander had stated, still lacked an identity.

The Dalyinese people were confused. They could not believe that their entire army, the finest that all of Thradon had ever seen, was completely gone. The Dalyinese Navy, that is, its few surviving ships, were far across the seas, waiting beneath the surface for a signal to return and fight. But the Army? Where were they?

The Dalyinese people desperately wanted to fight back but they needed guidance. They needed a leader. They needed a battle cry. Where were they going to find one?

Tonight was going to change all that.

The council was in deep hiding at a national forest preserve called Alvo Denor, some sixty clics east of Kasma Dor. In this heavily wooded, lightly mountainous region, Eberean spy probes were rendered ineffective. But while the preserve offered a safe haven for the rebels, it also hampered their ability to wage guerilla war. They were too distant from the enemy stronghold in Kasma

Dor, so that their already feeble supply line was stretched too thin, and raiders had too far to travel without risk of exposure.

Although Holak Ven had a well-earned reputation as a great pilot who was nevertheless hot tempered and easily bored, it was less than common knowledge he was also one of the most accomplished military historians in Dalyi. It was this strength alone that made him, although a mere colonel, an indispensable advisor to General Hederes. In between raids, he had studied indepth revolutionary movements throughout his planet's history. Unfortunately, he believed, so had the Ebereans, which would prepare them for anything the rebels might attempt.

Therefore, he had drawn on his knowledge of Earth history, and, in a private session with Nev Hederes, had put forth a strategy.

"There's an Earth nation," he had told Hederes, "a country called Ir-land. Eyer-land? Whatever. Anyway, Nev, they were occupied by a country called Bri-tan. And all they wanted was their freedom, a chance to become their own nation."

"And did they?" Nev had asked him.

"Here's what happened. For hundreds of years, a relatively small band of rebels would get together and pull some sort of stunt—kill some Bri-tan soldiers, blow up a Bri-tan government building. But they were too few, and their enemies were too strong."

"That doesn't sound very promising."

"It wasn't, and I'll tell you why. The *people* weren't united behind them. It quite frankly didn't occur to many Ir-land people that they were supposed to even *be* a free country. So, about a hundred or so Earth years ago, a group was formed, a group determined to fight for independence. They called the group Ourselves Alone."

"Ourselves Alone? I sort of like that."

"Well, you see, the Ir-lands spoke the same language as the Bri-tans, but the Ir-lands actually had an ancient language of their own, which the Bri-tans had outlawed."

Nev glared in distaste. "How do you outlaw a language? I've never heard of anything so ridic—"

"Well, like it or not, they did. In their own language, their group was called, what was it? I don't know if I can pronounce it—Shin Fin. Shine Feen? Oh, Sinn Féin. That's what it was."

"You are going to get to the point eventually, aren't you, Holak?"

"Yeah, it's simply this. The people had to be educated—they had to be given the rationale: Hey, we're our own people, we need our own country. Well, a lot of the members of the group wanted action, military action. But the smarter leaders said, 'What's the point, if the people don't support it? First, let's celebrate our own language, our own culture, even our own sports. Give the people the *identity* of Ir-landers. Once you accomplish that, then the people will say, "Hey, what are these Bri-tans doing here? Who are they to tell us what to do? Let's kick 'em out!"' "

"So, Holak, did it work?"

"Well—"

"*Did it?*"

"Well, yeah, after a fashion. Because a lot of the hotheads still used violence anyway, and it got really bloody and took a long time. But did they win their independence? Yes. Earth is full of history like that."

Hederes sighed. "So, I'll ask you one more time: What's your point?"

"Anything we do, Nev, has been done before. But not this. Not a revolution like there has been on Earth—in fact the Ebere-ans don't know a thing about Earth. They can't put anything we pull like this in the databanks for comparison and analysis, because it's never been done before."

"So what do we do then, Holak?"

"We go to the people. That is, you go to the people. You speak to them whenever you can, wherever you can. Stress *Dalyi* and nothing else. Our national pride, our history, *our* culture and *our* sports! Then, when we complete that phase, we'll be ready to fight!"

Nev Hederes considered that for awhile. "It sounds as if this could take awhile," he said finally.

"It could take a long while," Holak said. "But look at what we're fighting; a powerful, ruthless enemy, one who is in control of all propaganda. If we just hit them with raids, they can get on the comm-channels and make us look like animals. That's where you come in, Nev. And that's why we can't use violence until we're sure the people are ready for it."

Nev Hederes took a long look at his friend, unable to shake the eerie feeling that he was seeing him for the last time. He gripped Holak by his shoulders.

"Holak," he said. "I beg you. Be careful."

Holak affected his usual devil-may-care grin but the effect was a hollow one. "Forget it, Nev. I'll be fine. Just make the most of what you are about to do."

The single-use jump-packs attached to Holak Ven's feet had undergone a great deal of development since their use at Mount Ugon sixty years before. Although their basic function—that of powered airborne descent—had not been altered, it had been expanded. The jump-packs were now able to sustain lateral airborne movement for a short distance, depending upon wind current, the height of the drop, and the distance to the landing zone.

In this case, fifty-nine clics from Alvo Denor's highest point to the roof of the Kasma Dor Central Comm Building, total flight was possible, but only for a highly experienced pilot like Holak Ven. But Holak would have to use every bit of his intimate knowledge of local wind conditions, the topography of the land, and his ability to sight and avoid detector arrays.

Much of it depended upon a successful lauch from the peak of Alvo Denor, some forty-four hundred meters above sea level. He would jump off at dusk, at a point one thousand meters below the peak, circle the mountain on the wind's back, and ride the tidal wave of air that blasted toward the city. He would then glide for twenty-three clics to conserve power until he reached the outer marker of the Kasma Dor exburb, Duprana. Then he would have to jettison the small energy sources and shoot straight into Kasma Dor and onto the roof of his target building.

A sound and simple plan. Which was why Holak Ven *always* had a backup. He had lived through too many missions, in both peace and war, to fully trust any single plan. Because in his experience, they seldom worked.

In this case, he was absolutely correct. The launch around

Mount Alvo went off swimmingly, although Holak felt like a leaf caught in a whirlpool. He shot out of the mountain pass at a speed that plastered his face to his skull. He was feeling a sense of self-congratulations, tempered with caution, when it happened.

A faint blue light, the telltale trace of a detector array below, had just become barely discernible when the jump-pack on his left leg malfunctioned. Like the effect of a windmilling propeller on a twin-engined aircraft, the faulty pack began to pull him downward. He desperately battled a growing panic as he fought to locate the release mechanism.

Yet, Holak Ven was not renowned throughout the planet for nothing. Even as a young pilot, when he wisely ignored his ADF signal over Mount Ugon, Holak's instincts had been virtually flawless. In this instance, even as he plummeted groundward, fighting the release mechanism and trying with all his might to remain on course toward the city while desperately avoiding overflight of the detector array, even with all this threatening to consume him, a part of his mind was humming away, consolidating his alternate plan.

Holak finally activated the release button. The jump-pack was blown away into the slipstream at once, the remaining pack shooting him all about the sky like a deflating party balloon. He was just able to right himself when he looked below and saw the Kasma Dor Flyer, the evening commuter-monorail, passing beneath him. Without another thought, he jettisoned the pack and launched himself groundward, racing both the commuter-liner and the detector beam in a last desperate effort.

With a painful thump that jarred his teeth, he slammed into the monorail's rear section just as the detector array was about to emit an intruder alert. He smiled with grim satisfaction as the rail passed Cabwerlon station, from which point it would run nonstop.

"And just think," Holak shouted into the wind as he clung with all his might to a tiny handhold, "that was the easy part!"

•   •   •

Captain Groula Feeh, aide-de-camp to General Nev Hederes, approached his commander and saluted.

"Any news, Feeh?" Nev asked.

"None at this time," Feeh replied. "All seems to be going according to schedule." Feeh was still somewhat awed by his new job as aide to the great man himself. Only two years out of Tira Gen, Feeh, who was a second lieutenant when the Ebereans made their move four months before, had been promoted to Nev's staff by virtue of the simple fact that there was no one else left. At the time of the invasion, he had been AWOL, trying to track down a girlfriend who had dumped him for another. Had he been where he was supposed to be, he would now be dead like everyone else in his unit. It was a powerful sense of guilt that was turning him into something he had never been before: a good soldier.

"Is the comm-channel ready?"

"Aye-aye, sir. We're just waiting for Colonel Ven's signal."

"Very well, Captain. How do I look?"

Feeh was momentarily taken aback by such a question, as it was posed by the most senior officer in the army to the most junior and probably least worthy. However, the one thing Feeh could do well was butter people up.

"You look like a general, sir," Feeh replied smugly, overjoyed that he had come up with such an answer on short notice.

Nev had been greased by oilier customers than this young pup, but he decided to let it pass. There were more urgent matters at hand.

"Very well," he said. "Let's get this Revolution off the pad. We've got work to do."

The commuter-rail, once it entered the city proper, climbed a five-clic track skyward until it reached the perimeter rail girding all of Kasma Dor. The track circled the city once and then darted in and out at various neighborhoods. High-speed lifts brought debarking passengers safely to street level.

For Holak Ven, whose fingers were now in agony because their rapidly depleting strength was all that stood between him and eternity, the climb up the rail merely prolonged his own inevitable doom. But he couldn't think about that now. He was currently working out a math problem in his head. A problem he tried to solve as if his life depended upon it, because it did.

The mono rounds the Grevas Circle going, what seventy, eighty? Okay, I weigh—I must have lost fifteen or twenty since going into hiding. So that means I have to—Oh, God, here we go . . .

Because it was off-hours, the mono was able to round the circle at a much higher speed than normal, a speed so high that its slipstream supported Holak's body parallel off the rear section.

The fashionable Grevas Theatre, where he and Ket had spent so many enjoyable evenings together in her private box, loomed up ahead. That meant that the Central Comm Building was drawing near. *Just around this next curve,* Holak thought, *and then I can . . . now!*

Holak released his deathgrip and was tossed like a pebble into the mass of buildings below. Praying fiercely that his calculations were at least somewhat correct, Holak rolled into a ball and let the impetus carry him past the highest windows of Kasma Dor's tallest buildings. Had it not been dark, he would have provided dinner conversation for every office worker in the Grevas district.

He struck the roof of the Comm Building with such force that he thought at first that he had broken most of his limbs. But after a few minutes, he realized that he was more or less whole and slowly rose to take on the job at hand. The famous Dalyi Comm Channel rose high into the air before him. From this one spot, as well as another in Sha'n Res and two more in Kuran Il and Lansa, the government could speak to the entire nation. When activiated, every home would receive a signal to turn on their viewers. It was much like a television with only one station, or a video security camera. That was the extent of video on Thradon.

Holak worked quickly, programming the channel for its remote broadcast. *Just a little longer and . . . ready! Okay, Nev, you're on!*

• • •

"Signal, General Hederes!" said Captain Feeh.

"He actually did it," mused Nev. "All right, am I on?"

"Right . . . now," a technician said.

"Brothers and sisters of Dalyi!" Nev began. "Tonight, we begin our journey on the long road back to freedom!"

Okay, that was fine, Nev thought to himself, but is that what my countrymen really need to hear? What journey?

Nev saw that the captain and the technician were both signalling to him frantically. What for, he thought. No one's going anywhere.

"My friends," he said, removing all traces of oratory from his voice, "as you all know, the absolute nightmare of national nightmares has occured. Your nation is in the hands of the most ruthless and despicable enemy we have ever faced. I think we can all agree that our situation is beyond desperate.

"All is lost. Many are dead. A hated foreign flag has been raised atop our sacred soil. Be assured, we are at the very nadir of our eight-thousand year history . . ."

"Interesting," Celin Kwa remarked. "The Resistance finally speaks."

"Get a search-and-destroy team to the Comm Building at once!" Pasa Henz shouted to her aide, just as the military governor's private comm-line sparked into life. If there was any truth to what Kwa had told her before, the occupation of Dalyi had just reached its high-water mark. It would be all downhill from here.

"Wait," commanded Celin Kwa. He spoke into the line on his desk. "Who is this?"

"Celin Kwa, long time, no hear, you miserable sack of sh—"

"Well, Colonel Ven!" Kwa replied heartily. "I was wondering when we'd hear from you. I see General Hederes is emerging from Ket Mhulhar's considerable shadow at last. How long do you expect to keep him on line?"

"As long as it takes, Celin. And tell Pasa Henz not to bother sending an S&D team, or I'll blow the whole comm channel."

"Why would I care if you blow it or not?"

"Come on, Celin, how would it look? How are you going to

spread enough propaganda to counter what Nev is doing right now if you're off the line?"

"You know you're a dead man, Colonel Ven," Pasa Henz said.

"Pasa? Pasa Henz? Is that you? Hey, did we ever—"

"Please, Colonel. What do you hope to accomplish?"

"I've already accomplished it, sweet-cheeks. Listen!"

". . . but this fight is not over," Nev continued. "The question now is, how can we possibly win? My friends, the answer is that we have *already* won. It is against Thradonian nature to be ruled by force. It may take time, but in that time, they grow weaker and we grow stronger. It doesn't happen overnight, but take it as a given, it does happen. We must first begin by going against our very nature, and understand that when we win this war, we and the Ebereans can never be reconciled. They have chosen the path of hatred. Therefore, you must believe that once we chase them from our shores, our nation will shut them out forever. There will be no diplomatic ties, not in our lifetime. There will be no trade, no cultural exchange, no welcome for any Eberean through our doors anytime in the foreseeable future. Understand that. Any love or comradeship you have ever felt for Ebereans must be banished from your very souls!"

"He's talking as if they're actually going to win!" Pasa Henz exclaimed.

"Of course he is," Kwa said. "Because he's right."

"Then why are we here? Why don't we go home now and avoid a lot of pointless bloodshed?"

Kwa smiled ironically. "We've come this far, General. There are, after all, certain niceties to be observed."

Nev Hederes picked up a pulse gun and slammed the action home. "Yes, we will win. We have a hard fight ahead. But before we fight with this," he added, extending the gun toward his invisible audience, "we must first fight them with this, and with this," continued, pointing to his heart and his head.

"Therefore, from this day forward, the order of the day is Dalyi, Dalyi . . . DALYI! Speak no language but our own. Keep our culture alive! Our theatre, our poetry, even our silliest songs and filthiest jokes. Play no sport but those that originated here in this land. Dine only on our national dishes, wear only our native styles, and remember to fight! Fight with your heart, fight with your head, and fight with your spirit!

"My time with you is limited. Those who occupy our nation, those who worship dishonor, are at this very moment attempting to still my voice. But it is too late! The fight has already begun—"

"Good enough," Holak Ven muttered as he switched off the power-grid. As planned, the people of Dalyi would attribute sudden disruption as an Eberean attempt to silence Nev Hederes.

"You're off, General," the technician said.

"Good," Nev sighed in relief. "It's really not my forte."

Captain Feeh, who had been uncharacteristically spellbound, saluted his general. "I'm sorry, sir, but if you'll pardon the liberty . . . I think we've all discovered that this is *exactly* your forte."

"Colonel Ven," Kwa called, "are you still there?"

"Come and get me, you Eberean crud, I ain't going anywhere."

"You've finally said something I can agree with, Colonel," Kwa replied as the S&D team crashed through the roof.

Holak Ven nodded at the pulse guns pointing at his head. "See you in a few minutes, Celin. By the way, I could use a cold one . . ."

Holak Ven was thrown roughly to the floor at Celin Kwa's feet.

"Oh, don't get up on my account," Kwa said.

"Not a problem," Holak wheezed, trying to regain his wind as he struggled to his feet. "Pasa, my love. You're looking radiant as ever. Oh, I forgot. Nev said, from now on it's a no-no. My loss."

"I must congratulate you," Kwa said. "General Hederes's speech was a master stroke. Who would have thought he had such charisma?"

"Just about everyone who's ever met him," Holak retorted, even though he was every bit as surprised as Kwa.

"An ideological victory first," remarked Kwa, "quite an original idea. I wonder whose it was."

Holak shrugged. "You got me," he said.

"Still, there's something that concerns me. General Hederes's eloquence notwithstanding . . . I truly underestimated him and for that I apologize . . . but through all of this, where is the premier?"

"Who?"

"The premier. Your former lover. Your best friend. Ket Mhulhar. Where is she?"

"She's . . . around."

"Oh, come off it! Nothing! Nothing from her in four months! The highest ranking survivor of your government—Dalyi's most venerated officer alive . . . and she's nowhere to be found! *Ket Mhulhar*? In hiding? Not to have led a single action? Not to have made a single speech? Ket Mhulhar? Nonsense!"

"Well, she's the boss, Celin. We can't risk her."

"Perhaps. Or perhaps not. But I find her absence . . . significant. Guards! Take him below. Find out what he knows."

"There's nothing to find out, Celin. But you're welcome to try. Pasa! Maybe you'll drop by my dungeon some night."

"Get him out of here," Henz said.

"Oh, come on, don't be that way . . . " The guards led Holak from the room.

"This is serious trouble," Kwa said.

"Sir, it's nothing. One speech on the central comm does not make a revolution. Besides, Holak will soon talk and—"

"Henz, you're a fool! Of course he'll talk! He'll tell us where to find the leaders of the Resistance. But they'll be gone from wherever they are by the time the S&D teams get there. Who

cares? Until five minutes ago they were nothing. They led no
one. And now . . . the people of Dalyi have been invested with
the full-fledged *romance* of revolution!"

"But, sir—"

"I know these people, Henz! I was ambassador to this country for ten years! The Dalyinese are fighters! And because they
are generous winners, we consider them weak. But they are not!
Don't you realize that everytime a Dalyinese child says 'good
morning' in his own language, he will consider himself a freedom fighter? When a woman puts on a Duprana sash with
evening wear, she will be throwing a stone at us? When a gang
of boys and girls play Hokara-ball, they will be thumbing their
noses at us? Hederes has given everyone a stake in the Resistance! It's brilliant! And it's *never* been done before."

"So? What can we do? We can't execute everyone in this
country. We can't even arrest everyone. How can you fight an
idea?"

The governor turned to her suddenly.

"My God, Henz! You've just hit it! Although, knowing you,
not on purpose. That's it! How do you fight an idea? Only one
way: With *another* idea."

"And what is that other idea?" Henz asked, still smarting
from the governor's insult.

The governor sagged visibly. "That's the problem. An alto-
gether separate and different problem."

"Leave us," Pasa Henz ordered the guards outside Holak Ven's
cell.

"Pasa!" Holak smiled weakly. "Took me up on it after all!"

"Is that *all* you ever think about?" Pasa retorted, looking
frankly at the damage interrogators had wrought on Holak's body.
As usual, most of the injuries were internal, except for a considerable amount of dried blood on his face.

She pressed a code key and the air-barrier lifted. She went
in the cell and sat on the bed next to where Holak lay.

"How are you feeling?" she asked him.

"Oh, come on, General," he snapped. "You don't *really* care,
do you?"

"Very well," she replied briskly. "Forgive me for intruding." She tried to get up but Holak pulled her down by the arm. Then he let her go suddenly and chuckled to himself. "God damn," he said, "I *love* women! You creeps are torturing *me,* and yet I'm supposed to be apologizing to *you* for acting huffy!" He hardened. "Let's knock it off, Pasa. You didn't come in here to take my temperature. Your goons couldn't get me to talk, now they're trying the honey-trap? Get real!"

"You could save yourself a lot of trouble, Holak."

"You mean I could save *you* a lot of trouble."

"All right, yes, you could."

"And how would I go about that?"

"Tell us where we can find Ket Mhulhar."

Holak closed his eyes and turned away from her. "Oh, yeah. I'm just about to tell you that."

Pasa shook her head, even though Holak was facing away from her and the gesture was wasted.

"I'm very sorry, Holak," she said. "You were right, you know. I would have taken you up on your offer. I always did find you attractive. I remember, twenty years ago at Truska, you were—"

"Spare me, General," Holak said. "You have your orders. And if you enjoy carrying them out, well, that's an added bonus. Well guess what, General. If it were still an hour ago, you and I would have been bouncing off the walls of this dump. But I have my orders. You're an Eberean. End of story . . . end of romance."

"Oh, come on, Holak. That'll never stick."

"Maybe. But it will with me."

"You're a fool, Holak," Henz said, rising quickly. "A handsome fool . . . God knows, a sexy fool . . . but a fool. And I don't sleep with fools, not even for my country."

Holak leaned back and rested on his hands. "Well, I guess that makes us even, Pasa. I won't sleep with fools for your country, either."

The idea came to Celin Kwa in the middle of the night. "I have it!" he shouted, frightening his two concubines enough for them to fall out of bed. He shouted for his aide, who was somehow fully dressed and immediately available. Together they labored far into the night for the address they would give in the morning. After that, the governor would leave for a weekend of carousing in Srho, which had become just as popular with the Eberean military as it had been with the Dalyinese. He felt he had earned it.

"To my liberated brothers and sisters of Dalyi: I salute you," began Celin Kwa's address to the nation. "A matter of great urgency has just come to my attention, a matter that will shock and sadden all of us here in the Dalyinese Territory of the Eberean Sphere of Influence.

"Last night, you were no doubt as amused as I to hear the fanciful remarks of the cashiered General Hederes. The rants and raves of a poor lunatic are always listened to with a grain of salt. After all, the pathetic, deluded fool was once touched with greatness. And who can he harm? What damage can he possibly do? Precious little, we all believe, and so we listen with an amused ear.

"But, my brothers and sisters, there has been damage—grave damage, the way insanity can cause a murder—unintended, but still, there lies a body!

"My friends . . . this lunatic has wrought irreparable damage to all of us here in Dalyi. He destroyed a national resource we can never, ever replace.

"General Hederes has murdered Ket Mhulhar."

Earth

PRESENT DAY

7

The object of Celin Kwa's oratory was of course alive, but living in an incarnation no one on Thradon could possibly have envisioned. From the very height of the Dalyinese political and military world, her universe had shrunk to the cocoon of a film set. From a responsibility for millions, her life was now consumed with what would be considered mere trifles, the work of perhaps a supply coporal. And what no one, not even her closest friends could have possibly imagined, she was having the time of her life.

Becoming an army officer in Dalyi was no small achievement. Only the very best and the very brightest were even considered. If a candidate were selected, the Officer's Training Program that followed would put her or him through eight years of tortuous challenge. Therefore, by the time a newly appointed officer pinned on the single delta of a second lieutenant and arrived at his or her first posting, he or she knew that they were someone truly special. There was a swagger, a confidence, and a powerful aura that surrounded every officer. And when a group of officers were together, they attracted admiration and envy that was almost palpable.

For Ket Mhulhar, movie people radiated that same aura.

She couldn't figure out why, but it was true. Few of these people could have survived eight years—or even one year—at Tira Gen. Many were weak, indecisive, and completely self-centered. But despite these shortcomings, there was an intense commitment—not only to the film itself—but to the entire world of the movies. Like army officers in Dalyi, movie people had that same larger-than-life presence—a presence she had heard referred to as *star quality*. And like the Dalyinese Army, the film business was not an easy place to gain entrée for a career. Apparently, Ket had learned, her finding this position with Bobby Albertson was a stroke of luck not to be believed. Again, she couldn't understand what the big deal was, but it seemed true. The movies—or "show biz," as they called it, which also included the theatre and that thing called TV—was as difficult to become a part of as the Army was in Dalyi.

Frank Cosimo, Senior Master Chief USN (Ret.), was not the sort of fellow who was used to seeing a woman on a regular basis as "just a friend," but for an odd reason he couldn't figure out, it didn't bother him.

He had been dating Kathy Miller, Bobby Albertson's script girl, for over a month now. Well, it wasn't really dating, at that. Just occassional dinners or a few quiet drinks. He had yet to lay a hand on her, which he knew in his heart was something that was never going to happen. The question was, why didn't that bother him? Although he was fast closing in on sixty, he was in excellent condition and looked much younger, and except for his cruises at sea, he had never gone without female companionship. Especially now that he was a movie star, with a Golden Globe (best supporting actor) and two Oscar nominations (also in support).

It still handed him a pretty big laugh. If you went back thirty-five years, especially when he was a young seaman deuce on board the USS *Forrestal*, on that horrible day that still gave him the night sweats, the day a sidewinder from an A4 Skyhawk blew off on the carrier deck and turned the ship into an inferno—if you had told that frightened kid from East Portsmouth, Ohio, that he would not only live through this day, but that he would even survive to become a goddamned *movie star,* well, he'd have shown you straight through to the nearest shrink's office.

But it happened. The Big Warrant Officer in the Sky had rolled the bones and assigned a gangly kid from L.A. named Bobby Albertson to the USS *Algonquin,* where he would serve under Big Frank Cosimo, the meanest, toughest, smartest swingin' pole in the navy—and there the cocky bastard would get right under his skin.

Big Frank Cosimo was not actually all that big—he was of medium height, but with ropy muscles that gave him agility, endurance, and leverage. It was his quiet self-assurance that gave rise to his nickname. There was simply no situation that could possibly occur in which Big Frank wouldn't know exactly what to do, because Big Frank handled every situation exactly the same way, whether it applied to the navy or to show business: Shut up and pay attention. If you did that, you succeeded in the navy. If you did that, you succeeded as an actor.

He had so far shut up and paid attention to Kathy Miller. The woman fascinated him like no other in his life. In three short months, she had become indispensible to Bobby, subtly trimming away at all of the duties that had distracted him in the past and taking them on herself. She had a gift for organization, that was sure. Things just got done before anyone even knew it. Now Bobby gave his full and undivided attention to his directorial efforts, and the results so far were electrifying. This picture was shaping up to be his best ever. The dailies were becoming as crowded as premieres, with everyone on the set attending, just because they couldn't wait to see the day's work on the screen. If the film was edited right, the buzz on the set went, Bobby had a nomination in the bag.

That was probably crap, thought Frank wryly, but he did understand the effect of good morale, and that, he believed to be a good thing. And Kathy Miller, he believed, was the one responsible.

She had chosen him, Frank thought, because she thought he was safe. He wasn't kidding himself about that. That wasn't the point, anyway. The point was, why had she chosen him at all?

Why a platonic relationship with a man almost twice her age—
and why did the man twice her age put up with it?

The fact was, Kathy was a good pal. She seemed not to want
anything from him except his company. And in return, she was
okay company herself. It was funny, but that's what it felt like
when he was with her—like hoisting a few with an old service
buddy. She could knock them back like a real sailor, too, and
not ever show it. Always matched him drink for drink, and not
sissy-assed white wine, either, but real guy stuff—Irish whiskey,
nondesigner beer, even a little tequila when the mood hit. And
he could talk to her about anything—old war stories, the bars,
brawls, and brothels from the Med to the Phillipines, and she
took it all in like any old pal with hashmarks up to his elbows.
Kathy was even one of the few people in the world whom he
talked with about the USS *Forrestal* and the most harrowing
day of his life. And she seemed to understand. Well, Bobby had
said she had done a tour in the army. Maybe that was it.

They were shooting a scene in a particularly bleak, deserted
shipyard in Long Beach. Frank was not in this particular shot,
so he stood behind Bobby, Kathy, and the cameraman, as had
become his custom. Directing had always been a sweet mystery
to him, and it was interesting to watch the action from Bobby's
point of view.

But as usual, he found himself watching Kathy more than
the scene being shot. To him, she was more fun to watch. She
wore her usual work uniform of jeans, a denim work shirt, and
Reeboks. He had long since noticed that during a scene, her
head would cock slightly to the right when she was concentrating intently.

Everyone else on the set was watching her, too. The fact was,
no one could figure out what the hell was going on between her
and Bobby. Everybody knew that she was staying with him at
his condo in Santa Monica. At first, everyone of course took it
for granted that the two were sleeping together. It seemed obvious. Here was a guy who never delegated a lick of work in
his life—even in the navy the amount of work he took on for
himself had gained him Frank's appreciation and recommenda-
tions for promotion—and here Kathy had virtually taken on every
nondirectorial duty Bobby had. This, coupled with the fact that

the whole crew thought she and Bobby were busting the nightly bed, gave her extraordinary powers on the set. She had this incredible authority about her that still got things done even after she had begun spending evenings with Frank himself and the crew would have to revise their estimate about her sex life.

In the end, however, once the novelty wore off, people just stopped thinking about it. Ket got the job done, and that was that. They had even begun referring to her as simply *Bobby's Girl.* "Ah, don't worry, Bobby's Girl will take care of it." "Get ahold of Bobby's Girl, she'll clear this up." "Don't bother Bobby with this crap, get Kathy, you know, Bobby's Girl, she'll handle it."

Of course, there was one particular situation that no one would have expected Bobby's Girl to handle. Victoria St. Louis, the troubled, gifted, and difficult star of the film, failed to show up for a day's filming. A check of her trailer found her missing. No one quite knew what to do. Filming was halted as everyone on the set flew off in a thousand directions trying to find her.

Ket simply asked her friend and favorite gossip source, Bonnie the makeup artist, what she thought might have happened.

Bonnie held up a copy of the *National Enquirer.* On the cover was a picture of the actress's beloved, Chuck Hansen, entering a London eatery with a British supermodel.

"Is there any truth to this?" Ket asked Bonnie.

"Uh, yah," Bonnie replied. "But hell-o, it's the *Enquirer.* This picture is six months old, because everybody knows Maura is like mondo-preggers. And also, any moron would know, Chuck and Maura weren't eating alone. See the hand on her other arm? That's her husband on the other side, cut out of the picture."

"So, Chuck is still true?" Ket asked.

"I didn't say that. Just this picture is crap, that's all."

"Where can we go to find her, Bonnie. You've seen this before."

"The closest dive bar. Someplace where they'll land on her like a fuzzy-cheeked kid in C-block. Come on, I'll go with you."

Ket still had no legal driver's license, so she was glad that Bonnie had offered. The picture was now an hour behind schedule. Hopefully, she could clear this up quickly. She shrugged to herself. This too, was like the army; a typical situation for a young platoon leader or company commander, making a special, unofficial effort to get one of her troopers out of trouble.

"This looks like it," Bonnie said, "there's her car. Who'd be, like stupid enough to park a Lexus on the street in a neighborhood like this?"

"Thank you, Bonnie," Ket said. "There's no need for you to—"

"Nuh-uh!" Bonnie contradicted her. "You've obviously never seen old Vic when she's hammered."

" 'Hammered?' "

"Wasted. Loaded. Pissed to the gills? Drunk, Kathy."

"I see."

"If she gets half in the bag, we have to sit with her until she drinks enough to pass out. Otherwise, she starts screaming hysterically if you try to hustle her out of there."

The name of the bar was the Stupid Elf, illustrated by a neon logo of a rolling eyed, slavering-tongued imp overhanging the entry door. Once inside, Ket Mhulhar felt more at home than she ever had since the day she blasted off the pad at Cresvo Denor.

As a soldier, especially during her early years in the army, Ket had spent many of her off-duty hours in sleazy bars frequented by the tough customers who dwell at the lower regions of the food chain. It was all part of army life, a twelve-hour pass, all the liquor you could stand, maybe a brawl or two before a quick dalliance, and back to the base. This place seemed no different in character.

There was a long, scarred bar down one side of the room, and on the other was a pool table, an electronic dartboard, and a few tables. A long banner across the bar pronounced that *The Soviet Union didn't fall, it just moved to Sacramento.* Although it was midday, the place was doing a thriving business. From what Ket could make out, most of the characters in here seemed just barely on the other side of prison.

"Damn," Bonnie whispered to her, "this place looks like scumbag-heaven. I'll bet even cops don't come in here without backup."

"We'll be fine, Bonnie," Ket said. "Don't worry."

Victoria St. Louis was sitting alone at the bar, downing a shot and a beer. So far, the men were leaving her alone, although most darted furtive looks in her direction.

"Thank God," Bonnie said. "No one's hit on her yet. They're probably still a little nervous, 'cause she's a big star and all."

"Is that what usually happens?"

"At first. Then after she has a few more, she gets pissed that she's still alone."

Ket nodded and the two walked across the room and took stools on each side of the dejected actress. The bartender, a florid-faced ex-cop, placed drink napkins for them.

"Three lovely ladies, and all in one day! Should I be surprised that you're all friends?"

"Would it be a waste of my time," Bonnie began, "to ask if you have any white zinfandel?"

"It so happens, my auburn beauty, that my house zinfandel has won the plaudits of at least two people—though, perhaps not that many. You'll be amused at its impudence. And for the lovely blonde?"

"Just a draft, thank you." Earth spirits did little for Ket, which was why she could drink all night with Frank Cosimo and not show it. A cold beer, she had discovered, was at least refreshing.

The bartender nodded, and turned to fill their order.

"Hey!" Victoria St. Louis called. "What about me?"

The bartender turned and smiled inscrutibly at Bonnie and Ket. "We're old friends," he said. "Now, Ms. St. Louis, as I have often told you, and as you have every bit as often ignored— cheap, rotgut whiskey should be savored, or else how can you enjoy the experience?"

The bartender gave Ket and Bonnie another glance this time— the significance of which only Ket understood. The bartender was simply acknowledging that Victoria was under his protection, at least while she remained in control.

Oh, Holak, Ket thought to herself, here's something else that you should have included in your "Some Things Are Universal" lecture. Bars.

"So, Vic," Bonnie said. "How's it going?"

Victoria St. Louis, already a bit loaded, turned slowly to Bonnie, and then to Ket. "What the hell are you doing here?" she demanded.

"Thought we'd have a drink," Bonnie replied, as the bartender set their drinks down before them. Bonnie took a sip and winced. "Who were the two people?" she asked the bartender.

"Drunks," he replied.

"Victoria," Ket began, "you must get back to the set. Everyone is waiting for you."

"Don't give a goddamn," Victoria replied, downing a shot and pushing the glass toward the bartender.

Bonnie leaned back and caught Ket's eye behind Victoria. "Don't argue with her," she whispered.

"I heard what you said, Bonnie," Victoria mumbled. "Don't treat me like a goddamn drunk. Hey, Buzz! 'Nother shot!"

The bartender was there in a flash, refilling her shotglass. "Nothing personal, Vic, my pet—"

"What're you gonna say? 'Don't you think you've had enough?' Jesus! Get some new material!"

Buzz affected a hurt look. "Child! You've wounded me to the heart! What I was going to say was, 'don't you think you should get the hell out of here? I can only hold off these psychos for so long.'"

Victoria turned on her barstool and addressed the bar at large. "You hear that? He said you're all psychos!"

"Thank you, Victoria," Buzz replied cheerfully.

"Good one, Vic," Bonnie groaned.

One of the larger and less charitable-looking of the assemblage stood up and approached the bar. "You callin' me a psycho?" he demanded of Buzz.

"Oh, like you're not," Buzz replied. "Sit down, Stoney. You know better than that."

Stoney seemed mollified and returned to his seat near the dart game. All seemed to be back to normal when Victoria St. Louis suddenly screamed, "I HATE MEN!"

No less than a dozen customers stood and immediately made toward her. "I can change your mind," was the general rumble of conversation.

It was just at this moment that the door opened and in stepped

Bobby Albertson, Frank Cosimo, and Tom Courtland. All eyes swung in their direction and then back again.

Ket turned to the man nearest her, a heavy-set, tattooed biker-type, and said, "Gentlemen, please. Let us take care of our friend."

The biker put a hand on Ket's shoulder. "That's where you're wrong, Blondie. *We'll* take care of your friend. And maybe you too."

Frank and Bobby turned to each other. "Uh-oh," they said in unison.

"Like that night in Subic," Bobby sighed, girding for action.

However, what no one in the bar knew at this time, was that the biker had committed a grave sin. He had laid a hand on the Dalyinese high marshal of defense. No one laid a threatening hand on Ket Mhulhar. No one.

Without rising from her barstool, Ket turned to the biker and smiled slightly. In an action too quick for the eye to capture, she placed her hand under his chin and pushed.

The biker flew across the room, flipped over a table and struck the rear wall under the dartboard, which came loose from the force of impact and slid off its hook onto the biker's head. The biker lay unconscious.

"Holy shit!" Frank murmured.

"Battle stations!" Tom Courtland said, pulling off his belt and winding it around his hand.

"Oy vey!" sighed Buzz, who began storing breakables beneath the bar, lustily humming the "Hungarian Rhapsody" as he did so.

Another biker took a swing at Ket, who caught the fist in her much smaller hand and floored her assailant with a head butt.

"Kathy!" Frank called. "Let's get—"

"*Sit down!*" The order came in a voice that hadn't issued from her since Thradon, a low, powerful tone that cut through all of the noise in the bar. It stopped the action for a brief moment.

The general had spoken.

Frank shrugged, and he and Bobby and Tom moved to the

bar where they formed a protective wall around Bonnie and Victoria.

Now Ket faced three men in denim jeans and jackets. They all smiled dangerously. They were still smiling when Ket landed the first unconscious with a shot to the jaw, the second with a double in the stomach, and the third, who charged her, was sidestepped and flung over the bar.

"Beers all 'round," Frank said to Buzz.

"Comin' up," Buzz said. "Draft okay?"

"It'll have to do," Frank replied, leaning back as a gangbangerish type flew past him headfirst.

"Hey, no weapons!" Buzz shouted, as a slight man in coveralls advanced on Ket with a length of pipe. Ket turned sideways and into the man with pipe, kicking his legs out from under him and tossing the pipe over the bar to Buzz, who caught it deftly.

"Thank you!" Buzz called.

"Have you noticed something interesting about our script girl?" Frank asked Bobby. "Because I have."

"And what might that be?" Bobby replied.

"She doesn't fight like a girl," Frank replied, raising his beer as a hapless Ket-fighter slid along the bar past him.

"God, what a chauvinist pig!" Bonnie exclaimed.

"Now, Bonnie, you know that's not what I mean," Frank chided her, as Ket ducked a swing and decked her assailant with a combination. "Women are smaller than men, and they weigh a lot less. So when they fight men, they have to use speed, agility, and leverage. But look at Kathy there. She defies physics! She goes what—say, five-nine, a hundred thirty, thirty-five? And she's duking it out toe-to-toe with two-hundred pounders. And none of that kung fu crap, either. Incoming!"

Frank and Tom ducked as an aforementioned two-hundredweight unfortunate sailed over their heads and landed behind the bar with a crash of shattering glass.

"What do you think?" Frank asked Bobby, who had been staring openmouthed throughout the proceedings.

He stared at his friend with a bewildered face. "I think I'm in love," Bobby said.

8

"We're not going home," Ket said as Bobby zoomed up the ramp to the 10 Freeway, heading east instead of west.

"Damn right we're not," Bobby replied. He reached across her and opened the glovebox, extracting a handheld CB radio. New Highway Patrol methods had rendered his allegedly state-of-the-art radar/laser detector virtually useless, so he had to fall back on older but proven methods of getting around his old nemeses.

"Breaker one-oh, breaker one-oh," he said into the transmitter, "this is Flickmaster, looking for a westbounder on this here I-number-ten, come on." Ket wondered at the change in Bobby's accent as he spoke into the radio.

"Flickmaster, this is Smile Merchant comin' atcha on this here one-oh, do you copy?"

"Copy, Smile Merchant, need a smoky report, how's it lookin' over your left shoulder, come on."

"Flickmaster, you're clean and green all the way to the five-seven. Put a broomstick on the throttle, good buddy."

"Sure do appreciate it, Smile Merchant."

"Pleasure, Flickmaster. Keep the shiny side up and may all your ups and downs be between the sheets. We down, by-eee."

Bobby switched off his radio and eased the speedometer clockwise around the dial.

"I wouldn't do that," Ket said.

"Wouldn't do what?" Bobby asked stiffly.

"That man you were talking to in a strange voice? He was lying."

Bobby turned to her. "What do you mean, lying?"

Ket shrugged. "He was hiding something. His voice—something wasn't right."

"You got all that off the radio, did you?" Bobby asked.

Ket nodded. "But do what you want."

Bobby gave her another glance, then swore softly and downshifted, decelerating until he was just under the limit. He drove at that relatively sedate pace for several minutes.

"Son of a bitch," he barked suddenly. A Highway Patrol cruiser sat idling just under an overpass. "Smile Merchant," he gasped. He looked at Ket. "Is there anything else I should know?" he asked.

"As it happens," Ket replied, "quite a lot."

"Bobby! Kathy!" Shirley exclaimed as she opened the front door. She embraced Ket, who responded in kind and wondered why it was that she suddenly felt at home and safe. She embraced and kissed Sy as well. Then she noticed Bobby standing in the doorway, a serious look on his face.

"What brings you out here, sweetie?" his mother asked. "Not that we aren't overjoyed to see you. How's shooting?"

"Everything's great," Bobby replied tonelessly.

"Bobby? What is it?"

Bobby went into the living room and sat on the flagstone ledge of the fireplace. He waited until the other three joined him there.

"Mom. Dad. You never kept anything from me, not in my whole life. Even when I was what, ten years old and the store was in trouble and we had to tighten our belts, remember? I got a paper route, and I gave you all the money I made—which you put into a savings account for me. Hell, I even knew that. But guys, come on. Why didn't you tell me?"

"Tell you what, son?" Shirley asked.

"Hey, I love Kathy. I do, Kathy, I think you're wonderful. The work you've done for me is far beyond anything I ever could imagine an assistant could do. You're producer material, that's sure. And if it doesn't get too weird, down the road, yeah, I wanna start dating for real—maybe when you get your own place and it won't put a strain on either of us if it doesn't work out."

Ket felt a shiver—not a chill, but a thrill of adrenalin. Bobby had said one thing, but he meant another. And what he meant was simple—he was in love with her. Perhaps he didn't even know it for sure at this point. But it was there. She felt it.

Someone loved her. Only one other man in her life had ever made her feel that way, and that was Holak Ven. But not as strongly as this. Was it because she herself, now fundamentally a Terran, was weaker? It was a sweet dilemma, she thought.

After a long pause, Bobby said, "so I want to know, Mom and Dad. Who is she?"

Sy and Shirley turned to each other, the effect of which was not lost on Bobby. He was definitely onto something. But how big a secret could it be? Why would his parents keep it from him?

"What do you think she is, Bobby?" Sy asked.

"Oh, hell, I don't know," he replied irritably. "CIA? NSA? Military Intel?"

"What?" Shirley guffawed. "How would we know someone like that? We're retired furniture salesmen, for God's sake."

"Mom. Please. You know what my script girl did today? Care to guess? No? I'll tell you, then. She beat the living shit out of an entire bar, that's what she did."

"You can't beat up a bar," Sy argued.

"I can't. You can't. Most guys who aren't Seals or Special Forces or British SAS guys can't either. Because I saw my share of barfights in the navy, folks. And that's what you have to be to kick that kind of ass. And I'm not talking about some Hollywood action-adventure starlet who took tae kwon do for a year and learned how to knee a guy in the nuts. I mean like Muhammad Ali, with her fists, the kind of fights I used to see on liberty in dives from the Indian Ocean to the South China Sea. She *whaled* on these guys, almost a dozen, I kid you not."

"Kathy," Shirley said rushing over to her side. "Are you all right?"

"I'm fine," Ket replied. Her hands were slightly bruised, but they didn't hurt. "Bobby," Ket said, "why do you need to know? Why is it so important?"

"Because I want you to stay," he said. "I want you to work with me. I think we make a good team." He turned to his parents. "I've never felt so creatively free since I started this business. All I do is go on the set and direct. All the other crap, the stuff that gave me headaches and delays, it's all done, and done right. By someone I feel I can trust. I *love* working like this."

"So? What's the problem?" Shirley asked. "Why are you looking a gift horse, pardon the metaphor, Kathy?"

Bobby shook his head. "You're not getting it, Ma. Kathy has a brain like a Swiss watch, right? Engineering background, you said? Plus, she can kick the crap out of just about anybody. She shows up out of nowhere, on your doorstep. How do I know she won't just as quickly go back into nowhere? And how can I trust her if she doesn't trust me enough to tell me?

"Who are you, Kathy?"

Ket glanced over at Sy and Shirley. "Should I tell him?"

"It's your decision, Kathy," Sy said.

She nodded. "Very well." She got up and crossed over to Bobby, taking both of his hands in her own. "I am General Ket Mhulhar, High Marshal of Defense for the Nation of Dalyi."

"Uh-*huh*," Bobby said. "And where is this, uh, this nation of Dalyi?"

"On the planet Thradon."

Bobby nodded. "The planet Thradon. Yeah, okay, whatever. I mean, hey, I've been to the planet Endor, you know, on that ride at Disneyland, Star Tours? Bitchen ride, by the way. My favorite, next to Pirates of the Caribbean."

"Bobby!" Shirley said sharply.

"Oh, come on, Ma! General Mhulhar of the planet Thradon? Give me a friggin' break!"

"Oh, okay, son. You're right. We're just kidding anyway. She's really Agent Kathy Miller of the CIA, in deep cover to root out terrorist plots in the Hollywood film community! No, wait! She's a Russian spy! We have to help her or our house gets blown up! Oh, no, that's not it! She's 008, British Secret Service, and she's—"

"Why don't we just play him the tape?" Sy cut her off.

"Tape?" Bobby scoffed. "What tape?"

"You'll see. I'll go get it."

"A tape," Bobby sighed. "They have VCRs on, where was it, Thradon? Just how far is this alleged planet, anyway? How long did it take you to get here?"

"Two of your years," Kathy replied.

"Two of *my* years? And how long are your years?"

"A bit shorter," Kathy said evenly. "About three hundred of your days."

"Yeah, okay. And where's your rocket ship?"

"It burned up entering your orbit. I used an escape pod."

"And where's that?"

"It was programmed to bury itself under the desert, near where Oon—your parents found me."

"They found you? Like Jonathan and Martha Kent found Superman when he was a baby? You lift *their* car off the ground, too?"

"Bobby," Sy said, returning with the video. "You're being a jerk. Now pipe down and watch this."

"So this Polak guy—" Bobby began as the screen went blank.

"Holak," Shirley corrected him.

"Whatever, that's what everybody looks like on your planet?" Bobby asked.

"Does everybody on this planet look like you?" Ket answered.

"You know what I mean."

"Yes, that's what we look like."

"Sort of a cross between the Klingons and the Hulk. I like that Holak guy, though. Good actor. Even through all that makeup, you can tell he's supposed to be a real stud. Has he got a SAG card?"

"I don't think they have SAG cards on Thradon, Bobby," Shirley said.

"We don't have movies on Thradon," Kathy said, who was by now familiar with the various unions in the film industry. "Why would we have a Screen Actors Guild?"

"We're wasting our time here," Sy said. "Kathy, are there any special capabilities our planet has given you?"

"Yes," Kathy replied.

"What are they? Besides strength, I mean."

"Your planet gave me no strength. I was always strong, even back home. I'm a soldier, and in my earlier years I was in my share of barroom fights. No, the only gift I have from your world is that I feel."

"Feel what?" Bobby asked.

"Like today, with that policeman on your communicator. I could never do that before."

"You read minds?" Bobby said dubiously.

"No," Ket replied. "I just feel. I know. It's difficult to explain."

"Okay, Kath, I'm easy. What am I thinking? Or, what do you feel from me?"

"You're looking at my mouth. You're wondering what it would be like to kiss me," she replied simply.

"Hallelujah!" Shirley cried. "Bobby, I notice you're not saying anything. But . . . you're blushing!"

"Ma, please," Bobby said, shifting uncomfortably. "Guys always blush when women tell them they're blushing."

Sy regarded his son with an amused smile. "So after all your bullshit," he began, "all of your, 'who is she, I have to know,' nonsense, it still comes down to that, doesn't it."

"Down to what?" Bobby demanded.

"Oh, please," Sy waved him off. Then he turned back to his son and regarded him sternly. It was not easy for Sy to do, because Bobby had always been sensitive and generous, if a bit rambunctious, and had seldom required serious disciplinary action as a child.

"Now you listen to me," Sy began, "because this is the news. I don't give a hoot in hell whether you think this is all crap or not. Kathy needs our help. Her people need our help. We've decided to give it to her. If you don't like it, that's tough. So you can either bow out now, or treat her with the respect she deserves—whether you think she's crazy or not. And I don't honestly believe you do think she's crazy. I think, that you think, that she's beautiful, brilliant, and exciting—and that is what eventually is going to win out with you."

Shirley had been sitting next to Ket with her arm linked through hers. "Do you feel what I'm thinking, Kathy?" she asked.

Ket regarded her with affection. "Yes, I do, Oonah. And I can't think of anyone else I'd rather have for a mother-in-law."

"Are we about through playing let's embarrass Bobby?" Bobby said.

"That's up to you, son," Sy told him. "Now. Your mother and I are going to play golf. I think the two of you have a lot to talk about, so we'll leave you alone."

"Let's go for a swim," Bobby said after his parents pulled away in their electric golf cart.

"A swim?" Ket replied.

"It's a hot day, we've got a pool right outside. Be a shame to waste it. My sister usually leaves a suit here, and you're about the same size."

Ket looked at him archly.

"All right," Bobby said. "What I suppose you're *feeling* is—"

"There are no scars, Bobby. No evidence of surgery on my body. We're a little more advanced on Thradon than here on Earth."

"I figured as much."

"It's a little strange. I can pretty much tell what everyone is thinking, except you. Sometimes I can. But when you're all business, like that first day I met you, then I can't."

"Can you tell now?"

"Oh, of course. You want to see me in a bathing suit."

"You didn't need any special powers to figure that one out. But there is something I need to know."

She laughed softly. "Yes, Bobby, I do find you attractive. I never thought I would. I never thought I would find any Terran desirable. And if you saw me in a Thradonian body, you wouldn't be attracted to me, either."

"If I were surgically altered like you? Maybe I would, after awhile, just like you. Yes, I believe I would."

He stood over her and took her in his arms. "Now I'm reading your mind," he said.

"Oh," she replied, puzzled at the trembling she felt.

Bobby kissed her. She closed her eyes and gloried in the new sensation. This was one area where Terrans had it over Thradon. She felt a large flower blossom inside her, blooming all the way up into her head.

"You still haven't told me," she said finally, wondering why she was breathless.

"Told you what?" he replied, equally breathless.

"What was on *my* mind."

"Oh. That's simple."

"Is it?"

"Sure. You were thinking: Our lives just became a lot more complicated."

9

Bobby figured he had to be in love, or why would he have done the unthinkable: He was allowing Ket to drive his Porsche.

It was five in the morning, and they were on their way back to the set. Although Ket was at first unfamiliar with such things as internal combustion engines and five-speed manual transmissions, she proved to be an apt pupil. She was cruising at a comfortable eighty miles per hour through West Covina when the hair on the back of her neck stood on end. She carefully reduced her speed, lining up the dial at precisely sixty-two miles an hour.

"Jeez, hon," Bobby exclaimed as they passed a Highway Patrol cruiser waiting for trade on the shoulder, "you're better than radar!"

"Could you do me a favor, Bobby?" she asked.

"Sure."

"Could you call me Ket? It's been so long since I've heard my own name."

"Ket," he said. He smiled apologetically. "Sorry, but in all honesty, you look more like a Kathy. Anyway, there's something I want to ask you."

"And that is?"

"Well, you're a general, right? And, since all the problems on your planet began, you've been the top gun—premier, you said."

"That's right," she replied, downshifting as Bobby had taught her, as they entered a heavy traffic pattern.

"How do you stand it, then? Being out of the loop, doing something as mundane as working in the movies, after all that?"

"It's my second half, Bobby," she replied matter-of-factly. They had spent most of the night talking, Bobby wanting to know everything about her planet and her own life. She had only briefly touched upon the two-career life of the average Thradonian.

"But does everyone start at the bottom again?" he asked incredulously.

Ket nodded.

"But I don't get it. What if you were some high muckety-muck in your first half? Isn't that going to give you an edge over the average schmo for your second half?"

"Only up to a point. It may help you get in, admittedly. But you still have to perform your job well, you still have to take orders from your boss, and you can't use your past achievements to lord it over your fellow workers."

Bobby considered that with a dubious expression. "It sounds good in theory," he said, "but does it really work? I mean, what were you going to do?"

"I had thought of teaching, perhaps," Ket replied. "At the University of Kasma Dor, in the city where I live. Or at Tira Gen—that's our military academy. That's where I went to school."

"Your version of West Point," Bobby acknowledged.

"But that was before," Ket smiled.

"Before me?"

"Yes—and before movies. I'd like to bring movies back to Dalyi. Or even all Thradon. How exciting that would be! Could you imagine what that would be like? Seeing people watch a movie for the first time?"

"I saw you," he reminded her. "Or right afterwards, anyway. If I only knew. *Valley Kingpin* was the first film ever viewed by an extraterrestrial. What was it like for you? I mean, how much did you understand?"

"More than I thought I would. You see, when I was on the ship, there was nothing to do but learn. First, your language—"

"How long did that take? I took French for three years in school, and I still couldn't find my way around Paris without an interpreter."

"Well, the assimilators helped, but—"

"Assimilators?"

"While you sleep, the brainwaves—"

"Cool! But didn't it keep you awake?"

Ket laughed. "They don't work that way. I learned the basics of your language rather quickly, although to be fully comfortable with your vernacular took somewhat longer. But Holak did a good job—"

"Now, wait a second," Bobby interrupted. "Holak's been here before, you said?"

"Several times," Ket replied.

"But how did he avoid being seen?"

"That's his *job,* Bobby. Holak was—is—a pilot. Escape and evasion are important tools of his trade."

"I know, but come on. A Thradonian on Earth? Someone would have seen him."

"They probably did," she admitted. "But be serious. Your planet dismisses encounters with extraterrestrials as flights of fancy. No one really believes it. Are you hungry? I am."

"Pull off at that ramp up ahead. There ought to be a Denny's or something. But I still don't understand. How did Holak learn so much about Earth? Enough to teach you—"

"Have you ever visited a foreign country, Bobby?"

"You know I have."

"Maybe you didn't speak the language, but you did have common ground, didn't you?"

He directed her into the parking lot of a Carrow's. She did a creditable job of pulling into a parking space, but let out the clutch before switching off the engine, causing the car to jump forward before it stalled. She smiled apologetically, and he nodded to let her know it was no big deal.

"You have a word," Ket said after they settled into a booth,

"I believe it's called 'dovetailing.' That is part of Holak's genius. His lessons walked me through a day in the life of a Terran. Of course, each aspect of life has its own components, the dovetailing of each area, and he planned my lessons accordingly. Bobby! You're not paying attention!"

"Am too," he retorted.

"You're thinking of me naked, just like everybody else."

"Can you blame me?"

She grinned. "Not really. But, Bobby, we must talk."

"Oh, Jesus! Do women say that on your planet, too?"

"If necessary," she replied, not understanding the crack. "If we are to become lovers . . ." she trailed off, noticing that a waitress was standing over them.

"Hey, I can always come back," the waitress said, snapping her gum.

"Sure, but we'll need some coffee," Bobby said.

"Yeah, I guess you will," the waitress said, and went to fetch the pot.

"You were saying," Bobby prompted Ket. " 'If we are to become lovers . . .' Which by the way, I don't want anyone on the set to know about, until shooting is done."

"Then why don't we just not sleep together until the filming is over?"

"Can you wait that long? I can't. I'm having trouble keeping my hands off you right now."

"Bobby, I owe it to you . . . and to your parents. I can't—" The waitress returned and placed steaming coffee mugs in front of them.

"You folks clear everything up?" she asked.

"We're working on it," Bobby replied.

"Well, good luck." She turned to leave, but first whispered to Ket, "Keep your own bank account."

"What do you owe me?" Bobby asked.

"Bobby, I'm in danger. Maybe not right now, but sooner or later, someone will come after me. They're going to try to kill me."

"They have to get past me first," Bobby declared.

"And they will," Ket argued.

"Screw 'em!" Bobby snapped. "We'll outthink them, then.

Why wait? Come on, Kath—I mean, Ket, I thought you were this hotshot general! You just gonna wait for them to come charging through the door someday? Not me."

Ket sipped her coffee thoughtfully. "And how would you go about outthinking them?"

"How will they go about finding you?"

"Oh, it'll be quite simple. They'll find the escape pod—or at least where it buried itself in the desert. That'll give them my body signature—like your DNA, but it'll be even simpler because they'll be looking for a Thradonian signature, and there's only one on this entire planet, and you're looking at her. From there it'll be nothing at all to pick up my trail."

"Oh my God!" Bobby gasped.

"What?"

"My parents!"

"Yes," Ket said thoughtfully. "When the time comes, we'll have to get them to move out, at least temporarily."

"When the time comes! When will that be?"

"Not soon. It took me two years to reach Earth. I've been here three months. The Ebereans have no space-travel capabilities, which means they'll have to use ours. But we won't have any rockets, either, because Cresvo Denor will have been destroyed. Unless there's a prototype hidden somewhere—"

"Oh, hell, it could be years, then."

"Yes, but it will happen, Bobby. We'll have to give your parents an emergency plan for rapid evacuation."

"I imagine," Bobby began, "that when it does happen, we'll all be evacuating rather rapidly." When he saw that she didn't get the irony, he said, "What about us?"

"Us?"

"Okay, technically, there is no us. Look, shooting ends in a week. Why don't we go away for a long weekend or something? Separate rooms, of course?"

"Separate rooms? Why? Aren't we going to sleep together? Isn't that the point of going away for a long weekend?"

"You have long weekends on Thradon?"

"Of course we do."

Bobby looked at her, and his smile widened as he once again realized the identity of the woman he was with. "This is *so* bitchen!" he exclaimed. "Ooh, come on, come on, tell me some more Thradon stuff. No wait! I got a better idea. Tonight, when we get home, we'll watch some space movies! *Star Wars, Aliens, Star Trek, Close Encounters, Independence Day*! I can get your take on it, see if we've even come close!"

Bobby and Ket arrived on the set at their usual time, each carrying their usual burden. Now that their relationship, although unconsummated, had crossed a wide boundary, each wondered if anyone else had noticed.

Son of a bitch, thought Frank Cosimo, they've been to bed together. Well, good for them.

"How ya doin', slugger?" Frank greeted her, kissing her on the cheek. He nodded to Bobby, who immediately understood that he was onto them. Not that Bobby was surprised; even in the navy, nothing ever got past Big Frank.

"What're you doing next week, Frank?" Bobby said.

"After the shoot?" Frank replied. "Thought I'd play a little golf. Why?"

"I'm calling a war council. I need you and Tom and my parents to meet with me and Evander Holyfield over here."

Ket had perked up at the phrase *war council*, but it was merely Bobby's term for a meeting of the people he most trusted in his life. Bobby called a war council when he needed help with an important decision. Only this time, it really would be a war council.

Big Frank immediately registered concern. "Count me in, boot," he said. "Where? Your place?"

"That's as good as any."

"Fine with me. What's on the agenda?"

Bobby smiled grimly. "It's a war council, Master Chief," he said, calling Frank by his most senior rank. "We may really be going to war. Again."

Thradon
ONE YEAR AGO

10

Holak Ven had seen better days.

For months, he had undergone physical and psychological torture that would have driven a lesser man insane, or killed him.

It was all done in a very civilized fashion. Holak had been moved under guard to a comfortable apartment in the middle of the occupation headquarters. During the evenings, he was well fed, allowed plenty of rest, and given expert care for his wounds.

But during the day, as if going to a job like anyone else, he was transported to the interrogation room and his agonizing, terror-filled day would begin.

Celin Kwa personally oversaw these sessions. They would begin with a beating. Nothing too strenuous at first, just enough to get things rolling. After that, Holak would go on the brain machine.

The brain machine, or Personal Interrogator A2000, had been designed by the Ebereans for the express purpose of psychological torture. Its simple function was to implant memories in the subject's consciousness—memories that never happened, of course, but the subject had no way of knowing that. Over time, it would create a life for the subject that was so filled with traumatic events that eventually the interrogator would be the only person left for the subject to trust. Sometimes the machine worked so well that weaker subjects often gave up valuable information without being asked, so much did they come to trust their interrogator.

But strong minds like Holak's, although not impossible, were tough nuts to crack that took longer and tried their captors' patience. Which was why Holak usually received more physical torture before Celin called it a day.

What Celin Kwa and his henchmen didn't know, and in fact, couldn't have known, was that Holak Ven had long since prepared himself for the brain machine. He had heard of the PI-A2000 long before the Eberean invasion, and it had scared him to death. He therefore visited the Psychological Warfare Division in Sha'n Res, where he had consulted a physician he could trust. The physician had told him that if he was ever confined, before being subjected to the machine, he should create points of retrieval within his personal living space.

And so Holak did. During his first day on the machine, Celin had convinced him that his mother was a drunken prostitute who conceived him during the course of a transaction, and that her pimp had molested him all through his youth. He had spent his childhood in shame and degradation, and his first sexual experiences had given him nothing but humiliation.

When Holak was returned to his confinement space after that session, dazed, whimpering, and suicidal, his eyes lit upon his pillow—the point of retrieval for his childhood memories. And there it all returned. He had grown up in a poor but stable and happy home. His mother was a chambermaid at Kasma Dor's finest hotel, and his father washed down the city's monorail cars. His first sexual experience had been a dream come true, and he had been in love with women ever since.

The point of retrieval had worked its magic. But he had to pretend that it hadn't. And every day, he had to summon what appeared to be his final reserve of defiance, an act that gave him injuries to nurse overnight.

Still, the harrowing schedule was taking its toll. Holak had lost a quarter of his body weight, his coloring was pale and unhealthy, and he suffered frequent problems with his digestion and urinary tracts. But that was all worth it, he believed. Having the reputation of being a shallow hothead was doing the trick for him; not even Celin Kwa believed that he was working on a plan of his own.

Holak was brought to the interrogation room and placed in his usual spot, on the other side of a desk, behind which sat Celin Kwa. The procedure was of necessity polite and informal until the actual violence began.

"You look awful, Holak," Celin Kwa greeted him.

"Yeah, well, so do you. You been torturing me for months, Celin, what the hell am I supposed to look like?"

"True enough," Kwa nodded sadly. "It doesn't have to be this way, you know."

"Of course it does," Holak countered.

"You can end it all right now, Holak. All this unpleasantness, I mean. Just tell us what we want to know."

"Sure. Then you'll have no further use for me."

"Holak. Why are you allowing me to turn into a monster? I don't understand you at all."

"Celin. Do what you have to do. No hard feelings, all right?"

"There never were hard feelings, Holak. Not all Ebereans are revenge-crazed psychopaths. Play the game, I beg you. You tell us where she is, she'll be gone by the time we get there, but at least I will have tried and you won't have to suffer anymore."

"Of course not. I'd be dead."

"We wouldn't do that. I give you my word. You'll have your own little apartment anywhere you want—Srho, perhaps. Nothing fancy, of course, but livable. And a comfortable stipend, some walking-around money, maybe an occasional bonus to enjoy at the gaming tables."

Interesting, thought Holak, a new tack. The folks back in Eberes must be getting impatient for results. "That's very generous of you, Celin."

"Oh, I can be a generous man," Kwa replied. "When I was ambassador, don't you remember my parties? Was there a better host in all Sha'n Res? Look, I'll even sweeten the pot for you."

"Oh? How sweet?"

"You'll see. Don't decide now. We'll take today off, and you can go home and think about it."

When the guards let Holak off at his quarters, Pasa Henz was waiting for him in his bed.

"Oh, come on!" he exploded, although there was a hint of laughter in his voice at the transparency of the ploy.

"Hello, Holak," Pasa whispered.

"Where've you been, Pasa? It's been months."

"You didn't know? I was promoted. I'm the military governor of Kuran Il."

Kuran Il was Dalyi's fifth-largest city, a booming industrial town on Dalyi's north coast. "Military governor? Royalty! Congratulations, Pasa. What brings you back here?"

"You," she said.

"Uh-huh. Well, go home, Pasa. It ain't gonna happen."

"Damn it, Holak! I've wanted you ever since Truska—before that, even. The first time I saw you on the Comm-Channel after that voyage to Kranor."

Kranor, Holak remembered. No life then or ever, inhospitably bleak, cold, incapable of ever sustaining life. A dump. But it was the first time a Thradonian had ever visited another solar system, so it was big news, and so was he. The thought of it still embarrassed him.

"Pasa. Get lost."

"Why? Am I unattractive to you?"

"Yes."

She snickered. Pasa Henz was a good-looking woman and knew it well.

"Go ahead and laugh, Pasa. But I'd prefer an old hooker with a headcold. Get it through your skull: You're an Eberean. Take a walk."

"I'm in love with you, Holak."

Holak doubled up and laughed until it hurt, which didn't take long, considering his condition. When he finally recovered, he became serious. "I've got two problems. One, you're my enemy, I'm a soldier, and I have orders from one of the few generals

in the world I actually respect. The other problem is—none of
your business."

"What is it? I'll do anything—"

"Right. You'll help me escape?"

She looked around the room as if to ensure confidence. "Yes,"
she said.

Holak fell about the room in hysterical laughter.

"I'm serious," she said. "Why do you think I came all this
way from Kuran Il?"

He waved at her and couldn't stop laughing.

"I am," she insisted.

"You getting all this, Celin?" Holak shouted at the ceiling.

"He's not listening, Holak. No one is."

"Nice pot-sweetening, there, Celin," he shouted.

It struck Holak, quite suddenly, that if this was indeed an
eleborate ruse, he might as well see just how far he could push
it. That could well prove to be an advantage.

Holak sighed and dropped onto the bed next to Pasa. "Rub
my back," he said. "I've been dreaming of a massage for months.
If you really love me, you'll rub my back."

She straddled him and began kneading his shoulders. "What
was the other problem?" she asked him.

"What other problem? Oh, the *other* problem. Aaaah, that
feels good, right there. It's a little embarrassing. My body has
undergone some stress recently, and I don't think I can—well,
perform up to my usual standards. Or anyone's, come to that."

"Holak. I'm a general. Generals get what they want. Why do
you make me chase you like this? It's humiliating!"

"Pasa, you're an Eberean. You people are scum. You ate our
bread, married our sons and daughters, and all the time you were
planning to kill us! How could I possibly want anything to do
with one of you? No, don't stop, feel that knot? Yeaaahh, that's
it."

"That's true," she said. "And it's also true that when you colonized Eberes, you treated us all like dirt. My father was a respected businessman, wealthy and charitable, and yet, there were
places in his own city he couldn't go because he wasn't a wonderful and golden Dalyinese!"

"It stunk," Holak admitted. "A lot of us in the army didn't

like it. And even before Hilva, we all wanted to get out, give you back your country."

"Ah, yes, the famous petition," Pasa remarked, enjoying giving the massage as much as Holak enjoyed receiving it. "But the damage had already been done. And anyway, who were *you* to give *us* back our country?"

Holak turned over onto his back beneath her. "Then we both were wrong. That makes it even worse. So we've no future, Pasa."

She stared down at him and rubbed his chest. "Let me ask you one thing," she said. "Answer it and I'll go, if that's what you want."

"All right," he said, cursing himself for weakening.

"If there were no war, no hate," she began, "if we were just a couple of soldiers, a man and a woman . . . would I stand a chance then? I know I'm no Ket Mhulhar or Geras Haug," she added, the latter being a famous Dalyinese actress with whom Holak had often been romantically linked. "But even you have to admit, I'm not all that bad."

He thought for a moment. "You're the youngest in your family, aren't you?" he asked suddenly.

"Ye-es. Five sisters. What has that to do—"

"Your sisters were all beautiful, right? Real go-getters. Daddy's girls. None of them went into the army, right? You're the first in your whole, probably extended family to even think of the military, right?"

She climbed off of him and turned away. "Why are you doing this?"

"I'm an honest man, Pasa. I like honest people. My friends keep nothing from me; I keep nothing from them. You're an Eberean. You've smiled at us for years, and the whole time you had a knife behind your back. Now you want me to trust you. Fine. Make me trust you."

"I said I'd help you escape. What do you think will happen if—"

"No, no, later. This other stuff is too good. Oh, God, Pasa, you're reaching me! I can see it all now: Poor little Pasa, the baby of the family—but not a baby who's doted on and spoiled. Not with the hard-chargers you've got ahead of you in the birth order. What do they do now? Surgeons? Politicians? Successful merchants? And here's poor little Pasa—all she wants is Daddy's approval, hell, not even that, just a little attention once in a while. But there's four ahead of you. Gotta wait your turn, only your turn never came."

"Stop it, Holak! Just stop it!"

"Oh, I *am* close! So, what do you do? You've got to show those bitch sisters and that inattentive, maddeningly oblivious daddy of yours, right? So you work. And you struggle. And you fight. And you sacrifice. And lo and behold, you make it. You get into the academy. That'll show 'em, right? Could any of those four princesses have gotten into the academy? Could your fabled daddy? Hell no! So, you got 'em! Finally! And now they have to respect you. Now they have to give you the attention you deserve. I'll bet you came home on your first leave after plebe year—that indescribable hell that only the absolute best could even hope to survive.

"I'll bet they didn't even notice, Pasa," he told her sadly. "Didn't even care, did they?"

Pasa was weeping softly.

"You might not think so, Pasa, but I do remember you twenty years ago at Truska. I thought you were kind of cute even then. Your first battalion command—that all-important early promotion to light colonel. You served under Ket, her first action as a theatre commander. She always liked you, you know. You know what she said? She said, 'Colonel Henz will go far . . . she's got something to prove.' And you sure did prove it, didn't you? Three Bravery Clusters and a Wound Medal. Oh, I remember you, Pasa, indeed I do. What did your family say when you came home from Truska, a national hero? Probably, 'oh, that's nice, dear. Look, your sister's baby just cut a tooth.' I'll bet you haven't seen them in years, have you? I mean, what would be the point, Pasa?"

"Oh, you are a bastard, Holak!"

"Of course I'm a bastard, Pasa. I've committed the unforgivable sin of caring about who you are."

"And just who the hell are you?" she demanded in tearful defiance.

"Just who I've always claimed to be, Pasa. A poor kid from

the wrong side of Kasma Dor, whose parents tried as hard as they could to raise him right. I'm not as interesting as you, Pasa. My parents were poor, and maybe not real bright, but they loved me, and I never doubted it for a minute. I was a fun-loving kid who laughed a lot. And that's what makes us different, Pasa. You'd die to prove a point—that you're better than your stupid family. Well, I can save you the trouble—you *are* better than your stupid family . . . and always were. I won't die to prove a point—I have nothing to prove."

"What about Ket Mhulhar? You wouldn't die for her?"

"That's different. That's dying for a friend, and for a cause I believe in. I'm sorry to disappoint you, Pasa, but I'm a happy man. I always have been. That's probably why you like me. I mean, why would a gorgeous senior general, who can get any-one she wants—and probably has—why would someone like that want a lowly colonel who's never going to make general? Because I'd make you laugh? Well, I guess there are worse rea-sons."

Pasa attempted to draw herself up to full dignity. "Why are you telling me all this? What's the point?"

"*Because you want me to love you,*" he answered bitingly. "Well, that doesn't come for free. But it comes without reser-vation. If you're a scared little girl inside, I want to love that scared little girl. Because I can trust that little girl. If that little girl has grown up and now has nothing left to lose by saving me, I want to love her, too."

"Then you *can* love me," Pasa said.

"It's possible," Holak replied. "Of course, it's also possible that I might have to kill you. In which case, the love stuff goes right out the window. You know that I'll be committing treason by simply having you with me."

"Don't talk to me about treason, Holak. The instant we leave this room together, there'll be a price on my head."

"Join the club," Holak replied. "It's actually a sort of ego boost."

"I'll never be able to see my family again."

"And here you were looking at only the dark side!"

• • •

Celin Kwa's clever gambit had failed. If the downfall of the Da-lyinese had been that they had misjudged the Eberean thirst for revenge, the Eberean failing was that they had overestimated the esteem in which the Dalyinese held their conquerors. The simple fact was that no one believed Celin Kwa.

And there was another reason. The people seemed to have forgotten all about Ket Mhulhar. The name Nev Hederes was becoming known throughout the land, the rallying cry of the Resistance.

The past few months had been exhausting for Nev Hederes. He had travelled the country incognito, disclosing his identity only to those in the Resistance who seemed trustworthy.

Captain Groula Feeh was soon in a constant state of amazement at his general's ability to easily win the hearts and minds of the people. The general, while held in high regard for years as a planner, had never been what could be considered charismatic. But he listened more than he spoke, and he seemed to remember everything and everyone.

Of course, had anyone ever told Nev Hederes that he was becoming the face of the Revolution, he would have denied it. In his own mind, he was keeping the seat warm for Ket Mhulhar. He felt that he owed her a united Dalyi, ready to join her in ousting the hated Ebereans from their shores forever.

The Dalyinese had become united more rapidly than anyone had ever dreamed. Nev Hederes, while pleased, was also puzzled. What was it that had brought his countrymen together, a nation of individuals, who, while generous to a fault, were also highly motivated by self-interest? His answer came soon. And the answer did not come from his own world.

It came instead from a poem Holak Ven had brought him— a verse that Holak Ven had read once, when he had broken into a library in an isolated California town under the cover of deep night, and he had never forgotten it.

"Read this," Holak had told him. "I translated it as best I could. The next time you address the people of Dalyi, tell them that is how you feel about the dawn of the fight!"

"What is it?" Nev had asked. "Who wrote it?"

"It's from Earth. A poet named Roo-pert Broo-ke. He wrote

it at the very start of the worst war Earth had ever seen up to that time. A war that decimated an entire generation."

Nev glanced down and skimmed the powerful words once again. "Then why is he thankful?"

"He didn't know it then, obviously. His country had been at peace for almost a hundred Earth-years. The poet believed that they had gotten soft and fat and that this war would wake them up and shake out the chaff and get them back on the right moral track. Naive, I know, but well done."

"What happened to this Broo-ke?"

"Oh, he died in the war, less than a year later."

> *Now, God be thanked who has matched us with his hour,*
> *And caught our youth, and wakened us from sleeping,*
> *Who made sure, clear eye, and sharpened power,*
> *To turn as swimmers into cleanness leaping.*
> *Glad from a world grown old and cold and weary,*
> *Leave the sick hearts that honor could not move—*

Nev Hederes paused to dry his eyes. "Now, God be thanked," he repeated, "for he has awakened *us*. And until our freedom is won, we shall never sleep again!"

The millions of Dalyinese who witnessed Nev's address were deeply affected by Rupert Brooke's moving if misguided words. It was almost as though the words had been written for them, for their own time and place, instead of long ago on some distant planet most of them had never heard of.

And on the streets all over Dalyi strangers greeted each other with a new resolve. It became the watch-phrase of the Resistance: *"Now, God be thanked."*

Getting past the guards had been a doddle. When a stern look from Pasa Henz didn't erase all the guards' curiosity, her incredible quickness with a compact pulse gun finished the job. She and Holak were on the street. A quick monorail ride to the Grevas district, and soon they were standing in front of one of the most fashionable apartment buildings in all Kasma Dor.

"Let's go up," Holak said.

"You live *here*?"

"On a colonel's pay? Don't be silly. I'm house-sitting for a friend." Holak passed his hand over the code-lock and the air-barrier vanished. They whooshed up to the tenth floor, where Holak passed his hand over another code-lock.

"Whose place *is* this?" Pasa wanted to know.

"Just a friend. Okay, a close friend. Okay, a friend I sleep with whenever I can."

"Uh-huh," Pasa replied. The apartment's owner was obviously a woman. The effects were all feminine without being frilly. A woman of wealth, power, and taste.

"I usually keep some extra clothes in here. And I need a shower. Mind waiting? Or, perhaps, join me?"

Pasa stared out at the breathtaking view of Kasma Dor Harbor and the clean blue ocean beyond. Then it occurred to her exactly whose apartment this really was.

"Holak!"

"Yeah?" he called from the other room.

"Get in here!"

"What?" he said, towelling his head. Ket's bathroom had an air-dry, but it was disconnected, as she preferred heavy soft towels on her skin.

"This is Ket Mhulhar's private quarters!"

"Yeah, so?"

"How could you bring me up here?"

Holak smiled. "Are you jealous, my little Hilvan blossom?"

"Knock it off!"

Holak removed the towel from around his waist and began drying his mid-section. Pasa tried not to look, then tried not to be caught looking. Holak had lost a great deal of weight, and his body was scarred from abuse, but Pasa didn't care. He'd gain back the weight and the scars would heal.

"Listen," Holak began, "Ket is my best friend. Has been since Transitional Barracks at Tira Gen. Two Kasma Dorans among the country kids, although she came from Grevas and I grew up in Bhuhara. No rich kids at the academy, though, none of that snob crap. We hit it off right away. I asked her to become mates at least three times when I was sober. If it was going to happen, it would have by now. But we're still two ends of the same cloth."

"I can't help feeling a little strange, Holak."

"I told you before, Ket always liked you. She'd be glad you were here."

"Can we go?" Pasa's skin was crawling, as though Ket Mhulhar would storm in at any moment and throw her out the window.

"All right. We have to be someplace anyway."

"Where?"

"I need a good strong cup of zafra. How about you?"

The cafe was located near the old naval base, a rundown place reputed to serve the best zafra in the city. Before the navy was virtually destroyed by the Eberean invasion, the little shop had been a cash cow, furnishing strong morning zafra to workers on their way to the shipyards. Now the naval base was deserted and the cafe barely made its operating expenses.

A stooped and wizened old pensioner wordlessly poured two cups and placed them on the counter.

"How's business, Ia?" Holak greeted the old man.

"Stinks! Why do you think I'm here all alone? Who needs help nowadays?"

"This is marvelous zafra," Pasa said politely.

"What's the point? No one's left to drink it."

Holak chuckled. "Don't mind old Ia here. When he was making money hand over fist, he bitched that he didn't have time to breathe. There's no pleasing some people."

"I notice there's no pleasing you, Colonel Big Shot."

"Me? What do you mean?"

Ia nodded toward Pasa. "Dalyinese girls ain't good enough for ya? You have to get some off the enemy now?"

"How do you know I'm Eberean?" Pasa asked.

"Do I look like a moron? Don't take this the wrong way, ma'am, but if you weren't with Holak—"

"Let's not be rude, Ia," Holak interrupted. "This is my fiancée you're talking to."

Ia put up his hands in a surrendering gesture. "Hey, it's your life. I mean, she's a looker, all right, but if you wanna wake up with a Goula knife in the back of your head some morning, be my guest."

"Fiancée?" Pasa nudged Holak.

"Naah," Holak said. "Well, maybe. Who knows?"

"That's treason, Holak." Ia reached up and tore off the wrinkled wig and pulled the mask off his face.

"You always were a tightass, Nev."

Pasa gasped. "Is this . . . General Hederes?"

"General Pasa Henz. I salute you."

"I salute you, General Hederes."

"Thank you. Is she armed?"

"Of course I'm armed," Pasa snapped. "I'm a general in an enemy city." She removed the compact pulse gun from her hip and slapped it onto the counter.

"What have you done, Holak?"

"I took a girl out for some zafra! What's the problem?"

"She's the enemy, Holak. How are we supposed to convince the people of Dalyi to hate the enemy when one of our most trusted officers is b—"

"Wait a minute, Nev. Pasa, are you defecting?"

"I have no choice, now, do I?" Pasa retorted.

"If she's defecting, let her prove it."

"She had a weapon, Nev. She could have killed us both in a heartbeat, and she could've gotten away clean. Why didn't she?"

"Maybe it's part of a plan."

Pasa stood up. "That's it. I'm out of here." She turned and headed for the door.

"Pasa! Wait!" Holak called.

She stopped and glared at both of them. "I'm a marked woman and for what? S&D teams are probably combing the city looking for me right now, but unlike you, Holak, I've got nowhere to hide. Well, the hell with both of you."

"Wait!" Nev Hederes had entered the room. "Thank you, Sergeant-Major. Well done. You are excused."

The man who had pretended to be Nev came to attention and saluted. "Thank you, General." He turned stiffly and marched out of the room.

"My apologies, General Henz," Nev said. "We had to be sure."

"Sergeant-Major Pandof was an enthusiastic volunteer," Holak said. "He's been the general's batman for more than twenty years. Not that we would have let anything happen," he added quickly.

Pasa nodded in understanding. "I would have done the same," she said. "In fact, I can't believe I didn't think of it."

"Let's all have a cup of this execellent zafra," Nev said. "Then we'll see what we can do about this mess."

"Mess," Holak demanded. "What mess?"

"The sergeant-major wasn't far wrong," Nev said. "We're at war with Eberes. You have brought an Eberean into our midst. What do you suggest we do?"

"She can't go back," Holak argued. "Anyway, it's too late for that. She can join us."

"Hey! Dummy!" Nev exploded in a rare outburst of temper. "The Ebereans did join us. For sixty *years,* remember? She's a ranking general! She knew what was going on."

"She fought a war," Holak countered. "She didn't murder anyone in their beds."

Pasa Henz picked up her compact pulse weapon from the counter and slammed it down in front of Nev Hederes. "Either you kill me now, or help me get a passage to Taray."

"Taray?" Holak asked with distaste. "What the hell would you do with yourself on Taray?"

Pasa rounded on him. "I'd live. Where else can I go?"

"Oh, come on, not there! It's a hole." The island nation was in fact, a blistering hot wasteland, with nothing to recommend it except for those in flight for their lives or freedom and those who enjoyed debauchery in extremely tawdry surroundings. It was also used as a threat to frighten unruly children: "Stop hitting your sister or we'll dump you off in Taray." Taray had no extradition agreement with any other nation on Thradon and was therefore peopled with many unsavory types. Because it was so far from the other major nations of Dalyi and had no strategic or agricultural value, it was ignored by would-be conquerors. Which was why the surviving vessels of the Dalyinese Navy lay anchored just off its shores.

"Wait a minute," Nev Hederes said, suddenly in furious thought.

"What?" Holak said.

"Shut up. I'm thinking." He ruminated for another minute. "Okay. Holak, maybe it would be a good idea if Pasa did go to Taray."

"Now, hold on a sec—"

"And an even better idea if you went with her. Yes. Just the ticket. You're both S&D bait if you stay here. And someone has to coordinate with the Navy. It's also the only place where—forgive me, Pasa—an Eberean and a Dalyinese can be seen together without attracting too much attention, or causing problems."

Pasa glared at him angrily. "Isn't this a bit much, general? You Dalyinese aren't like us—you can tell your people to hate us, to despise us, have nothing to do with us, but will they? Is it really in their character to do so?"

"I don't know, General. And at this point, I don't care. Your—the Eberean—track record isn't so great. Okay, so maybe someday we will all hold hands and dance in a circle together, but it won't be soon, and you know it. I've got three objectives right now. One, to organize a revolution; two, to chase every Eberean back across the ocean. Three, to eliminate your Central Authority and your military infrastructure, to ensure that you never hurt us again."

"My God," Pasa said, "you're talking as if it's actually possible."

"It's not only possible. It's inevitable."

"You can't win," Pasa told him sadly.

"Of course we can," Nev replied. "And now I know why. Holak, it was as you told me on Ear—I mean, as you predicted. I went to a meeting last night. I go to a lot of them now, you know. Five people at someone's house. Thirty in an apartment hallway. A few hundred at a small theatre. On a monorail car once. Everywhere. I've been over the length and breadth of Dalyi, from Kasma Dor to Kuran Il—yes, Pasa, I was in Kuran Il right under your very nose. And everyone I meet is ready to fight. No exceptions. Do you know why?"

Pasa tried not to be angry with herself. Her own flying squads in Kuran Il, having received intelligence that Nev was in town, had fruitlessly searched the entire city, block by block.

"Just out of curiosity," Pasa said, "where were you hiding?"

Nev smiled. "You know I can't tell you that. There are other lives at stake. Maybe after the war is over and it doesn't matter anymore."

"Understood. Why? Why are they ready to fight?"

Nev grinned at the memory. "I was in Srho, of all places. Even went into a casino and played the tables for awhile, made great pals with a couple of your elite assault troops. I ask you, is there a stronger, and briefer, friendship than the ones made gambling? But I digress."

"You always do," Holak cracked. "Always have."

"You are insubordinate, Sir," Nev replied. "I met with some friends a little later on. It was a big meeting, and that surprised me. I mean, the only thing that has changed in Srho is the flag on the roof and the clientele. But Srhovians are making a fortune—even more than they did in peacetime. Why would they care, they of all people?"

"That is a shock," Holak admitted.

"Yes, it was. And yet it was the largest meeting I've ever had. As I often do, I opened by asking for comments from the floor. 'Why are you here? What made you get involved?' And the answer is usually the same—although it never gets tiresome. 'Because Dalyi is my country, not Eberes.' It's often as simple as that. All but one fellow; his answer impressed me the most."

"Must have been a hell of an answer," Holak remarked.

"It was honest, so honest and so visceral that it made everyone in the hall gasp. I recognized him from one of the casinos, where he was a dealer. Making an incredible living off of Eberean suckers. I found out later he was ex-army, a corporal in the Truska campaign."

"What did he say, already?"

"He stood up, looked around, gave a kind of a sneer, stared right into my eyes and said, 'because for the first time, this bullshit is actually going to be *fun*.'"

Pasa said, "How erudite. I can see why you were impressed."

Holak waved her off. "No, no, I see your point. And everybody else did, too, right?"

Hederes nodded. "Nothing personal," he told Pasa, "but an Eberean wouldn't understand it. Because Ebereans don't share the Dalyinese sense of humor—or morality."

Pasa drew herself up, insulted.

"I'm sorry, Pasa, but it's true. And I'm glad you didn't understand it. Because that means Celin Kwa and the others won't, either. And that's why we'll win!"

"Will somebody tell me what the hell that dealer was talking about? Goddamnit! All he said was that it was going to be fun."

Nev and Holak glanced at each other and shook their heads.

"I'm sorry, Pasa," Nev said. "We've been rude. But the dealer was right. Not that it was going to be fun in the sense of entertainment; he meant that now when we fight, we answer to no one. The rules of engagement are off. The articles of war are off. The military code of conduct is off. For the first time in our nation's history, we don't have to be the good guys anymore. We can't afford that luxury. And so the worst part of the Thradonian nature, the most murderous and most brutal, is about to be unleashed. Because there's no one to whom we have to answer. And our enemy has proven that he deserves no quarter."

Pasa's hand flew to her cheek. She was still an Eberean, and it dawned on her what was about to happen.

Holak shrugged apologetically. "What did your people think would happen, Pasa? That we'd stay bent over forever? I'll tell you one thing, though. That Celin Kwa, and all those other creeps from your government? I almost pity the poor bastards. I really do. *Almost.*"

Pasa Henz choked, put her hand over her mouth, choked again, and fled from the room.

Holak turned lazily and faced Nev. He asked, "Was it something I said?"

"Never mind that. I want to talk to you alone anyway."

"Are you serious about Taray? Damn it, Nev, what the hell good will I be all the way down there?"

Nev looked around and lowered his voice, even though the shop was empty. "I wasn't kidding about you being the liaison to the Navy. I've come up with a battle plan. The other three objectives I mentioned to Pasa are only part of it. Unfortunately, Kasma Dor will be the final battle ground, unless we can force the killing ground to shift to Cresvo Denor."

Holak's eyes lit up and his pulse began to quicken. This was what he had been waiting for! "Well, don't keep me in the dark, Nev."

"Once we commence violent action, it has to have a direction. It can't just be random."

"Tell me something I don't know."

"Okay, listen up. We begin with a few overt acts. Take out the comm-grids. Seize their supply convoys. Take out key commanders. The more havoc we cause, the more recruits to our side and the bigger our army."

"So far, so good."

"But here's the ultimate plan. I want all of the action we take to draw their manpower in one direction."

Holak thought quickly. "You want to draw them into one pitched battle, a final showdown."

"Right. But it has to be on Cresvo Denor or a coastal town."

"Ah," Holak nodded, getting it. "You want the mass of their troops within range of our naval guns, is that it?"

"You always were a hell of lot more intelligent than you let on, Holak. That's why I need someone I can trust to coordinate with what's left of the Navy."

"I hope those bubbleheads have been keeping up with their training," Holak said. "Morale must be pretty lousy, so far from home, nothing to do, worried about their families."

Nev's eyes widened. "Which gives me an idea . . ."

Holak's jaw dropped. "That's a very good idea. It's brilliant! I'm glad I thought of it."

"You thought of it?"

"All right, we both did. I'll need authorization from you to give to the commodore in person. I hope she's not completely wrung out from partying in Taray."

"This ought to wake her up," Nev said. "Unfortunately, you'll have to make it to Taray on your own. I can't help you there."

"Not to worry, old son," Holak replied expansively. "As you almost said, I'm smarter than I look."

Pasa Henz shouldered open the door of the water closet and slammed it shut behind her. What had she done? What had she heard? What was she *doing*?

She stared at her reflection in the stained and blurry mirror.

She looked the same, a little worse, given the type of day she was having, but not bad at all. Not bad for a traitor.

But a traitor to what? To a nation still so mired in its past that it had lost all sense of love and decency? A government that was risking the flower of its youth to occupy a country that would soon rise up and destroy them? A traitor to whom? A commander who took pleasure in inflicting misery on an entire country full of innocent people? A family that had no use for her, despite the honor she had brought upon them?

If she was anything, she was a soldier who fought with honor on her side. And this occupation of Dalyi was no honorable calling. She was a soldier, not a jailer.

It was all madness. The Eberean thirst for revenge, and the Dalyinese war of vengeance that was soon to follow. A war that her nation would deservedly lose. Everything she believed in was gone, or proved hollow. All that was left was the one thing she had always done without: Love.

From now on, her nation would be Holak Ven. Everyone else could go to hell for all she cared. She reached behind her and removed the flat, razor-sharp fighting knife she had secreted in her waistband.

Gritting her teeth against the pain, in one quick motion, she sliced deeply into her thigh. A tear stung her eyes as she rooted inside the wound until she found the fleck-sized identity chip that had been implanted in every Eberean soldier. With that chip, the wherebouts of any soldier could be determined instantly. She regarded it briefly and then dropped it into the Personal Waste Unit. In another moment, the chip headed where all waste on Thradon went—to the core of the planet, where it would burn so hot that it would disintegrate.

The wound was clean enough; it would soon stop bleeding. It hurt, but who cared. She was free, for the first time in her life. And she and Holak would soon be heading off to Taray, far, far away from the havoc that was soon to follow. Not an ideal spot for a romantic getaway, but who cared? It was far enough, and there was no going back.

Earth
PRESENT DAY

11

There were six of them in Bobby's apartment the day after film-ing ended; in addition to Tom and Frank, Sy and Shirley had driven in from Rancho Mirage. They had brought Holak Ven's VCR tape with them.

As the tape wound on, Bobby went into the kitchen, where Shirley was putting the finishing touches on a guacamole dip.

"Mom," Bobby began, "there's something I have to ask you. I mean, you're a woman—"

"Very astute observation there, sonny-boy."

"C'mon, Ma, you know what I mean. It's about Ket—I mean, Kathy."

Shirley looked up at her son pointedly. "I never thought I'd live to see the day."

"What day?"

"The day where you finally meet a woman who has you all at sixes and sevens. So you haven't worked up the nerve to sleep with her yet, have you? Well, good for you, son. It'll be a new experience, getting to know someone first."

Bobby threw up his hands. "I don't know what to do, Ma. I feel all . . . intimidated."

"You? Intimidated? You?"

"Yeah. But I don't know *why*."

Shirley mashed up another avocado. "I do. Bobby. I said it was a new experience for you, a girl like Kathy. What you seem to forget, being male and therefore, completely self-involved, is that you are a new experience for *her*."

"I don't get you, Ma."

Shirley stopped mashing and looked directly at her son. She loved all three of her children equally, but there was something about Bobby that always kept her on her toes.

"Bobby, you keep thinking of Kathy as a woman."

"A lucky thing, as a matter of fact."

"That's not what I mean and you know it. This may well be the twenty-first century, and we're all very enlightened, but the fact is a woman is still severely limited compared to a man. Men still have the option of making the first move—"

"And women still have the option of telling men where to stick it—"

"Yes, and some women never get asked. Don't change the subject. It's still a man's world, and men are the ones who make the moves."

"*Once* they get the signal from the woman."

"Maybe, but it's still up to the man to make the move. Now, all of a sudden, along comes Kathy—Ket. Her planet has a completely different social dynamic—gender is out of the equation. Kathy has been a soldier all her life—not just a soldier, but a commander of millions of soldiers. She goes after what she wants. A woman general is still a general—if there's a guy she finds attractive, she goes after him. There's no stigma of being pushy, or desperate, or a man chaser. There's none of that Sadie Hawkins crap about it."

Bobby took a chip and dipped it into the guacamole, earning a light slap on the back of the hand for doing so. He grinned. "Aren't you going to say, 'that's for company,' like you used to when I was a kid?"

"That's for company. Is any of this getting through to you?"

"I guess so, Ma. What you're saying is, we've got a Mexican standoff here romantically, is that it?"

"Not really, but I guess it'll have to do, won't it?"

Bobby put his arms around his mother and gave her a kiss.

"You're the best, Mom. Now, I've got to get back in there. I can't wait to see Frank's and Tom's faces."

"This is a joke, right?" Tom was saying when Bobby entered the room. The tape was on pause, and Holak Ven's face was frozen on the screen. "It's a gag, it has to be. Bob, did you get Rick Baker to do this guy's makeup?"

Bobby sat on the arm of the couch next to Ket. He reached down and put his arm around her. To his great pleasure and satisfaction, she responded by sliding in closer to him.

"No tricks, nothing up my sleeve," Bobby said. "This here is the original *ET*, but she hates Reese's Pieces and couldn't phone home if she tried."

Tom shook his head. "Kathy, you know I love you, but come on! This is bullsh—"

"No it isn't," Bobby said. "It's all true."

"Tom," Ket said, "is there any way I could prove it to you?"

"It doesn't matter," Big Frank said.

"Why doesn't it matter?" Tom wanted to know.

"Do you love Kathy? You just said you did. Do you? Or was that Hollywood crap that we all swore we'd never become?"

"Of course I love her," Tom said.

"All right then. I love her, too. So do Sy and Shirley and especially Bobby over there, if body language is any indication at all. So it seems to me, it doesn't make a goddamned bit of difference whether we believe her or not. She's in trouble, she's ex-military like everyone here, and she's asked us for help. That's good enough for me."

"Bravo," applauded Sy. Frank raised his beer in salute.

"I guess it's good enough for me too," Tom admitted. He went over to Ket and took her hand, the one that wasn't on Bobby's shoulder. "Forgive me, Kath? I'm sorry I don't believe you're from another planet; it's just too big a leap for me. But I'm there for you, no matter what."

"Thank you, Tom," she replied, squeezing his hand. "I understand. I'd have trouble believing it, too."

"So, we're okay, then?"

"Of course we are." Mollified, Tom went back to his seat

near the television. "Uh, Tom," Ket said. "Don't you think it's time you forgot about Bonnie? She loves her husband, and you have no chance, movie star or not. So I wouldn't bother asking her to go away to Morro Bay with you this weekend."

"What the—how did—" Tom sputtered.

"'Nother planet," Frank acknowledged drily. "Kathy, you say it might be years before these people can come for you?"

"Yes," she replied. "But I want to be ready now. I know our space program was working on a ship much faster than the one I used. What if the Ebereans captured those plans and forced our technicians to build it? What if there was a prototype and they found it?"

"She's got a point," Shirley said, entering the room with a tray of guacamole.

"It's not only that," Ket continued. "Once the armed resistance begins, events will proceed more rapidly. Everything will speed up and become more critical. Including the need to find *me*."

"You'll have to move out of the house," Bobby told his parents. "They'll trace Kathy there first thing."

"I suppose you're right," Sy replied.

"I'm so sorry," Kathy said. "I know how much you love that house."

"Kathy, it's a house. Lives are more important. Especially yours."

Big Frank went out on the balcony to light a cigarette. He had been doing quite well with his efforts to quit, but every now and then his willpower gave out. Bobby noticed his exit and nodded to Tom. The two joined Frank outside.

"Nice job of quitting," Tom said.

"Shut up," Frank replied.

Bobby glanced sideways at Frank. "You don't really believe her, do you, Master Chief?"

Frank blew out a puff of smoke. "It doesn't really matter, does it? I believe that she believes it, and you, and your parents, who I respect—unlike the rummy losers who brought me into this world—they also believe it. And if Kathy is in trouble, we owe it to her to help her out, because that's the kind of men we are."

"What do you really think she is, Frank?" Tom asked. "Just out of curiosity, I mean."

"What's the diff? I don't know, you don't learn to fight like that at a karate school in a strip center. That's obvious. And she might have been military once—it's in the walk, you know that. We've all got it. My best guess? Some kind of cop, probably. Most likely DEA, maybe the Cartel put a price on her head? CIA? You never know what *those* shirt-lifters'll come up with."

"We're gonna be hanging it out a lot farther than the Gulf, aren't we?" Tom asked.

"The Gulf wasn't personal," Bobby said. "This is."

"Okay, so how do we organize this?" Tom asked Frank.

"What're you lookin' at me for?" Frank said. "We got a general in there. Let's go ask her."

"Mom, Dad," Bobby said, "you don't have to be here for this."

Shirley drew herself up in her seat. "I beg your pardon," she said with dignity. "I worked at the Pentagon. That means I'm the one qualified to be G-2."

"G-2?" Ket asked.

"Intelligence," Shirley said. "G-1 is personnel, G-3 is operations—"

"Oh! I understand," Ket said. "Basic command staff table of organization—it makes perfect sense! I can't believe your military is structured so much like ours."

"Makes sense to me," Sy spoke up. "It's all the same principle. Anyway, Kathy, you're the ranking officer here—in fact, you're the *only* officer here, so you might as well take charge of the briefing."

"I'll take notes," Shirley said, jumping up for a pad and pen.

"Wait a minute," Ket said. She had grown to love everyone in this room, and it suddenly hit her that they were ready to risk their lives for her. It moved her . . . and it troubled her.

"There's one thing I must say," she began. "My life is in danger. Those who will come for me will not stop until I'm dead. And they will kill anyone who stands in their way. Perhaps it would be better if I just went away—"

A chorus of dissension immediately exploded in the room.

"Don't even think it, Kathy," Shirley chided her.

"Forget it. Next!" Frank said.

"You're all very kind, and very brave," Ket said, "but this a serious business. I won't let you put your lives in jeopardy—"

"Our lives are in jeopardy," Sy said, "whether you go it alone or with all of us around you. Trained killers from your planet are coming to our planet. We can't ask for help from the police or the government—they wouldn't believe it, and you don't want that kind of attention anyway. So we are on our own. We might as well do this thing together."

"But you all have such wonderful lives," Ket insisted. "Why would you—"

"Kathy," Sy interrupted her, "Long before—" He stopped and chuckled to himself. "I was going to say, 'long before you were born,' but of course, it wasn't, was it? Anyway, almost sixty years ago, I was at an airbase in northern England, at the briefing before my first combat mission. I was scared to death to begin with, and I was also exhausted because I wasn't able to sleep the night before—don't know who could have. We're all in this big assembly room. Up front there's a map the whole length of the wall, but it's covered up by curtains. Well, the CO comes in, and he starts drawing the curtains back.

"There was a thick piece of black tape across the map, starting at where we were in England and extending all the way to the target. So, the CO draws back the curtain, and keeps drawing it back and drawing it back, and that damned tape just kept going and going and going . . . and when it finally stopped there was this big gasp, everybody in the room all at the same time. You know where that tape stopped?"

"Berlin," Frank said quietly.

"The squadron lost five planes that day. Fifty men. We lost an engine, and the turret gunner got hit bad, but we made it back. And after that I still had twenty-four more to go.

"Well, Kathy, as I've told you before, since that day I've been on borrowed time. And I've used it well. Maybe more than my share. So now it's payback time."

There was a moment's pause as the Terrans in the room returned from Berlin with Sy.

"Let's get to work, Kathy," Shirley said, her pen poised and ready. "And no more about this other thing."

Ket leaned forward. "All right. The first rule of Dalyinese combat tactics is 'know your enemy.'"

"Where have I heard that before?" Frank said.

"Unfortunately," Ket continued, "it's not a rule we follow as often as we should."

"And where have I heard *that* before?"

"It's not a mistake I'm ever going to make again. So I want you to know all about those who are coming. And here's something in our favor; the Ebereans are good fighters—but they make lousy soldiers. Even the Elite Assault Force—who we'll probably run into sooner or later—are only effective as shock troops. If you survive their first attack, the chances are you'll beat them because they lose discipline under pressure."

"But these guys are killers, right?" Tom asked.

Ket nodded apologetically. "Yes, they are."

"How many can we expect?" Frank asked.

"Our ships carry a crew of ten. Ebereans like comfort, so it's doubtful there'll be more than that. But that's ten very dangerous people."

"I wish I liked those odds," Tom said.

Ket smiled tightly. "It's not that bad," she said. "We've got the advantage."

"We do? How?"

"We know the terrain. We're at home here. They'll have to remain hidden and travel by night. They'll have to stay close together for protection. That's not the way an elite team operates; they like to go in without being detected, execute their mission, and be gone before anyone knows what's happened. An elite team uses stealth, shadows its prey, and stays completely hidden but in constant visual contact for hours—sometimes days. I doubt they can do that here—for one thing, they won't be able to simply blend into the population. The shortest one of them will be at least six-foot-six."

"Jesus, they're huge!"

"What about weapons?" Frank wanted to know. "Any phaser/disruptor/Jedi-sword things? I'm not being flip," he added,

"I really want to know what we'll be up against—and I'm also curious."

Ket met the eyes of everyone in the room. The inventory of the Eberean Elite Assault Force ceased to be simply a matter of the standard soldiers' issue—Supply/Weapons/Personal/Anti-Personnel-for-the-Use-of—they were now instruments of possible death of the people in this room.

"Very well," she said softly. She cleared her throat. "The standard issue longarm of the EEAF is the MK240-AP Pulse Rifle. It is capable of firing five-hundred compressed-air pulses per minute. It is charged by a pulse shell capable of delivering up to fifteen hundred rounds—"

"An *air gun,* for Christ's sake!" Tom hooted. "They're gonna come at us with airguns?"

"I've seen those air guns, as you call them, blow a hole right through a man," Ket said sternly.

It was the same voice she had used in the bar, the voice of command that had once been her natural tone. It got everyone's attention.

"Sorry," Tom gulped. "I didn't mean to make light of it. It just sounded—"

"Silly," Frank said. "Now shut up. What else, Kath?"

"Sidearms are the M2K-Compact. Virtually the same gun, just smaller and with less of an effective range. They'll also be armed with . . . Goula knives."

That got everyone's attention.

"I don't think anyone likes the sound of that one, Kath."

"It's a three-bladed fighting knife," Ket said, trying to keep her voice instructional. "A weapon of last resort. It takes some mastery, because the blades are for different uses—hacking, slashing, and stabbing—and considerable skill is needed to switch the blade quickly in a fight. The haft is heavy enough to be used as a club."

Ket stopped speaking and saw that everyone had virtually frozen. She understood immediately; the goula knife was a weapon that struck terror even in the hearts of Thradonians.

"That's why all Dalyinese soldiers are given sidearms," she continued, not adding that the Goula knife was a weapon of Eberean origin and their favorite method of dispensing death.

"We have a saying in the army: 'Never go to a knife fight without a pulse-gun.'

"Sounds like a plan," Bobby commented.

"What kind of weapons are available to us here?" Ket asked. She could hardly come up with a successful battle plan unless she knew what weapons she could use.

Tom and Bobby smiled archly at Frank. Frank still had plenty of connections in the military, especially at the all-important senior NCO ranks.

Frank leaned back comfortably in his chair. "What's available? Or what's legal? 'Cause there's a big difference. Tell you what. I'll take a little drive down to San Diego next week, visit some old friends. I'll see what I can come up with."

"I haven't fired a rifle since boot camp," Sy said. "And that was an M-1."

"These are all the M-1s children, Sy," Frank said. "Only, they're a lot easier on your shoulder—and your thumb."

"Oooh," Sy winced, " 'M-1-thumb.' I forgot all about it. Thanks for reminding me."

Frank grinned and looked over at Bobby. "You're pretty quiet, all of sudden."

Bobby shrugged. "This is the first time in awhile that I haven't been in charge. It's . . . different."

"It's Kathy's province, Bobby," Shirley said. "You know that."

"You've been pretty quiet, too, Mom. I know how you feel about guns. This can't be too pleasant for you."

"I don't know about that, son. I'm a mother protecting her children—who in their right mind would want to go up against that?"

"Not me," Sy commented.

"All right, then."

"Oonah," Ket said, momentarily dropping her command voice, "we're going to have to do some training. If you are not comfortable with the idea of using a weapon—"

"One moment, General," Shirley cut her off. "The Ebereans, they'll be coming after you, won't they?"

"Yes."

"And, Bobby, you'll be with her the whole time, right?"

Bobby gazed evenly at his mother. "Forgive my phraseology,

Mom, but . . . *nobody* fucks with Bobby's Girl." He stood up, strode purposefully over to Ket, kissed her on the lips, and then turned around and sat down again.

"Damn right," Tom agreed.

"Ditto," Frank added.

"Then I guess we're all agreed," Shirley said. "Nobody . . . messes with your girl, and nobody messes with my son, or my husband. Or our dear friends. So, one of you will have to teach me to shoot, and shoot well."

"My pleasure, Shirl," Frank said. "I suggest we all meet in Vegas a few days from now. I'll bring the hardware . . . you bring the beer."

A short time later, Bobby noticed his father standing on the terrace alone. He opened the screen and stepped outside to join him.

"Daddy? Are you all right?"

"I'm fine, son," Sy said heavily.

"No you're not," Bobby replied, putting his arm around his father's shoulder. "You're not okay with this, are you?"

"No, son, I'm not. You know, Bobby, your movies are pretty graphic, lots of gunshots and ketchup."

"I was in a real war, Pop."

"Yes, you were, and I'm not belittling that. But your war, for you, at least, was a clean one. And thank God no one on your ship was touched. But, you pushed a button, and hundreds of miles away—"

"I know what happened hundreds of miles away, Pop. I've never hidden that from myself."

His father let out a sigh. "Bobby, I've seen blood. Lots of it. And I've spilt blood. I was credited for three FW190s, and God knows how many guys I shot that didn't get knocked down, or maybe someone else took credit for. It doesn't matter. I thought I was through with all this."

"I'm sorry, Dad."

"We're past that, son. We're in it now. I'm just making peace with that part of my life that has just changed irrevocably."

He turned to his son with sudden fury. "Remember that, son.

You're entering a new life, now. It's going to change you. It's already changing me. Everything will look different. You'll be acutely aware of just how precious life really is, because you've become that most short-lived of God's creatures—a soldier."

The two locked eyes until Sy was sure that his message had hit home. Then they both turned and looked out over the rail at the Pacific Ocean.

"Say, uh, Pop. You want to do me a favor?"

"Sure."

"Would you mind not calling me a soldier? I'm a swabbie, for God's sake. My life might have changed, but not that much. *Never* that much."

Bobby awoke sweating profusely.

He knew why, too. He remembered every detail of his terrifying dream: Giant, hugely muscular aliens were attacking him with strange three-bladed knives, and he was armed only with a handgun that refused to fire.

It was a long way from filmmaking.

He switched on the light at his bedside and started in surprise. Ket was sitting at the edge of his bed, watching him.

"Kathy!" he said, trying to collect himself.

"I heard you tossing in your sleep. Are you all right?"

"I'm fine. Don't worry. Come on up."

She crawled up the length of the California-king-sized bed until she was next to him at the headboard.

"There's something I've been meaning to ask you," she said.

"Shoot."

"Why haven't we slept together yet? You obviously want to, and I just as obviously want to."

"Well, that's good to know," Bobby replied.

"Bobby, I've gotten everything I've ever wanted in my life. I wish I was more interesting, but I'm not. I've had no great heartbreak, no traumatic incidents, nothing to cause any sort of neuroses that would make me doubt I'd ever succeed. My life has always worked. So, I'm puzzled, Bobby. Is it Earth? Is it me? Why haven't you come into my room?"

"Because you haven't asked me. You're a guest in my house,

and you're entitled to your privacy. I was well brought up, Kathy. I don't go scratching at bedroom doors."

"Of course you were. You were blessed with your parents."

"What about your parents?"

"They're both gone," Kathy said.

"I'm so sorry."

"Not at all," Kathy said. "They were both second-halfers, you know. My father was a soldier, a colonel when he retired. My mother ran a small gown shop. They were both confirmed bachelors living entirely different lives. They met completely by accident; Father was trying to find an old friend's house and stumbled into her shop."

"What did they do with their second halves?" Bobby asked.

"My father helped my mother. Mother had spent her life quite happily running a small shop, catering to an exclusive clientele. When she married my father, she suddenly had a new enthusiasm for life and wanted more. Father approved and used management skills he had learned in the army. In a very short time, there were two shops, then there were ten. When I was born, there were fifty."

Bobby grinned. "Rich kid, huh?"

"I suppose I was. I went to . . . you'd call it 'private school.' I had my own transport—"

"Ooh—not to change the subject, but I have to know. Do they fly or anything? Do they run on lasers?"

"You just did change the subject, no they don't fly—don't be ridiculous—and they run on compressed air and solar energy like everything else on our planet. And oh—they're much more boring than your vehicles. No five-speed transmissions. Now, where was I?"

"You went to private school."

"Yes. And then I was chosen for Tira Gen. Our 'West Point,' I believe you said. As soon as I went into the army, money became a nonissue. Officers are paid well, and our needs are few. Especially when we're young. All I required was enough to keep my dress uniforms up, especially when I was in a Guards Regiment. I didn't really need my parents' money. There's a kind of a code in the army, sort of an unspoken agreement; officers are competitive enough within the army, and showing off with unearned, nonarmy advantages is frowned upon.

"That's for the navy," she added with a mischievous grin.

"Don't look at me," Bobby said. "I was just a petty officer third class. I worked for a living. Unlike now. Did you ever get ahold of the folks' moola? Just curious; I obviously don't need your money."

"Well, when I made general I could finally afford the apartment I always wanted in Grevas, the part of town where I grew up. It's kind of like your place, on the ocean. To tell you the truth, I never thought about their fortune until the will was read. I was having a great career, and that was all that mattered to me. Anyway, it's only money—who cares?"

She slid into his arms and rolled on top of him. "You know what, Bobby? You make me talk too much."

"Jesus!" Bobby exhaled heavily.

"God!" Ket sighed deeply, wiping a tear from her cheek and regarding it with surprise.

"I didn't disappoint you, did I?" Bobby asked, too exhausted at the moment to really care one way or the other.

"Are you serious?" She wiped her eyes again. "This never happens to me. Crying, I mean. I never cried from . . . pleasure before."

He pulled her into his arms. "I'm glad. I was worried that I might not be up to Thradonian standards. Even though, I must admit, I've never been *that* good in my life."

"My body's human, Bobby." She ran her finger down the muscles of his stomach. "You'd make a good Thradonian. Especially in Dalyi."

"I'm flattered, but what makes you think so?"

"Well, I think so. And I'm the toughest judge there is."

"There's still something I don't understand, Kath."

"What is it?"

"Kath, why me? You've had a long career, known lots of decent guys you obviously respect, and even Holak Ven . . . Kath, why me?"

She kissed him. "What about you, Bobby? You have a brilliant career, lots of women would love to be with you, you could certainly take your pick. So, my question is, why me?"

Bobby chuckled. "I guess I see your point. So, I suppose a more logical question should be, 'why *not* me?'"

A little over a hundred miles away in Rancho Mirage, Sy sat in bed reading a book about golfing in Hawaii. Shirley was out of bed practicing with an automatic putt-return.

"Sy," Shirley said as the little bell on the machine tinkled, signifying a perfect putt.

"Mmm-hmmm?"

"You think they did it, finally?"

"Who?" Sy asked, not looking up from his book.

"Madonna and Prince Charles, who. Who do you think?"

"Oh, Bobby and—"

"Yes, Mr. Deductive Logic. Bobby and Kathy. Your son and his lovely girlfriend, the general from another planet."

"Oh. Probably."

"Good." She set up another putt. "Sy."

"Mmm?"

"Would we have to go there, or would her family have to come here?"

"When?"

"If they got married. How would we get everybody to—"

"Shirl," Sy said, looking over his book at her, "aren't you being a little premature, making seating arrangements already? How do you know they even can do it? And if they do, is it the same? And if it is the same, is it as good?"

"Well, I guess we'll know the next time we see them."

A little less than one hundred miles away from where Sy and Shirley were having their discussion, Frank and Tom were heading south on the Santa Ana Freeway in a rented sedan. Frank did not want to use his own car for the trip they were taking.

"Think they did it?" Tom asked, breaking a seventy-five mile silence.

"Absolutely," Big Frank replied.

12

Ket disliked Terran air travel immediately. The air transports were uncomfortable and looked ungainly, unlike the more sharply lined aircraft of her own planet. The entire airport and its environs reeked of the primitive fossil fuel Terrans used, and the engines were so agonizingly loud, she couldn't understand why they were tolerated. Holak Ven must have had a good laugh when he saw Terran air transport.

Not only that, a mere 400-clic voyage took almost an hour. Still, no one seemed to mind. Everyone on the flight to this Las Vegas place seemed to be enjoying themselves, and she was glad to be with Bobby and Oonah and Sy, who had met them at the airport and flown with them.

But Ket did have to admit that she liked Las Vegas immediately, perhaps because she knew exactly what to expect: a Terran version of Srho. She wondered if every planet with life had a Srho, concluding that they probably did. Every planetary race needs somewhere that they can indulge their fantasies, she thought. Or even overindulge them without guilt. Why not?

Unfortunately, they were not in Vegas for those reasons. In fact, they would not be in Vegas very much at all.

Frank had prevailed upon an old navy friend who owned a

ranch-turned-shooting range near Nellis Air Force Base to rent them its exclusive use, including the comfortable lodge, for the next several days. As he was a fellow master chief, he agreed without question, although he also accepted Frank's generous cash offer with equal alacrity.

The range was twenty miles north of town, on a barren stretch of land with a few shacks and picnic tables covered by wooden roofs for relief from the hot Nevada sun. There were targets set up in front of dirt hillsides and several portable johns nearby, which Shirley regarded with distaste as she resigned herself to their inevitable, uncomfortable use. She instinctively knew that she could not look to Ket as a fellow woman for commiseration; as a career soldier, Ket was probably used to lavatories that were far less than sumptuous.

In addition to the weapons and ammunition with which they would be training, Frank had also looked ahead to all contingencies. He had arranged for several large coolers worth of food, water, and juice drinks; and he gave particular thought to Sy and Shirley by setting up a tent with two cots in case the sun became too much for them. For now, though, the early morning was still pleasantly cool, and it would be a few hours before the sun became much of a problem.

"Okay," Frank said. "Let's get started. I want everyone to do two things right now. First, put on your ear protection and switch it on. You're all wearing shades so we don't have to worry about eye protection."

The earphone-like headsets were like normal ones except that they were electronic. Normal hearing was not only possible, but improved, as other ambient noises were filtered out. When sound reached a certain decibel level, as with a gunshot, the channel would automatically close, deafening the explosion to an easily tolerable level.

"I want all of you to keep these in a place where you can grab them in a hurry when the shit comes down," Frank said. "You see all this crap in the movies—you know, like the movies *we* make—where guys throw shots at each other in a house or from a car. Excuse me! This is real life. You fire a gun from a car or in a closed room, and it's the last thing you'll hear for at least a couple of days. The other advantage is, you wear these in an indoor gunfight and the bad guy won't be able to hear anymore, but you will. Keep that in mind."

Frank stopped until a pair of fighters streaking toward the Nellis gunnery range zoomed past.

"Okay, everybody holster up." There were belts and holsters laid out for everyone.

"Why can't we use our own belts?" Shirley wanted to know. "Not that these aren't nice—lovely brown leather, Frank. And my size, too, flatterer."

"Shirl, I know you've got style. The belts and holsters are Bianchis, kind of the Gucci of gun-leather. Nothing says you can't be lethal *and* fashionable. To answer your question, you need a good strong belt that won't sag or tear, and they have to be thick enough so that the holster doesn't ride up when you draw."

"Now, I want everybody to go to the table, take a pistol and holster it. Kathy, today's handgun is a Glock 19, nine millimeter. Not my first choice but a good gun. I chose it for both you and Shirl because there's no exterior safety to fool with, no hammer to get snagged, and it's an easy gun to use and use well."

"Is it loaded?" Bobby asked.

"What?"

"Is it loaded?"

"What?" Frank repeated, reddening.

"Is it lo—"

"What's the first rule of firearms, pissant?"

Bobby winced. "Oh, Christ, I forgot. It's been a long time, Frank, give me a break."

"What's the first rule of firearms?"

"Guns are *always* loaded," Bobby recited contritely.

"General," Frank asked Ket, "I bet you have the same rule in your army."

Ket smiled, feeling comfortable with a weapon on her hip. "Close enough. We say, 'no pulse-shell is ever empty.'"

"What we mean, Shirl, is—"

"I know what you mean, Frank. I'm no dummy. You mean that every gun should be treated as if it were loaded whether it's loaded or not. Right?"

"Gonna be a hell of a shooter, Shirl," Frank said.

"Frank," Ket said, "I mean, Master Chief, sir, could you show

me the ammunition? I've never seen it up close." Ket had seen
enough movies by now to understand the principle of firearms,
but she didn't know the theory of how ammunition actually
worked.

Frank handed her a nine-millimeter round. "You've got four
elements to a round of ammo, or cartridge. Some people call it
a bullet, but technically that's wrong. The bullet is that smooth
missile-shaped thing on the round end. The other three are the
shell, the primer, and the powder. When I pull this trigger, the
hammer strikes the firing pin. The firing pin hits the primer, which
ignites the powder, which then explodes and fires the bullet out
of the barrel."

Ket was dumbfounded. Such a long and involved process—
how could it work? How effective could it be?

"Can this defeat a pulse-gun?" Ket wondered aloud.

"Everyone stand behind me," Frank warned, "Eyes and ears
on. Firing downrange." He pointed at a target, which had a full-
sized bad-guy drawn in color. "Watch the center mass of that target, Kath," Frank said. He crouched and drew his weapon
smoothly, rapid-firing all seventeen rounds of the magazine.

The middle of the paper was completely gone; the wood target stand was visible behind it.

Ket gaped in astonishment. For a primitive weapon . . . it would
certainly do. And that was just the compact version. It was not
as powerful as a pulse-gun, but it didn't have to be—it just had
to be powerful enough.

"That's nothing, Kath," Frank said with a touch of pride. "Okay,
a little later we're gonna familiarize ourselves with the Mini-14
semiautomatic rifle and the Winchester 1300 Defender 12-gauge
shotgun. But first let's get really comfortable with the Glock."

"That's a lot of hardware, Frank," Sy observed.

"Nahhh. That's just the *legal* stuff. The real fun comes later."

Ket fell in love with firearms.

Adapting from Thradonian to Terran weapons proved not to
be a problem; as a soldier she had spent her entire career transi-
tioning from one upgraded version of a gun to another. Her hands
were still strong and quick, her eye was still keen. Once again,

there was that maddening Earth characteristic of noise and more noise—even the biggest pulse-rifle was quieter than the smallest Terran firearm—but there was no mistaking the satisfaction derived from placing a round exactly where she wanted it to go.

No one was really surprised at Ket's aptitude; she was a soldier, and it was expected of her. The big surprise of the day was Shirley, who proved a natural markswoman from the very first. Frank secretly thought that there was no way he would allow either Shirley or Sy in any combat situation, but he was relieved to know that Shirley would be able to handle herself in a dire emergency.

"I've got a special surprise just for you, General," Frank told Ket on the morning of their third day at the ranch. Ket could not imagine what the surpise could be. The shotgun, Mini-14 rifle, and the little Glock seemed to her to be all that could possibly be needed. But Frank went over to the picnic table and removed the oilcloth from an odd-looking weapon, a gun with a short barrel and a long magazine.

Frank picked it up with a proud expression. "*Regardez*! The H&K MP5, nine-millimeter automatic weapon."

"Jesus," Bobby exclaimed. "Isn't that illegal?"

"Few things are as illegal as this little honey," Frank affirmed. "You see, Kathy, it has been against the law for a private citizen to own an automatic weapon in the United States since 1934, when everybody was killing each other with Thompsons. The only exception is if you have a Class III license, but to get one you have to submit to a proctoscopy by the BATF."

"What about all those drug dealers who have guns like this?" Shirley wanted to know.

"They didn't buy them at the local gun shop and go through a Brady check, Shirl. And they sure as hell don't have Class III tickets. To my knowledge, there has never been a crime committed by a Class III holder. It would be stupid; every gun is too carefully monitored. Bobby, if she has this and the two of you are driving somewhere, you'd better slow it down. You don't want to get pulled over with one of these."

"Where'd you get this?" Bobby asked.

Frank shrugged. "Don't ask."

"Oh, man, it was gross!" Tom groaned. "This real low-rent

trailer right near the Mexican border, we're talkin' serious beer
can pyramids, mounted rattlesnake heads white trash, and this guy,
ex-navy, with more tattoos than—"

"Kathy," Frank smoothly cut off Tom, "there's a seventy-five-
round mag in there, but don't let that fool you. It'll be gone in
seconds. Stay light on the trigger."

Kathy could not believe the firepower available from this relatively small gun. She had pressed the trigger for only a second,
but the center of the paper target was gone.

"Think that'll stop your Elite Assault creeps?" Frank asked
smugly.

Ket nodded. She thought briefly of Holak Ven, and what he
might say given a weapon like this. "I think so," Ket replied. She
fired again, completely destroying what was left of the target and
its wooden mount. "I almost pity the poor bastards," she said.

"We've got one other problem," Ket said to Frank. "There's nothing I hate more than being on the receiving end of a surprise."

"You mean, how will we know when they're here? Before they
find you?"

"Yes. Now, they'll probably have their sensors out just before
they enter. The sensors will pick up my escape pod, so they'll
probably land there. Is there any way, short of stationing someone out there to keep watch, to alert us when they land?"

Frank nodded. "That is a problem."

Shirley joined them. "Why don't you set an alarm? One of
those burglar things they have at mansions."

"We could program it so it won't go off if some desert rat
crawls over the spot. Turn it up so only something really heavy
will set it off," agreed Frank. "Nice going, Shirl."

"Well, I am G-2. I should know these things."

"Okay, our initial training phase is over," Frank said. "Tonight
we'll all be in Vegas where you'll all be my guests for dinner at
Michael's in the Barbary Coast, a graduation present from your
instructor."

"Michael's," Bobby commented. "You are generous." He turned

to Ket. "It's one of the best restaurants in Vegas," he told her. "Costs a fortune and is worth every nickel. The best food, and unbelievable service, one of those four-waiters-per-table deals. Thank you, Master Chief," he added.

"It's my pleasure," Frank said. "You've all done well, and I'm not just saying that. I want to add, though, that I believe we should train like this at least once every six weeks, preferably more often. In addition, you want to go to the range with your handguns at least once a week. Take the rifles and shotguns to the ranges at Angeles National Forest as often as you can. And Kathy, we'll have to schedule someplace where you can blow off that MP5. This might have been fun, but we're here for a serious reason. Let's not forget just what it is we're training for."

When they returned to Los Angeles, Ket took all of the money she had earned so far and went to one of the most reputable custom jewelers in town. The shop owner was intrigued by the order, a design that he had never seen and never would have thought of himself.

Several weeks later, at a break in postproduction of Bobby's film, another meeting took place in the Santa Monica high-rise apartment. This was a catered sit-down dinner.

At each guest's place at the table, as well as Bobby's, Ket had placed a blue jewelry case, with the name of the recipient embossed in gold on the lid.

The other five diners all glanced significantly at the cases and at each other, but made an unspoken agreement not to touch the cases until they were invited to do so.

Dinner was a relatively subdued affair. Frank was between films, but Tom was scheduled to begin another picture in England later in the month. Most of the talk centered on reassuring Tom against his own self-doubt, as he was appearing for the first time in a classical British costume drama with actors he had long since held in awe. But mostly the guests were concentrating on the blue boxes and wondering what was inside.

Finally, when the main course was over, Ket stood up.

"In my country—on my planet," Ket began, "gratitude is expressed once, with our Dalyinese Embrace of Thanks, and usu-

ally that is enough. However, in this case, I do not find it suffi-
cient. How can you really ever thank people who have taken you,
a complete stranger—an *alien*—into their homes and hearts without the slightest question or doubt? How do you thank people
who have given you a new life, a new career . . . and a new love?"

"Come on, Kathy," Bobby said. "It's no big—"

"Yes it is, Bobby. It's very big—as big as it can get. The answer is, you can't. And yet, that isn't even the extent of the
debt—"

"Kathy!" Shirley interrupted sternly. "There is no debt. We love
you."

"And I you, Oonah. But there is. Because you have given me
even more. You have—" She stopped until the lump in her throat
receded. "You have now determined that you will risk your lives
for me. And that is something for which no amount of gratitude
is ever enough.

"So, while I can't give you the gratitude you so deserve, I
refuse to turn you away empty-handed. Therefore, feel free to
open your cases."

"Kathy, you shouldn't have," Shirley scolded, although she was
dying to know what was inside.

In each box was a gleaming platinum delta on a platinum
neckchain. On one side of the delta was a gold Duprana sword;
on the other, a golden sun with a diamond set in the center. Ket
ordered platinum upon discovering that it was the earth's most
valuable metal.

"Would you all please stand up," Ket said.

They did so, immediately understanding her solemnity, if not
her purpose.

"The last office I held was high marshal of defense. In this
position, one of my duties was the final authorization of com-
missioning and promotion. As far as I know, I still hold that office. Therefore, as is my right—because you have all proven
yourselves and proven for all the world that you merit this honor,
I now commission you colonels in the Dalyinese Army Reserve.

"You may now don your insignia of rank."

Thradon

NINE MONTHS AGO

13

The Battle for Dalyi began as a war of wits. In this first phase,
Dalyinese freedom-fighters used every possible method to
frighten their Eberean occupiers out of theirs.

The Dalyinese solar grenade, an explosive device using stored
power from the sun, could be either deadly or just temporarily
incapacitating. One never knew. It was said that the one you
heard wasn't the one that would kill you.

Nev Hederes had given inviolable orders that no Eberean was
to be killed in this phase—at least not yet.

"Our aim in this phase is to get the swagger out of their
stride," he told his staff. "The first thing I want is to ruin the
morale of their ordinary soldiers. My aide-de-camp, Captain
Feeh, has come up with a plan to be coordinated by Resistance
cells in every major city. I have approved it. And now I give it
to you."

That was how Groula Feeh had come to be tending bar in
this noisy soldiers' pub in the working-class Bhuhara district of
Kasma Dor. There were ten other undercover freedom-fighters
dispersed throughout the room disguised as waiters and prosti-
tutes of both sexes.

Groula was an inept bartender, but no one seemed to notice.

The Ebereans in this room were mostly young privates, home-sick and gullible. At eight o'clock precisely, as in bars like this in thirty other major cities in Dalyi, they would be frightened to death.

A very drunk Eberean was leaning on the bar trying to bend Groula's ear.

"I miss my girl," the soldier said.

"I don't care," Groula Feeh replied, filling a trayful of drinks and spilling most of it.

"She's the most byoo-ful—"

"Not interested, pal," Groula cut him off.

The soldier dropped his head in drunk suprise. "Bu' yer a bartender. Yer s'posedta be inress-ed."

"Well, I'm not, fella. I don't want to hear your personal prob-lems."

"Wha' kinda bar'nder you, anyways?"

"This kind, sport." Groula looked around to see that no one was watching and conked the Eberean on the head with the jack the real bartender kept there. The drunken Eberean went face down on the bar.

Groula checked the time; it was hard by eight on the dot. He made eye contact with each member of his team throughout the room. When he was sure they were all watching, he nodded. That was the signal to begin a silent ten count and jump for cover.

. . . Three . . . two . . . one! Groula ripped the grenade from where it had been hidden under the bar and tossed it into the center of the room. Then he ducked beneath the bar.

The grenade exploded with a deafening roar. It stunned each and every Eberean soldier in the room. Groula and his team, who had taken cover in time, had drawn their hidden weapons and taken positions covering their enemy.

The Ebereans began to recover from the shock of the grenade.

"Okay, everybody shut up and pay attention!" Groula shouted. He fired at an Eberean who had opened his mouth to protest. The shot was nonlethal but effective nonetheless.

"I said shut up! Now!" He fired several more rounds un-comfortably close to the nearest Ebereans. "Corporal Sani!"

A provocatively dressed young hooker stood to attention. "Sir!"

"Find me the ranking Eberean piece of crap stinkin' up this room. Now!"

"Aye!" The corporal ran through the crowd of soldiers, roughly grabbing at shoulders for rank insignia. She stopped at one petrified youth, yanked him to his feet, and placed her pulse-pistol next to his head. "I do believe we got us a sergeant-third here, Cap'n!" she called.

"Bring him up here, Corp."

Corporal Sani roughly shoved the young sergeant through the crowd.

"Well, Corp," Groula pronounced, examining the young soldier with contempt. "We got us a brand new baby sergeant. How much ass you kiss to get promoted this early, jerkoff?" Feeh marvelled at how his own grammar and syntax had automatically deteriorated to fit the situation.

Frightened as he was, the soldier was at least aware enough of his responsibility in setting an example. He tried to maintain a bit of military dignity.

"Sir, I must—"

"Shut up! Corporal, make him shut his mouth!"

Corporal Sani was about to strike the young sergeant when Groula held up his hand. "What? What'd you say, cream puff?"

"*Youcanhurtmebutnotmymen,*" the kid said in a rush. Groula could not help but feel sorry for the kid and admire his moxie.

"Oh, you a brave little soldier boy? Is that it?"

"Let me take this Eberean pissant outside and blow his nuts off, Cap'n," Corporal Sani urged.

"What you think, Sarge?" Groula asked. "Do I let the Corp here blow your nuts off? See, that way you get to live, only without no nuts. What? Hit him again, Corp!"

Coporal Sani grinned and smacked the soldier on the back of the head. He wobbled, but remained standing. Groula nodded his approval. "Maybe you a real soldier after all," he told the Eberean. "Now, you gonna listen to what I have to say?"

"Yes," the Eberean gritted his teeth.

"Yes? YES WHAT! You talkin' to an *officer,* turd-brain!"

"Yes, sir," the boy amended quickly.

"Good. Now you tell everybody here to pay attention. You tell them to listen to my words. Okay?"

"Yes, sir."

"Well, do it then!"

The sergeant turned to his fellow soldiers. "Pay attention to what he has to say." The soldier turned back and faced Groula.

"All right, then," Groula said. "I am Captain Groula Feeh of the Dalyinese Army. That's right; the Dalyinese Army that you all thought was deader'n Celin Kwa's woodie. Well, guess what? We are very much alive, and your behavior in the next few minutes will determine whether *you* will be very much alive. That's right, kids, the army that kicked your primitive, arrogant asses before is now ready to do it again! Now, I want all you boys and girls from Eberes to know, right now you are witnessing history. We have just started a war, and *you are it.*"

The buzzing in the room started immediately.

"WHAT'D I SAY! WHAT'D I SAY! CORPORAL!" Groula shouted at the sergeant. Corporal Sani slugged the sergeant with her pulse-gun again. This time he did go down, but Groula dragged him to his feet. "What'd I tell you! What kinda sergeant are you! You're a disgrace, boy! Now tell those dipshit friends a yours to keep their mouths shut."

"Ten-hut!" The sergeant tried to shout, although he had no voice left. But it was enough to call the rest of the troops to order.

"That's better," Groula said. "You hurt, boy? Corp, you hurt this kid?"

"Not as much as I could have," Sani replied curtly.

"Ooh, you are strict, Corporal. Sarge, you'd better make these puds stay at attention, or I'm gonna let the Corp here have you for lunch. Now, give me your identification."

"Sir?" the sergeant asked, bewildered.

"Am I wearing a sign that says, 'it's safe to piss me off even more than I already am?' Well, am I?"

"No, sir." The soldier presented his ID wrist-ring.

Groula ran his scanner over it. "Sergeant third-class Ures Pon. That you?"

"Yes, sir."

"You're from ... what the hell is this? Ka-pa-no ... what kinda name is that?"

"Kapanogh, sir. Sixty clics outside Hilva."

"Sixty clics outside Hilva. You got a family there?"

"Sir?"

"Are you stupid? Have you got a family there?"

"Sir. Mother and father, sir. Baby sister."

"Mother and father *and* a baby sister," Feeh announced to the room. "And what do mother, father, *and* baby sister do in Kapanogh, sixty clics outside Hilva?"

"They have a small inn, sir."

"An inn? What the hell for?"

"It's a ... scenic spot, sir."

"Would I like this ... scenic spot?"

"It's very beautiful, sir. Most people do."

"*Most* people do. You got a girlfriend, Sarge?"

"Sir. Yes, sir. She's my fiancée, sir"

"You miss her?"

"Very much, sir."

"What's her name?"

The sergeant winced, then gulped. "I refuse to answer that, sir."

"Her *first* name."

"Biras."

"She pretty?"

"Yes, sir. Very pretty, sir."

"Don't *lie* to me, boy!"

"Nothing special, sir."

"I said, don't *lie* to me, boy."

"Sir. She's ... not particularly attractive, sir."

"What you doing with her, then?"

"I'm happy when I'm with her, sir."

Groula looked past the sergeant at Corporal Sani, who signalled that time was growing short.

"Stand at ease, Sergeant," Feeh ordered. "You want to know why I asked you all those questions, Sarge?"

"Yes, sir."

"Good. Because it's important that you and all your friends here know why. I'm gonna tell you why. I know who you are, and by now we've got the vital stats on every one of your friends in this room. I know about you, Sergeant Ures Pon. That your mom and dad and baby sister have a small inn in a beautiful place they love. That you love. And that you have a plain girl-friend who makes you happy and you've got sense enough to miss her so much it hurts. You know what this means, Sarge?"

"Sir?"

"It means, this war is personal. It means, if I kill you, I don't just wax some poor nameless, faceless dumb-ass in the wrong uniform. It means I waste Ures Pon, a boy who loves beauty and can find it even when it's hidden. It means, I waste you, a warm country inn becomes a hellhole of tragedy for a couple of decent parents who raised their kid right. And it means, I waste you, some poor sweet plain girl might spend the rest of her life all alone 'cause she may never again find a man with enough heart to see how beautiful she really is inside her."

The sergeant's eyes were wet. "What do you want, sir?" he said raggedly. "Why are you doing this?"

"Because this war, son, isn't like any war you ever thought of," Groula said almost kindly. "This war . . . is personal. We un-derstand your Eberean vengeance . . . you waited sixty years and then you struck. But what you didn't realize was this. We Da-lyinese have never lost before. And guess what? We don't like it! And what you don't understand is, we hate losing *more* than you hate us! And we just ain't gonna do it anymore!

"So, kid. Go home. You've got a free pass tonight. So do all of your friends. But under one condition. You leave. You de-part. And you do it *now*. There is a Truskan freighter shoving off tonight. We've negotiated with the Truskans—they'll only intern you for a year. Then you'll be free!"

"But then we'll be dishonored!" the sergeant exclaimed. "We won't be able to go home!"

"Yes, you will. We're going to win, yes, I believe you know that now. And we will set the rules from now on. No one at home will dare hurt Ures Pon, son of innkeepers, beloved of Biras, the world's most beautiful woman no one's ever noticed. Don't make me kill you, Ures Pon. Don't make Captain Groula Feeh, who graduated at the bottom of his class at Tira Gen, son of a political hack from the farm country in Nagnel, don't make

this theatre-lover kill you. Because I will, son. And I'll hate myself and probably turn into a basket case for life, because I'm
a soldier, not a murderer, but you'll still be dead, and those who
love you will still be in agony.

"That is the war you have just seen begin. There is no glory
in this war, young Ures, and even worse, there will be no honor.
This is war in its most basic form—organized murder. For we
are going to murder everyone who won't go home. And you will
have to murder us in return. You will try to hunt me down, but
you'll never find me. I'm too good. And when you can't find
me, you'll murder my sick grandmother, Ures Pon. You will be
ordered to murder my two nieces. You will be forced to murder the poor chump who cleans the bathrooms at the transport
central. Is that why you joined the army, Ures Pon? To murder
old ladies and children and sad stupid men? And when you're
done, how are you going to look Biras in the eye? 'I'm back
from the war, hon, let's go to the scenic place we both love and
I'll tell you all about old pensioners I greased in cold blood.'

"Is that a soldier's honor, Ures Pon? I have no choice! This
is my home. But you do have a choice! Go! Or tomorrow night
that inn sixty clics outside Hilva will be a house of pain. For
tomorrow, if you are still in Dalyi, I will find you, and I will
kill you. And it *will* be personal. Go!"

"Sir . . ."

"GO!" Groula screamed. "EBEREANS OUT! NOW!"

"Go on!" shouted Corporal Sani. "You heard the captain! Get
out!"

The young Eberean soldiers fell into an orderly exit line and
quick-marched for the door in twos. At the end of the line, Ures
Pon looked back at Groula Feeh.

"Go," mouthed Groula Feeh. "*Please.*"

The soldier's eyes widened at the word *please,* and then he
turned forward and followed his comrades out the door.

"Are you all right?" Corporal Sani asked Groula when the
Ebereans were gone.

"I was always prepared to give up my life for Dalyi," a trembling Groula said. "I just didn't know I'd have to give up liking myself as well. How're you doing?"

"I need a drink. I didn't join this lash-up to bully homesick babies."

Groula reached over the bar and grabbed a carafe that felt full. "Here. You know what our problem is? We're too damn decent for this business."

"No, not here," Sani replied, refusing the carafe.

"Where?"

"My place."

"Is that an invitation, Corporal?"

"That whole time, Captain, I was wondering if I could do it. Now I feel rotten."

"Why?"

"Because I found out I could do it. Come home with me, Groula. We'll have a few drinks and go to bed—"

"We'll go to bed? On our first date?"

"Yes. I need someone to hold me while I vomit. And then I need someone to hold me while I weep."

"What do you mean, 'they just disappeared?'" Celin Kwa shouted at his aide. "How do seven hundred of our soldiers throughout Dalyi just disappear?"

"Sir, there's no sign of them! They're just gone!"

"Are they dead? Where are the bodies? Evidence! A torn, bloody shred of uniform? Anything!"

"Nothing, sir! They're just gone!"

Celin Kwa cursed. "Very well. Send an Elite Squad into the Market District. I want thirty hostages. Men, women, babes in arms, I don't care. Release word that if our soldiers aren't returned by dawn, the hostages will die. Publicly. Is that clear?"

"Yes, sir." The aide stopped and considered a moment, then decided to risk it. "May I speak freely, sir?"

"No, damn you! All right. *What?*"

"This hostage-taking . . . is it really a good idea, sir?"

"No! It's a terrible idea! It may be the *worst* idea of my military career! But have you an alternative?"

The aide paused. "N-no, sir."

"Then get out of my sight!"

•   •   •

Nev Hederes scanned the map table with his staff.

"They took them from the Market District here," Groula Feeh said. "They're holding them at the old comm building here. It's too heavily guarded for a rescue."

"We can't stage a rescue," Nev said, hiding the pain he felt. "Anyway, that's not the message we want to send. General Col?"

A young general looked up from the map. "Sir?"

"Have you got a good precision-pulse team ready?"

"Good to go, sir."

Nev pointed to the map. "I want snipers placed here, here, and here. Make them two-man teams, and for God's sake, be sure they have their escape routes ready."

"Of course, sir."

"I want them in place in one hour. Clear?"

"Clear, sir."

"Have them fire exactly on my signal."

"Sir?" Col asked. "What is our target?"

"It'll all be explained."

Fifty-five minutes later, Nev tapped into the Eberean command-channel.

"This is General Hederes for Celin Kwa."

"Whyn't you go soak your head, pal?" the corporal on comm-watch replied.

"Why don't you pull your head out of your ass, soldier, and do as I say?"

Celin Kwa's private channel piped in. "Governor, forgive the intrusion, sir. There's a guy on the channel here says he's General Hederes."

"Put him through," Kwa commanded. "Well! General Hederes! We finally meet!"

"Let's cut out the phony part of the meeting, shall we, Kwa?"

"As you wish, General. What can I do for you?"

"You can release the thirty hostages you took this morning."

"And you can release the hostages you took last night."

"This is not open for negotiation," Nev replied evenly. "Free them now."

"Or else what?"

Windows shattered at several points in the headquarters building. Kwa's aide rushed in.

"The Dalyinese are attacking!" he shouted. "Three soldiers dead, another badly wounded, right in the next office!"

"Quiet!" Kwa snapped. "What does this mean, General Hederes?"

"Do you remember what it was like, Kwa, when we were the government and you were the rebels?"

"Heady days, General, heady days."

Windows in the building shattered again. Kwa's aide demanded a report. He listened a moment. "Six more dead, sir!"

Kwa held up his hand for silence. "Just what do you hope to accomplish, General Hederes?"

"Free the hostages, Kwa. *Now.*" The channel closed.

Kwa glanced at his aide. "Release the hostages," he ordered.

"But sir—"

"Our soldiers are gone. Casualties of war. We've nothing further to gain either keeping them or killing them. Killing them would have been stupid anyway; why make the people think they have nothing to lose anymore? We'll give an address on the comm-channel that the civilians were merely held for questioning in the matter of our missing soldiers, and then released."

The aide started in surprise. "You're not letting them go unpunished, sir?"

"Who said anything about letting anyone go unpunished?" Kwa paced for a moment. "It would appear that the cavalry charges have begun. And yet, Ket Mhulhar is still conspicuously absent. I find this all very difficult to credit. And where is the greatest cavalier of all, Holak Ven? Where is Holak Ven through all this?"

"He is missing, sir. Along with General Henz. We lost her locator—"

"Ah!" Kwa replied dreamily, "dear Pasa. So love finally triumphs." His tone became stern. "Find him. I don't give a damn what it takes. Search all of Thradon if you have to. If we find him, we find her. Get Holak Ven back, and do it now!"

14

The island nation of Taray was enjoying a booming economy, as it always did during a war. Wealthy refugees from Dalyi had infused millions into local businesses, as had deserters from both armies, spies, quick-buck artists, and criminals from both countries. In addition, the suriving vessels of the once-mighty Dalyinese Navy, four capital ships with crews of nine thousand each, were adding even more to the Tarayan economy; the crews had to be fed, clothed, and equipped, and the ships needed refitting and constant maintenance. All of which the Tarayan government was happy to supply on credit. If the Dalyinese won back their country, it would all be repaid at the standard usurious Tarayan interest rate. And if the Dalyinese lost, there'd be just as much to be made supplying the rebels with weapons that had originated in their own country.

The business-minded Tarayans knew that there was nothing to be gained by taking sides. That was sheer foolishness, a myth perpetrated by those destined to die or starve or live out their lives in servitude. The Tarayans welcomed misery elsewhere on Thradon; it always spelled profit for them. If they had taken sides, they would probably root for the Ebereans to conquer the whole world; just imagine the money that could be made then!

As expected for a country that profited so much on the misery of other nations, the vices in Taray flourished. There were more fleshpots in Taray per city than anywhere else on Thradon. There were more desperate people and places where life was worth a pittance.

Holak loved it.

"My kind of place," he told Pasa Henz. "Everyone is as big a lowlife as they seem. There's a strange sort of integrity about it."

What Holak really liked about Taray was that it was an easy place in which to get lost. There were too many people on the run for anyone to be interested in the business of others. And spies were easy to detect, if anyone had bothered; most just assumed that the other fellow was up to no good and left it at that.

Because Taray was closer to the sun throughout the year than any other nation on Thradon, it boasted a vast surplus of solar energy. And because it was an island, its water supply, thanks to the planet's most advanced condensors, was inexhaustible. Energy and fresh water on Taray were virtually free, which kept down the costs of construction and allowed for perpetual irrigation, leaving the island completely self-reliant.

Therefore, one had an island of garishly sumptuous yet inexpensive luxury.

"It's cheap to live well in Taray," the saying went, "but then, you're living in Taray." The island had thousands of bars, brothels, and casinos but not a single museum, theatre, or university. Tarayans weren't interested in culture or education. They were interested in business and pleasure.

Holak and Pasa spent three days in their hotel room when they arrived in Tan Wo, the capital of Taray. For three days they forgot about Dalyi, Eberes, and everything else. It was only when news of the first strike against the occupiers and the subsequent release of the hostages was announced that the real world began to make its presence known. Then Holak remembered his critical errand.

"Where are you going?" Pasa asked from bed as Holak began to dress.

"Just out for a little stroll, my love. I'll be back."

She held out her arms. Holak went to her. "Don't be long," she said.

"Just a mere twinkling, my pet. Feel free to luxuriate in my absence."

"Will I ever see you again?"

Holak tossed her his trademark devil-may-care grin and left. But alone in bed, Pasa Henz began to wonder.

The four surviving vessels of the Dalyinese Navy were capital ships; the *Kuran Il,* the *Kasma Dor,* the *Lansa* and the Navy's flagship, the *Sha'n Res.*

These were the world's four most powerful ships afloat. The Ebereans had long wanted them captured or destroyed, but each ship was so fast and and so heavily armed that the cost of its capture or destruction would be far too great to bear. The Ebereans believed they were safer keeping them at extreme distance.

Each ship was armed with pulse-guns twice the size of those that had controlled Mount Ugon decades before, making it sheer folly for any ship or aircraft to attack it. What made the ships even deadlier, however, was the fact that their incredible size allowed the ships to each carry several squadrons of fighter-bomber aircraft. Each ship was the equivalent of a dreadnought, submarine, and carrier rolled into one.

They were outrageously expensive to keep afloat, but then, Dalyi had been the wealthiest country on Thradon.

Therefore, the small fleet was a valuable prize and security was heavy. The ships were submerged off the coast of Tan Wo and were impossible to find without an escort; security was so heavy that anyone who did stumble upon them was interned on board. But Holak wasn't interested in getting near any of the ships.

All he really had to do was jump into a hired transport and ask the driver for the nearest flyboy hangout. At the price of an enormous tip, the driver kept his word and dropped Holak in the least reputable quarter of the world's least reputable town.

Holak felt at home immediately; nobody partied like a fighter jock. You could cut the arrogance with a Goula knife—any blade would do. But this crowd was missing the usual high spirits en-

demic to fighter jockdom. The air was permeated with home-
sickness and frustration.

What Holak had intended to do was to unobtrusively strike
up a quiet conversation with one pilot at a corner of the bar.
But all he had to do was enter the room and all conversation
stopped. He had forgotten that as the most celebrated pilot in
the history of Dalyi, he was known to flyboys and -girls everywhere.

"Hey, fellas, you know who that is?"

"Holy crap, I don't believe it!"

"Damn, guys, it's Holak freakin' Ven!"

"Does this mean it's started? When do we get to fight?"

The young pilots all gathered around him, slapping him on
the back, shaking his hand, voicing their surprise at his presence. Normally, such effusive greetings by Navy pilots to a mere
Army pilot would be inexcusable, but this was for God's sake
Holak Ven. The guy who was so cool and in command that he
had made the entire battle for Mount Ugon possible in the first
place. But mostly they asked about home.

He saw the sincere, worried faces around him and decided
they would not be denied. He would tell them everything. But
first things first.

"Who's the senior officer in here?" he asked.

A very junior commander stepped forward. "I guess that'd
be me, sir," she said.

Holak took her aside. "Which ship are you from?"

"The *Kuran Il,* sir. Second Ground Attack Wing."

"Anybody here off the *Sha'n Res*?" The *Sha'n Res,* named
for the nation's capital, was the Navy's flagship.

"That tall, skinny flight lieutenant over there, sir."

"I'd like to speak to him alone."

Her brow furrowed, but she knew better than to question his
orders. "Right away, sir."

The flight lieutenant stood a head taller than Holak, who wondered how he could fit comfortably into the cockpit of a navy
fighter. But he had to be a damn good pilot, or he wouldn't have
been one of the hand-picked aircrew for the fleet's pride and
joy.

"Flight Lieutenant Rigas reporting, sir."

"Nice to meet you, Rigas. And now, I have to apologize. I need you to cut your liberty short."

"That's quite all right, sir. How may I help the colonel?"

Ven put a hand on the young pilot's shoulder. "I just want you to get back to the ship. I have a chain of command order for you."

The flight lieutenant's eyes widened at the request. A chain of command order was one that had to be given in person. It was accompanied by a code word, so that no one would know for sure just whom the order was for. But it had to be *big*.

"Is this it, sir? Are we finally—"

"You'll know soon enough. Just keep it to yourself. The code is *Lightning Six*."

"Aye-aye, sir."

"Hey, don't 'aye-aye' me, flight lieutenant. I'm a land-lubber."

Rigas grinned. "Nobody's perfect, sir." He saluted and hurried out of the bar. As soon as he reached the ship, he would deliver the code *Lightning Six* to his immediate superior, who would relay it to his immediate superior and so on up the chain of command, until the officer who actually was Lightning Six received the order and acted upon it.

Therefore, as Holak Ven was narrating slightly embellished tales of the newly begun revolution to the rapt young pilots who refused to let him pay for a round, the fleet commander was receiving the Lightning Six order.

"Commodore!" the fleet commander's exec burst into her stateroom. The commodore was completely nude, having just stepped out of a shower.

"Well, come on in, Aldes. Put your feet up—pour yourself a drink, why don't you?" Everyone was cranky from long months of frustrating inactivity and the commodore was no exception.

"Sorry, ma'am."

"This is important, it better be!" The commodore stepped into the air-dry, then exited and put on a robe with the ship's crest emblazoned over the left collar.

The exec stood to attention. "Ma'am! The order is, chain of command—Lightning Six!"

The commodore motioned for the exec to sit down. Then she

went over to her stateroom bar, which she had resolved to avoid until the moment her sailing orders finally arrived. She poured two stiff shots and handed one to the exec. They clinked glasses.

"It's about goddamn time," she said.

"I'm afraid it's true, sir," said Celin Kwa's aide.

"There's no mistake?" Kwa demanded.

"No, sir. The *Sha'n Res* left the territorial waters of Taray sometime yesterday morning. The *Lansa* is reported to be on the move although still in Tarayan waters."

"What of the *Kuran Il* and the *Kasma Dor?*"

"Nothing yet, sir. They may have gone too deep for our ADF to pick them up. We know they're still somewhere off the Tarayan coast. Where could they be heading?"

"Idiot! Here! Where else? Alert the Navy." Even as he gave the order, Kwa knew it was useless. The Eberean Navy in its full complement couldn't hope to lay a glove on any one of the Dalyinese ships of the line. But that wasn't what was worrying him. What was the Dalyinese Navy after? They couldn't hope to engage a land-bound enemy from the sea, not for a decisive victory. What was their motive? He had to find out.

The trouble was, there was no one he could ask. The most senior admirals had been eliminated in the early days of the invasion. There was no one left to torture for information, no one who could tell him anything he didn't already know. He would have to find his clues elsewhere. He would send out search teams again, just as he had at the hour of victory. Once again, they would search any building formerly housing Dalyinese military authority and report any findings they could. They might have missed something the first time around.

"Major," he told his aide, "I want information retrieval teams ready to go now."

"Yes, sir. Where shall I send them?"

"The old Admiralty Building, to begin with. The government security building. And . . . oh, yes. The old space program headquarters, Cresvo Denor."

"Sir, Cresvo Denor was destroyed. It was blown up just before we took Kasma Dor. It's just a lump."

"Then search the lump. You can blow up anything. Destroying it is another matter."

Comm-watch piped in. "Sir, secure from the Central Authority."

"Very well." Kwa motioned with his head for everyone to leave the room. This was a call he'd have to take in private.

The speaker of the Central Authority glowered over him from a long wall.

"Don't even start with me," Celin Kwa warned.

"I may be your cousin, Celin, but that still doesn't mean—"

"Shut up! Just shut up! I told you morons *years* ago that this would never work. I warned you, a year at most, then all bets were off. The Dalyinese would never stand for being occupied—"

"What are you talking about? We won! We defeated the great and powerful Dalyi—"

"We won a battle—just as the Dalyinese won a battle at Ugon. We can take this country, but we can't *rule* it."

"You can't put down a little rebellion?"

"NO! You bloody idiot! Doesn't history teach you anything? No rebellion can be put down once it starts. Because once people decide they would rather die than be ruled by you, you've lost. You might as well go home."

"Well, you haven't been giving them that choice," the speaker glowered. "You've been far too lenient with the Kasma Dorans. Armed rebellion! Citizens flaunting Dalyinese customs in your soldiers' faces. You let them get away with it?"

"Of course I do, you simpleton! My soldiers are mostly children! They know nothing of history. They're far from home in a place they don't understand. Do you know how simple it would be to undermine their morale?" Also, Kwa didn't add, he was not about to be branded a war criminal in a losing fight.

"Now, I told you a year and a half ago—I could hold Dalyi for a year and probably no more. The old army units would begin to reconstitute themselves. And once the Dalyinese have an army again—"

"Celin! Are you saying that the Dalyinese are better soldiers than—"

"Of course I'm saying that! They *are* better soldiers. Any fool could see that. If they pull together, we're fu—"

"Celin. You are speaking treason."

"As opposed to what? Loyalty and self-deception in a dream-world?"

"Celin Kwa! I command you to find the ringleaders of this . . . *this,* and kill them. I want Hederes, Mhulhar, Ven, and Col, dead! You are ordered to contain this terrorist movement! Fail, and your life is forfeit. Do you understand?"

"Our family isn't very close, is it?"

"DO YOU UNDERSTAND?"

"Yes, Your Excellency."

His cousin vanished from the wall. Celin Kwa breathed a sigh of relief. He remembered how he used to beat the hell out of his cousin as a boy; now he no longer regretted having done so.

"Sir," his aide entered the room. "It turned out you were right about blowing things up as opposed to destroying them. Our search team just reported in from Cresvo Denor. You're not going to believe what they found."

"Try me," Kwa said tiredly. "I've had a long day and it's still morning. Get to the point, major."

"They've done it, sir. They've found her."

"Found who?"

"General Ket Mhulhar, sir. We now know where she is."

Kwa suddenly came to life. "Why, that's wonderful! I'll lead the assault team myself. I want a flying squad of transports—"

"Uh, sir. We know where she is, all right, but that really isn't much help."

"Are you going to tell me where she is? Or do I merely look quietly forward to the end of the business day?"

"Sorry, sir. She's . . . on her way to Earth, sir."

Celin Kwa did a double take that was positively vaudevillian. "You mean to say . . . she's on another bloody *planet*?"

"Yes. A very far planet, sir. It's way across—"

"I know where the Earth is, Major. I sat in on Holak Ven's lectures after his last trip. The closest planet to Thradon in livability and basic characteristics ever discovered. Holak said that the people are really quite warm and amusing, if primitive, and that they are not ready for contact."

"Well, they're in contact now, sir. Or they will be, when General Mhulhar lands in about six months or so. But, sir . . . that's not all we found."

"Well, don't keep me in the dark, Major."

"A prototype, sir! My exec, Captain Huul, he's an engineer. He told me this prototype could be the fastest ship ever! And that's not even the good part. It hasn't been tested, but this one doesn't need an escape pod. It can enter the earth's atmosphere all by itself, make a soft landing, and take off again. And, sir! It doesn't even need a fuel supply! It's got a solar funnel that catches—"

"Get me everything, Major. Every scrap of information you've found intact."

"Yes, sir!" the major replied enthusiastically.

"And, Major . . ."

"Sir!"

"Well done." The major saluted and turned on his heel. My heavens, thought Celin Kwa, and here I thought this was shaping up to be a simply *rotten* day.

Earth

PRESENT DAY

15

A month before, Bobby had inexplicably disappeared into his office in the Santa Monica apartment. Ket instinctively knew not to disturb him, as she heard nothing but the tapping of a keyboard from dawn till dusk. He emerged only for meals and even slept on the daybed in his office.

Ket was far too secure with herself to even consider that he might have second-guessed the attraction he had for her. She simply gathered that he was inspired and that was that. He would come out when he was done with whatever he was working on.

Finally, after five weeks of this, he emerged from his office with a sheaf of pages, which he dropped into her lap. He kissed the top of her head.

"Read this," he said. "If you hate it, I'll burn it. If not, that's our next film, if I get it past the pants lizards."

She stared at the title page. "*Bobby's Girl*?" she asked incredulously. "Is this what I think this is?"

He flashed the mischievous smile she had so come to love. "Read it and find out," he said. "Take your time. I'll go and—"

"No, stay," she said. "It won't take long."

"All right." Bobby helped himself to a drink from the kitchen and sat down across from her. He usually hated to watch someone read his work, but this was different. Also, as Ket read about five times faster than the average person, this wouldn't take long.

And it didn't. Ket's expression was neutral as she read a virtual journal of her visit, starting from the moment she met Sy and Shirley to the last few weeks, and an extrapolated, slambang ending where the Eberean assault teams land and get annihilated by Bobby and Company.

"Well, what do you think?"

"Do you want the whole world to know about—"

"Kathy. The whole world knows by now that we're an item. But that's as far as it goes. You've been here long enough. Do you think anyone would really believe that you're from another planet?"

"No, that's true," she admitted. She put on her producer's cap. "This will be a costly film, Bobby. Will the studios back you?"

"The hell with them. I've made them enough money. It's about time they indulged me just a bit. Do you love it or not? That's the important thing."

"I love *you*," she said. "But the script needs work."

He crossed over and took her into his arms. "Later," he said.

"Much later," she agreed.

"I'm curious," Bobby said much later. "I mean, if it doesn't depress you to talk about it—but what do you suppose is happening on your planet—in your country, right now?"

"It doesn't depress me," she replied. "Bobby, when I awoke to find myself in deep space, in an entirely different body, knowing full well that I might never get home—I went through that whole psychodrama alone, back in the ship. That it was a well-intentioned but misguided effort to save me because our premier really believed our way of life was gone forever. It was a tough break, but I'm here now, Bobby. The second half of my life has already begun. A little earlier than I planned, but it's here. And I'm fine with it."

"Are you sure? I mean, you're a general, for God's sake."

"Is that what this is about, Bobby? You're still intimidated

because I'm a general? Well, forget it! I'm not a general anymore. That was my first half, and it was wonderful. And I've
no complaints about my second half, so far."

"Well, I'd be going nuts, if I were far from home and—"

"I am going nuts. But there's nothing I can do about it. I
had my orders from the premier. If I can ever get back to
Thradon—"

"Whoa! What do you mean, if 'I' ever get back to Thradon?
You mean, if 'we' ever get back to Thradon."

"Bobby. I wouldn't want to put that on you—"

"Hey, it's already there."

"What about your work? What about your parents?"

Bobby shrugged. "You yourself said you'd want to bring
movies back to Thradon. You wouldn't want to do that alone,
would you?"

"But what about your parents?"

"Do you have golf courses on Thradon?"

"No, but we could build one easily enough. In fact—" she
started laughing. "Oh my God! The contributions of the Albertson family! Movies and golf! You'd become absolute gods!"

"There you are, then."

"You'd really do that for me? Leave everything—"

"If we're together, I'm not 'leaving' anything."

They embraced then, and Bobby felt tears on his shoulder.

"Hey, Bobby's Girl," he said softly. "You all right?"

"Better than I ever thought I would be, Kathy's Guy."

"Then help me out," he said, jumping into work mode.
"You're a general. Your country is occupied by the Ebereans.
Tell me about it. How would you play it?"

"There's really only one way you can play it. First, you must
understand that no Dalyinese soldier is ever truly mustered out.
It's never happened until now, but once a national emergency is
declared, all soldiers are returned to duty and are part of the
chain of command."

"So everybody gets called up," Bobby remarked.

"Yes. The Dalyinese Army is the best trained in the world—
on Thradon. Our motto is, 'Training Is Everything.' So when a
soldier returns to duty, there's no need for him or her to get used
to being back in harness—they simply get back to work."

"So, all of the soldiers in the Dalyinese Army, the ones who are left, they're good to go?"

Ket nodded emphatically. "Oh, yes. And the chain of command is back in place. All they need is a coherent plan. The Ebereans should have known this, but it's too late now. They're really in for it." She looked at Bobby meaningfully. "That's why they had to practically force me to follow the premier's orders. I really wanted command of the Resistance. But Nev Hederes is going to do a great job."

"What do you suppose he'll do?"

"Well, he served under my direct command for most of his career, so I think it's safe to say that he'll do what I would do."

"And that is . . ."

"Match our strength against their weaknesses. Then build a trap and shove them into it."

"You make it sound so simple," Bobby said.

"Most good plans are. The very first lesson we ever learn in basic military science is, always fight the enemy on your terms. Never on theirs."

"You mean, never react, always proact."

"Exactly. That's why, Bobby, after this picture is done, we're going to do some serious training. If Ebereans ever land here, we're going to have to have a viable plan and we're going to have to follow it to the letter."

"Hey," Bobby said. "That's your job. I only make movies."

"And when we're making movies, I'll always listen to you. But you're also a colonel in the Dalyinese Army Reserve, and when you're called up—"

"Don't worry, hon. I'll be a good soldier. I promise."

But Ket wasn't so sure; the only thing Bobby took seriously was filmmaking. She hoped he meant it; she would need him when the time came.

The film *Bobby's Girl* was green-lighted almost immediately, despite its hefty price tag. The studio smelled box office, as it always did from a high-budget space thriller, and they also felt that Bobby had earned the right to move up to bigger-budget films. *Bobby's Girl,* which appeared on paper to be a slam-dunk, seemed just the ticket to push Bobby up to the A-list.

Because Bobby had also paid his dues as a writer as well as a director, they allowed him to take the script through development. During the first rewrite, Ket sat beside him at the computer every day. That was until Bobby discovered that she could type at least three times as fast as he could. Then Ket took over.

"There's another character I want to introduce," Ket said. "An Eberean, but interesting."

"They're not all boring, are they?"

"You'd be surprised. I'd like Victoria St. Louis to play her."

"You hate Victoria St. Louis!"

"No, I don't. I just . . . can't stand her. But I admire her as an actress, and I think she'd do well here. There's an Eberean officer I once knew quite well. She served under me at Truska and distinguished herself in combat. Her name is Pasa Henz. I'd be willing to bet she's a senior general by now, almost assuredly high up in the occupational government."

"What was wrong with her?" Bobby wanted to know.

"Oh, she was a good officer, honorable and decent. But she needed something. I never could figure out what it was, love, approval, I never knew. But I always knew one thing . . . she was hopelessly in love with Holak Ven. Had been for years."

"And what'd old Holak think? Did she have a chance?"

"Holak was never the sort to go looking. You had to almost jump out at him."

"Did you?"

"Are you jealous?"

"Of course. He sounds like a hell of a guy. Did you?"

She shook her head. "Holak and I were close friends from the instant we met at Transitional Barracks—those nightmare first weeks at Tira Gen. We always thought that the worst thing we could have ever done to our friendship was to ruin it by getting married. So we stayed friends—the very best kind of friends, and yes, when we needed love, we were also there for each other."

"What about your second halves? Do you think, in new careers, with the pressure of being military hotshots completely off, you would have finally married then?"

Ket dimly remembered the Five-Point Kiss. "Yes. I believe we would have done just that."

"Now I'm really jealous," Bobby said.

"Don't be, because I've got another casting suggestion."

"For Holak Ven? Who?"

"You."

Bobby barked a quick laugh of disbelief. "Are you kidding me?"

"I can't think of anyone else. I wouldn't want anyone else."

"But I haven't acted in years, not since *Valley Kingpin*!"

"And you were good, Bobby. Bobby, I've seen you run lines with Frank and Tom, and even Vic sometimes—and you *are* good. Plenty of directors act in their own movies—Quentin Tarantino, Sydney Pollack, why not you?"

"The studios'll never go for it. They'll want Bruce Willis, or somebody like him."

"He's not tall enough. Come on, Bobby, do it for scale, the studio'll be thrilled to save ten million dollars."

Bobby stared at her in disbelief. "You sure know your stuff, don't you? Really, Kath, you amaze me. How'd you get earthed-out so fast?"

"Did I ever tell you about my second-class year at Tira Gen?"

"No, but by all means—"

"It's the last big test. You pass it, and you cruise through final year, which mostly prepares you for graduation. But if you flunk, you have to repeat it. Flunk it again, and you're out. Know what we had to do?

"We had to go to a foreign country and live there. Take a job, establish a new life, and just be there, part of the neighborhood, for a year. Oh, you had to pretend to be a citizen of that country, too, with a whole history for yourself, learn the language perfectly and all that. You had to check in with a control every week, and if you got caught—"

"You were able to do all that?"

"Yes. Because if you're smart, you begin preparing for it in your first year. So I became a transport worker in Truska. I learned all I could about the country, found my way in, got a job, and lived there bored to death for a full year."

"What was the point?" Bobby asked.

"There was no point. It was the military, why would there be a point? However, it did prove to me that I could adapt anywhere, and to anything. And that's what makes a good officer."

"Just out of curiosity," Bobby asked, "where did you graduate in your class at Tira Gen?"

Ket mumbled an answer.

"What? I'm sorry, I didn't hear you."

"First," she muttered.

"All right," Bobby sighed. "I'll play Holak Ven." He put on a newscaster's voice. " 'And in the world of entertainment, Bobby Albertson played Holak Ven in his latest film. Holak Ven lost.' "

The final pitch session went well, up to a point. Bobby had insisted that Ket accompany him to the meeting, telling her that she might as well get used to dealing with the pants lizards.

The green-light guy was a well-dressed presentable fellow with a bad sinus problem that forced him to punctuate every sentence with a glottal *chhh*. The meeting was interrupted by a ringing phone a conservative average of twelve times per minute. Ket saw it for what it was, a tactic to let Bobby know just where he rated in this man's pecking order.

"Bobby! Chhh! Good to see you. And this must be the famous Kathy Miller, your new right arm, chhh! You're pretty enough to be *in* the picture. Sit, sit!"

"Thank you, Ed." Bobby then sat and waited. These meetings were by and large a game of flinch. Whoever talked first, lost. The picture was already a lock. The purpose of this meeting, Bobby knew from experience, was to take as much of it away from him as possible.

"Bobby, we've got a slight problem, chhh."

"Oh?" Bobby asked nonchalantly. "And what might that be?"

"My board doesn't get the whole girl-general bit. They want it to be a guy who comes from the other planet." He held up a protesting hand even though Bobby hadn't said anything. "I know, I know, chhh. It's 2K, we all should know better. But the fact is, a guy has a better shot at opening the picture. Who would really believe a girl could be that kind of general, anyway?"

Ket and Bobby glanced at each other.

"The way I figure," Ed continued without benefit of a chhh, "is figure Willis or Schwarzenegger or, don't laugh, but Stallone would kill for a hit right about now, that would give us an open that would knock *Titanic* flat on its ass."

Bobby looked significantly at Ket, made a slight motion toward the door.

Bobby stood up, and Ket followed suit. "I'm sorry it had to be this way, Ed."

The phone rang again, and Ed picked it up. "Wait, wait!"

But Bobby and Ket turned and went through the door.

"Wait, Bobby! Jesus!"

"I'm sorry, Ed. Looks like I go back to Warners."

"Jesus, Bobby. Chhh! It was just an idea!"

"Not the right idea, I'm afraid," Bobby replied evenly.

"Look, Bobby, it's your first A-list picture. We have to cover all the bases."

"The bases are covered. I've got a terrific story, and we're going to kick ass at the box office. Now, whether we kick ass for your studio, or someone else's, that's up to you."

"Look, let me talk it over with—"

Ket turned up the corner of her mouth so that only Bobby could see it.

"Good-bye, Ed."

"All right, all right! Jesus, Bobby."

"That's my name; Jesus Bobby. Do we have a deal?"

"Bobby . . . chhh . . ."

"Do we have a deal?"

Ed sighed. "I'll send the contracts around in the morning."

"Why, thank you, Ed. It's always a pleasure doing business with you."

"Goddamn it," Bobby exclaimed as they walked out to his car. "Now you know why I've stuck with indie films this long."

"I thought you did quite well in there."

He turned to her. "I owe it all to you. You knew he was bluffing, didn't you? You felt it?"

"Of course."

Bobby took her in his arms. "Why don't we get married?"

Ket looked at him in surprise. "You want to marry me?"

"Who better?"

She smiled. "All right," she said. "Close your eyes." Ket kissed his eyes his nose, his ears and his mouth.

"Is that a Dalyinese thing?" he asked.

"It's about as Dalyinese as you can get," she replied. "The Five-Point Kiss. It covers every sense."

"Is that what happens when you get engaged?"

"Engaged, hell!" she replied. "It means we're already married."

"Wow!" Bobby said. "I never thought I'd marry a general!"

"You didn't. You married Bobby's Girl, that's all."

Thradon

SIX MONTHS AGO

16

The coded message to Nev Hederes had gone through sixteen layers of security before reaching him. It was an appeal from the government of Truska.

PLEASE STOP SENDING US EBEREAN DEFECTORS. WE CANNOT POSSIBLY HANDLE ANY MORE. TRY TARAY OR BRUNEPA.

Nev Hederes chuckled briefly and handed the note to General Col.

"What are we going to do with them, then?" Col wanted to know.

Nev shook his head. "They'll take them in Truska. With what we're going to pay them after we win, they'll be glad they did."

"With *what* are we going to pay them?"

"Our infrastructure is still intact. It won't take long before our economy is up and running again." He paused and smiled inscrutably. "And let's not forget Eberes. They've looted trillions from us during this occupation. Well, now they're going to have to pay it all back."

In the months following the first hostile actions, Eberean defections had been fast, furious, and frequent. The simple message, leave or die, was taken seriously by the mostly young, in-experienced, and poorly trained soldiers of the occupation force. Defections, particularly from the lower ranks, were decimating the Eberean force far more rapidly than violent actions, which were also becoming more commonplace.

All Dalyi wanted in on the Resistance. It was now widely accepted among the Dalyinese populace that liberty was at hand, and even those with the most to lose, who in other cultures might have become easy targets for collaboration, were anxious to risk their fortunes, their safety, and even their lives.

The Dalyinese Army secretively but rapidly mobilized. In cities all over Dalyi, units big and small terrorized the Ebere-ans, forcing even the best army units to start in fear at the slight-est disturbance. They never knew just when pulse-guns would fire upon them, solar grenades would land on top of them, or even when children would throw rocks at them. But one thing they did know was that it *would* happen.

Reprisals were brutally severe. Ebereans would drag inno-cent but defiant Dalyinese out of their homes and round them up in the street. Execution squads would murder dozens for each Eberean life lost, but the cost was high; execution squads were themselves put to death, sometimes within minutes of a reprisal.

It wasn't long before many Eberean soldiers refused to par-ticipate in the murder of civilians. Some were summarily put to death, but many didn't even bother to protest; they simply ran away. Some were killed by vengeful civilians, but most were handed off to the nearest Resistance cell, where their defections were quickly accepted.

The first town in the entire country to once again raise the Dalyinese flag over its Civic Hall was Karig, a town of but a few thousand that had been administered by a small platoon of Ebereans. The Ebereans surrendered en masse to the town's only soldier, an ancient veteran with a rusted pulse-gun that he doubted could even get off a single round. But the word spread through-out Dalyi like wildfire—there was a small part of the land that was free!

None of this was done randomly. The well-disciplined Da-lyinese Army was following a meticulously planned order of battle and was ticking off its objectives one by one. The first was to take back their own territory, the smaller regions first. Therefore small towns in isolated areas were the first targets, and the easiest. The Ebereans simply did not have the resources to go through the difficult task of winning them back.

While the smaller towns of Dalyi began to fall, the cities were also undergoing vicious assaults. The purpose here was to create areas in which the average Eberean soldier would be too afraid to enter. These neighborhoods would expand outward until soon the Ebereans occupied only the tiniest section of a city, at which time their defeat would be inevitable.

The rest of the world was watching now, as they had been from the very first. As Thradon's richest nation, how it was governed, and who governed it, had a profound impact on the rest of the world. Dalyi's closest allies, Truska and Benepa, had long since placed neutral observers in the country. As the tide began to turn, they made contact with Nev Hederes and arranged massive arms and supply shipments. Even Taray jumped on the bandwagon; it was a country that always backed a winner, and winners were always generous in the glow of victory.

The first major city to fall was Srho. The gambling capital of Dalyi used temptation, rather than violence, to win defectors over to their side; soldiers simply walked from brothels to casinos to the Air Depot, where mammoth Truskan air transports were fueled and waiting. And as the defecting soldiers deserted the garrison, a Dalyinese assault team took the former stronghold in minutes.

The comm-wall at Celin Kwa's headquarters exploded into life.

"Where is Kwa? Where is Celin Kwa? I demand to know!" the speaker of the Central Authority shouted.

"Uh, he's not here, Your Excellency," Celin Kwa's orderly gulped.

"I can see that, you fool! Where the hell is he?"

"Uh, I'm not—that is, it's top secret . . ."

"Idiot . . . reconsider those last words."

"Uhh, Cresvo Denor, sir. He's been there for the last week."

"Cresvo Denor! It's a lump! Why is he there, when Kasma Dor is about to fall about his ears?"

"Uhh, don't know, Excellency." The orderly also didn't give a damn. All he knew was, he was off duty in two hours, and he was going to slip into some civvies, head for the Bhuhara district, and turn his scared Eberean ass over to the Resistance.

"Of course you don't know! You're an orderly!"

Celin Kwa had at first believed the Juma 97 prototype to be a heroic find. Now, with defeat close at hand, he began to see it as something else . . . a lifeline.

The rocket construction facility, hundreds of feet below the ground, had been untouched by the explosion when Cresvo Denor had been destroyed. The carefully concealed entrance had been found quite by accident, because a single defective charge had detonated much later, when the structure was seriously weakened. The unplanned, misdirected detonation had blown a hole in the wrong location, attracting the attention of the retrieval team.

"Captain Huul," he asked the engineering officer. "What are your findings?"

Huul had worked for the Dalyinese space program in the more cordial days before the occupation.

"It's a beauty, sir. If I can figure out these course headings and lay them in, we should be all right. But I'm not worried. This ship was obviously designed to travel to Earth."

"Any other problems?"

"This sucker's gonna really move, sir. Cut the voyage in half, at least. We'll have to be really careful when we program our suspended animation schedule. We don't want to be asleep when we enter the earth's orbit."

"Just do it. Major! Give me a progress report! How bad is it?"

"Oh, it's bad, sir."

"Give me an estimate."

"A week. Hardly more than that. The rebels have bypassed Sha'n Res. They're driving us into Kasma Dor."

"Is there anything left?" He knew the battle, once joined, was a losing one; he just hadn't thought it would all slip away so quickly.

"Kuran Il fell this morning, sir. The whole garrison just surrendered, even the generals. The Nagnel district can't hold out much longer. And Lansa is going to go any day now—our boys are completely encircled."

"I always said we were rotten soldiers."

"We're good soldiers," the Major insisted, "we're just rotten jailers."

"Perhaps. I find it difficult to believe one thing, however. Kasma Dor is the favorite city of Dalyi. I love Kasma Dor myself—why do you think I chose to command the garrison here, instead of the capital, Sha'n Res?"

The major nodded sadly. "It's a fine city, General. I'd hate to see it destroyed."

"Then why is Hederes pushing us here? For that is surely his plan, has been all along. Why would he risk a pitched battle here?" Kwa shrugged. "Oh, well," he said dismissively, "it's not our problem. Not anymore."

Just as Nev Hederes had planned, those Ebereans who had not been captured or killed were pouring into Kasma Dor. While this strengthened the garrison considerably, it also isolated the Eberean stronghold and made it a more visible target.

With their backs to the sea, the Ebereans wondered what would follow. Surely the Dalyinese valued their prized city too much to submit it to the destruction of a pitched urban battle. What were they doing? And what were they waiting for?

Celin Kwa had returned to his headquarters, more out of curiosity than commitment.

"Well, Major," Kwa said to his aide, "not much of a conquest, was it? A year and six months. Much less if you consider how long it took for the Dalyinese to begin fighting back."

The major stared dejectedly at the floor. "I don't understand it, sir. What was it for? If we knew we couldn't last, why did we do it?"

In a rare kindly gesture, Kwa put his arm on the young major's shoulder. "It's part of our painful evolution into a modern people, my boy. Look at what happened: Dalyi bent over backwards to help us assimilate into the modern world. How did we pay them back? With the most ancient, barbaric custom there is, revenge. Why did we bother? We were growing strong. We were growing rich! And now, when the smoke clears—although there won't be much smoke, because there will be no need for Eberes to be completely destroyed—we'll pay dearly for our arrogance. We looted their country; they will beggar us getting it all back. And we will be a pariah nation for decades to follow. The Dalyinese aren't kidding about that. We pushed them way over the edge."

"What will we do, sir? There'll be nothing to go back to!"

"Who said anything about going back?"

The comm-wall sparked to life. "Kwa!" the speaker shouted.

"God's teeth!" Kwa exploded. "Will I *never* be free of you?"

"Where have you been? What is your position?"

"My position? Damned uncomfortable. Now, go away."

"Kwa, you are in such big troub—"

The screen that was the comm-wall suddenly split in half. The speaker now shared it with Nev Hederes.

"General Hederes," Kwa greeted him. "What a pleasant surprise."

"Celin Kwa," Nev returned. "And Noreg Kwa, the speaker of the Central Authority. Well, this certainly makes things easier. I'll put this plainly: I order you to surrender at once. Celin, lower your flag, and we won't fire upon you. Noreg, dip the colors on the Government House."

The speaker hooted. "Never! Celin, attack at once!"

"Just ignore him," Kwa told Nev. "I trust my men will be well-treated?"

"Far better than you treated ours," Nev replied.

"I'm sure that'll be true."

"Celin!" the speaker shouted. "If you surrender, you die!"

"Noreg," Nev began, "I don't think you want to continue with that sort of attitude."

"Who are you to speak to me?" Noreg Kwa demanded.

Nev turned from the screen and nodded his head. In several moments, from the speaker's side of the screen, there was a loud explosion. The speaker's screen shook.

"Speaker, that was pulse-artillery from the *Lansa* and the *Kuran II,* currently submerged 100 clics off the Hilvan coast. Would you like another round? Maybe an air strike this time?"

The speaker's screen vanished.

"I take it," Celin Kwa said, "that the *Kasma Dor* and the *Sha'n Res* occupy much the same position off *my* little patch?"

"What do you think, Celin?"

"It doesn't matter what I think, does it?"

"Not really. So, General Kwa, should we avoid anymore needless bloodshed?"

"But, of course! My staff will be contacting you to discuss terms—although I seriously doubt that you'll be offering any terms other than an unconditional surrender."

"Your staff? What about you?"

Kwa smiled sadly. "Ah, there's the rub, General Hederes. I may be a libertine, motivated purely by self-interest, but nevertheless, I'm a supreme general and I love my country, misguided though it may be."

"We'll hunt you down, Celin. Where can you go?"

"Don't mind about that, Nev. The flag will come down in one hour. I'll order the troops to assemble near the transport line in each district, arms stacked before them. Is that good enough?"

"That'll be fine. Inform your troops that any show of resistance will be severely dealt with."

"Of that I have no doubt. There will be no trouble. I trust that my people will be repatriated without too much delay?"

"It's merely a question of transport facilities. You might tell your fool cousin that Eberean civil air transports will be permitted within our borders, on specified routes only, for the duration of the repatriation process."

"That's most generous of you," Kwa replied.

"Well, we're a generous people, Celin. You should know that."

"I do. Although I fear it will be some time before we Ebereans are once again recipients of Dalyinese largesse."

"You might also tell that idiot that any reprisals against Eberean soldiers who surrendered will be considered an attack against Dalyi. And we will take appropriate action."

"I shall do so. I thank you for sparing my troops. Well, General Hederes, the time has come for me to take my leave of you, and this fair city."

"Why don't you just surrender? It'll go much easier on you that way."

"And be tried as a war criminal, in the dock with money-grubbing, civilian administrators far more guilty than I? No fear."

"We'll see each other again, Celin."

"That would be extraordinary. Good-bye, General. Congratulations on your momentous victory."

Celin closed the channel.

"Major!" he called. "Time is growing short."

"Ready, sir."

"Take a last look around, Major," Kwa said with a trace of wistfulness.

"Will we ever return, sir?"

"That's up to fate. And whatever else we may happen to encounter." He paused and switched on the channel to the Central Authority.

"Celin," his cousin glowered at him, "the Central Authority demands that you flatten Kasma Dor at once. At once, do you hear?"

"Noreg. You were a contemptible little shit as a boy, and I see that age has not mellowed you one whit. Now, shut up and listen."

"You had bet—"

"I said, shut up. Now, you listen to me. General Hederes has agreed to repatriate our troops with the utmost dispatch. Our civil air transports have been granted leave to enter Dalyi to pick them up."

"Any man or woman who disgraces us by surrendering to that rabble will be sentenced to death!"

"Interesting. You mean to say that any Eberean soldier who returns home will be executed, like a common criminal?"

"Anyone who surrenders *is* a common criminal."

"Hmmm! I see. Is that your final word on the subject?"

"You know damned well it is!"

"Very well. Good-bye, cousin."

"Wait!" Noreg cried, but Celin had already cut him off.

"To Dalyinese high command. This is General Kwa of the Eberean Imperial Defense Force, Kasma Dor. I request an open channel to the captain of the *Kuran Il*."

A moment later, the commander of the *Kuran Il* filled the screen.

"Is that Arno Voc? Lieutenant-Commander Arno Voc?" Celin asked. "The former naval attaché in Hilva?"

"General Kwa," Voc replied. "It's Commodore Voc now, sir. What can I do for you?"

"It's more along the lines of what I can do for you, Commodore. I take it our pitiful navy has ceased to be an obstruction for you?"

From the screen, Voc stared at him neutrally.

"It's like this, Commodore. We all want peace. It's that damned Central Authority that is gumming up the works."

"I see," Voc replied evenly.

"Now, I have long since been aware that the Dalyinese Navy consists of honorable people, and I know that you don't want to fire those gigantic pulse-guns indiscriminately, killing innocent Eberean citizens."

"No, sir. It's not something we'd *want* to do."

"Of course not. So in the spirit of peace, I uncloak these secret coordinates, and present them to you now."

"And these coordinates are?"

"Why, the headquarters of the Central Authority, dear boy. Do with them what you will."

Earth

PRESENT DAY

17

U.S.S. *ARIZONA* MEMORIAL, PEARL HARBOR, HAWAII

As Bobby had predicted, Ket had fallen madly in love with Maui. Since they were married by virtue of the Five-Point Kiss, Bobby felt that they were entitled to a honeymoon of sorts. They had stayed for five days at his timeshare in Wailea, doing very little except laying out on the beach and swimming, occasionally snorkeling. Bobby was a true water rat, and once he was immersed in the warm, startlingly blue water, it was difficult to get him to come out.

The blueness of the water was a touchstone for Ket, as it reminded her exactly of the Dalyinese Ocean. The mischievous hot breezes made her think of her own favorite vacation spot, the tropical resort-city of Lansa. But most importantly, it was a place that made troubles seem to disappear far off into the horizon, at least for awhile.

She was glad Bobby had taken her here. It was a calming and precious feeling, to walk hand-in-hand along the beach in the sunset with the man she loved. She felt as if she could stay here forever.

But after five days it was time to return to "real life," as

Bobby called it, and so they boarded a small plane to Honolulu. Ket felt empty as the beautiful green island dropped away behind them.

"Two reasons why we're going through Honolulu instead of straight through from Maui. One, the damn plane from Maui to LAX is too small and uncomfortable. I don't mind it going there, because, hey, we're *going* to Maui, but on the way back I'll take a widebody, thank you.

"Second, there's something I'd like to show you. I think you, more than anyone, will appreciate it."

The Arizona Memorial is composed of a museum, a theatre, and the actual memorial itself, a partially covered rectangular viewing platform built across the actual wreckage of the ship that was sunk by the Japanese on December 7, 1941. There are twelve hundred American naval officers and men resting inside her; many of the survivors who have since passed on have had their ashes scattered over her so that they too may rest with their shipmates.

Ket immediately registered the change in Bobby's mood as they studied personal posessions and parts of the ship that had been salvaged for display. She was aware that this was a special place for all Americans, but the visceral effect that strikes so many visitors did not hit her until after the documentary, which explained the events leading up to the attack on Pearl Harbor, followed by footage of the attack itself and statements from those who had been there.

Bobby was silent; she had never seen him struck completely mute before. She could feel from him an incredible sense of grief that eclipsed all else but anger, a slow, controlled rage. And, she was even more surprised to discover, a sense of shame.

After an unapologetically stern warning from a park ranger about the unacceptablility of both cellular phone calls and screaming infants during the tour, they joined the other visitors aboard the launch to the memorial itself. Bobby was still inside himself, and Ket simply took his arm and allowed him his thoughts.

It wasn't until they were inside the memorial that Bobby spoke. They were standing in front of a wall bearing the names of all those who rested forty feet below them.

"Look at how many of the last names are the same," Bobby pointed out. "There were a lot of brothers and cousins serving on this ship. Even a father and son."

Ket waited for him to continue.

"I used to come here a lot when I was stationed in Hawaii," Bobby said. "Even now, whenever I go to Maui, I try to get over here before I leave. Maybe it's because I was a sailor, too, but I feel connected to these guys, as if I'm visiting the grave of someone in my family."

Ket nodded; she felt the same way when she visited the memorial in the Valley of Honor near Sha'n Res. It was where she had always thought she would be interred someday.

"The thing that makes me love these men the most, though, is the gift that they keep giving, even though they all perished almost sixty years ago: Whenever I feel down, or confused, or worried, or if any stupid thing at all bothers me, this place is the ultimate reality check. Because I owe it to these wonderful guys to take pleasure in being alive, if only because they can't."

He took her hand and walked her to the rail, where the wrecked hull of the ship was clearly visible below the surface of the water. A tiny black dot popped up and dispersed when it hit the surface.

"Oil," Bobby said. "After sixty years, the ship is still leaking oil. You'd think," he added, with a catch in his voice, "that the oil would have run out by now."

He turned to her and gripped her arms. "I know you love me," he said, "and for that, I'm happy. But I don't know if you believe you can depend on me if . . . when something happens."

"I never said that," Ket replied.

"No, but you thought it." When Ket didn't answer that he said, "well, I want you to know that you can. Even though you're a great warrior, and you could probably kick my ass in five seconds flat, I'm still going to protect you. They still have to come through me to get to you."

"I know you will, Bobby. I feel it. I feel it all through me."

"Do you know why? Because if you really can 'feel' me, you'll know I'm telling the truth. Because this is the one place on Earth where no one can tell a lie, even to themselves. It would be the worst kind of disrespect to show these men, breaking one's honor on this very spot. Any promise I make here, I keep."

"I believe you, Bobby," she said softly. "I'll count on you, I promise."

"Good," he replied. He turned and faced the rail, regarding the hollow funnel below. "General, stand to attention."

"Yes, Petty-Officer," Ket replied gravely.

"Salute." Bobby saluted like an American sailor, Ket as a Dalyinese general, which was not all that different; her hand went flat into her forehead, the back facing outward.

"To," Bobby said, and both hands came down. "Now let's get back to L.A. and make a movie these guys would be proud of."

Bobby's Girl would be a small-big movie, which meant that while it would boast exciting and expensive special effects and scenes requiring hundreds of extras, the story would not have too many principal roles, nor would it boast a star whose salary would cut too deeply into the budget. Extra care had to be taken with casting, which was why Bobby left the final decision up to Ket. Ket might have been new to movies, but on Thradon she had been an avid theatre-goer and understood the principles of good acting.

Big Frank Cosimo—stimulated by the prospect of playing a good guy for once—was the logical choice for Nev Hederes, and Victoria St. Louis had already been chosen for Pasa Henz. Ket still insisted that only Bobby could play Holak Ven, and in his deepest of hearts, Bobby was too flattered to refuse.

Because Ket had left Thradon before the actual fall of Kasma Dor, she had no real idea as to whom the garrison commander would be. Through extrapolation, however, and her knowledge of Eberean personnel, she was able to correctly guess at Celin Kwa. When General Kwa had been ambassador to Dalyi, he had been a generous host and always good company at dinner, and he plainly loved Kasma Dor. Yet, one can easily imagine what sort of enemy a certain kind of friend can make, and Celin Kwa easily fueled any speculation.

Tom Courtland, fresh from his triumph in England—all had

gone far better than expected, he needn't have worried, the Limeys weren't as stuck-up as he thought they'd be, they *really* knew how to party, et cetera and so forth—was anxious to sink his teeth into the role. He begged Bobby and Ket for the role, even made up and tested for it. He pleaded with Ket to specify exactly what she wanted, and Ket did so as if she were fine-tuning an electronic device. Tom got it right and in doing so, won the role.

Sy and Shirley would be played by John and Gemma Eldridge, a venerated husband and wife team that had dominated Broadway for much of the fifties and sixties, had a ground-breaking sitcom that ran through the seventies, and then had more or less retired, working again when the spririt moved them and when the offer was attractive enough. Bobby, who believed it nothing less than criminal that two such actors should ever be allowed to retire, was thrilled when they called to accept their roles.

The final two casting decisions were the most important; the choices for Ket and Bobby—who would, of course, not actu-ally be named Ket and Bobby. Ket gave Bobby complete free-dom to choose the actress who would play her; she believed the role was too close to her to make a truly objective choice. But she had faith in Bobby and trusted his decision.

The casting of Gwen Hayes for the role of Ket was difficult for Bobby on a variety of levels. First of all, he knew that Ket would consider his choice a reflection of the way he saw her; therefore he had to find someone whom Ket would give her un-restrained approval.

Secondly, Gwen Hayes had been Bobby's first "Hollywood" romance. They had begun dating shortly after his triumph with *Valley Kingpin.* Although a big star at the time, Gwen was a down-to-earth, generous, and warm-hearted girl, and Bobby had fallen for her deeply. Sy and Shirley had also approved of her. But Gwen simply had not had the same feelings for Bobby that he had for her, and the affair ended, somewhat abruptly for Bobby's taste. He felt raw for months afterward.

Third of all, Gwen's career was on the wane. A perennial Oscar contender solidly entrenched on the A-list at the time she dated Bobby, she had not starred in a full-fledged hit for several years, and her stock was dropping rapidly. Ed the green-light guy doubted her ability to open the picture. But Bobby fought for her over a barrage of emphatic *chhhs,* promising that the story and its special effects would put the film over the top and make big stars out of just about everyone.

Although Ket allowed Bobby the freedom of casting her character, she allowed nothing of the sort for the character of Bobby.

"No way!" he had argued, at first with some amusement. But the mood of foolery burst when he saw that she was dead serious. They had gone round and round for an entire night, until he had fallen asleep in the middle of a protest. They picked it up again the next morning. Bobby would give her any number of reasons why her choice was a mistake, and Ket would merely sit by, looking smug. She had bested generals and politicians in arguments of national policy; she certainly wasn't going to lose this one.

When she finally sensed that Bobby was near the breaking-point, she spoke.

"You're lying to me, Bobby," she said with a knowing smile. "And I love you for it, because you're doing it to protect me. That's why I want you to play . . . you."

"I can't play a double role! The PLIC (pants lizard in charge) is giving me enough flack just being in this at all! Now you want me to *carry* the goddamn thing!"

"No," Ket replied, as calm as Bobby was excited, "I want you and Gwen Hayes to carry this picture."

"Why, for Christ's sake?"

"I'll give you two reasons. The first is simple enough; you're a frustrated actor. Everybody knows it, they even laugh about it on the set—affectionately, of course, but it's no secret."

"Balls. Who says so?"

"Everyone. It's about time you did what you've always dreamed of doing. That's one reason, but it's not the best reason. The best reason is because, you're worried that if you do a love scene with Gwen Hayes, it'll mess up what we have."

"I am not!" He protested. "Well, maybe a little. What if I . . . what if I find I'm still not over her?"

"Then we're through, and you're back to square one with her, which may lead somewhere, but probably not. Bobby, wouldn't it be better if we found out now?"

"Kathy . . ."

"That's what I want, Bobby—I want that chemistry. Because it's true. Because it works. Because it'll explode off the screen. You're still afraid of her. Perfect! You were afraid of me! That's exactly what we want—and there's nowhere else we're going to get it." She folded her arms in punctuation. "Now argue your way out of *that*."

Bobby raised a finger and opened his mouth to protest, but nothing came out. "Next time," he said, "next time, I'm sticking with an Earth girl. So there."

Space

THREE MONTHS AGO

18

The babies were sleeping.

That was just the way Celin Kwa wanted it. The ten elite assault troopers would only be awakened in the final month before touchdown, during which time they could access the assimilators for instruction in language and basic living conditions on Earth.

Other than that, however, Celin Kwa's rule was, always know more than everyone else.

Terrans were scrawny little things compared to Thradonians, but Celin wasn't fooled. They were a violent people, clever enough to develop weapons that more than compensated for their size. These Terrans were so warlike that on Thradon, only one nation even came close to their barbarism, Eberes. He'd fit right in.

This country that seemed to fascinate Holak Ven so much, this *America.* It was plain to see why; it was rich, it was fat, it had delusions of its own moral leadership, and it seemed like the easiest country in which to get established. Although Celin had no misconception about one thing; his very appearance would certainly attract attention. The assault team would have to proceed carefully. Very carefully.

What about Ket Mhulhar? he wondered. Had she been in hiding all this time? Holak had so often stated that Earth was far from ready for contact—what had happened when Ket landed? Had the authorities captured her? Put her on display like an animal in a zoo? Or was she under a giant bell jar in a laboratory somewhere?

If that were the case, in fact, if that were the choice, why would Ket bother to go to Earth at all? She could have remained in hiding on Thradon, come to that.

He looked at the viewer and spent awhile enraptured by the stars blurring past. Space navigation was a sweet mystery to him; he couldn't even begin to guess at the ship's direction of travel, its speed, or even approximately where they were in relation to where they were going. But he did enjoy the view.

It was all one to Celin Kwa, as long as he got there. He turned on his lap unit to continue his reading. He was beginning to develop a taste for Earth literature now that he had mastered at least one of their languages. But he couldn't understand this Scrooge fellow. If someone broke into Celin Kwa's house in the middle of the night, interrupted his night's sleep, and tried to point out the error of *his* ways, well, ghost or no ghost, he'd be so full of pulse rounds he'd be blasted out of this world *and* the next.

Thradon
SIX WEEKS AGO

19

One of Nev Hederes's strong points as a general was that he not only knew how to manage a war, he also understood the equal importance of successfully administering the peace that followed. In the final period of the struggle for freedom, Nev Hederes had worked day and night on Dalyi's postwar administration.

When the last victory celebrations were concluded, Nev Hederes, somewhat surprised to find himself the interim premier, quickly went about the business of restoring Dalyi to a peacetime footing. The army's first task was to return public utilities and services to their rightful Dalyinese administrators; those services whose managers could not be located continued to be under the aegis of the army.

Nev implemented a six-month plan, during which time the constitution was in full force, but the government was for the most part run by the army. In six months, free elections would be held and the army would relinquish its temporary power of government.

It was a daunting task for Nev Hederes, who had always believed that the military should answer to a civilian authority, and he vowed to make the transition as smooth as possible.

One official act he did not hesitate to perform as temporary premier was to finally promote Holak Ven to the rank of general. Holak had returned from Taray with Pasa Henz to resume his work on the space program; getting Ket Mhulhar back was now a national priority.

Bringing Pasa Henz, an Eberean, back to Dalyi caused Nev no small concern. However, it soon became apparent that the Dalyinese character had no provision for enforced emnity. Apparently, there *were* Ebereans who were decent and kind and had been merciful and mannered during the occupation, particularly among the younger soldiers in the regular army. The Dalyinese were simply not ready, or were perhaps too far advanced, to tar and feather every Eberean on Thradon. Many felt, since the *Kuran Il*'s "lucky" hit that destroyed the Central Authority building and killed most of its members, any real threat to Dalyi was now virtually nonexistent. Nev's aide, Major Groula Feeh, and Feeh's new wife, Sergeant Sani, had even voiced a desire to honeymoon at a scenic inn in Kapanogh, sixty clics outside Hilva.

With the Central Authority now defunct, a new, moderate provisional government was set up to govern Eberes. It was as if the Eberean people had finally realized that the time had come to join the rest of the world and leave old, self-destructive ideas in the past where they belonged. But, the Ebereans were also being pragmatic; their economy was simply not strong enough, nor was their country rich enough, for Eberes to survive as a pariah nation.

The new government made every effort to return Dalyinese loot to its rightful owners, and although they were aware that Nev Hederes wanted no diplomatic relations with Eberes, they nevertheless sent a group of observers to their former consulate in Kasma Dor. After much wrangling back and forth, Nev finally relented and permitted the restoration of diplomatic ties with Eberes. However, there were two strict guidelines from which he would not waver; the carefully monitored behavior of Ebereans in Dalyi would have to be above reproach, for the slightest action taken against Dalyi or any of its citizens at home or abroad would be considered an act of war; and the Ebereans had to appoint General Pasa Henz, the only Eberean he trusted, as ambassador to Dalyi.

Nev Hederes worked tirelessly at helping his beloved Dalyi to reemerge and take its rightful place as the premiere nation of Thradon. And something else was happening, although the self-effacing Hederes would be surprised to hear it; he was becoming beloved by Dalyi. He had no idea at the moment, but it was in the wind. Nev Hederes was the odds-on favorite in the next free elections. He was going to be the premier of Dalyi for a long, long time.

For the first time in her life, Pasa Henz was a joyful woman.

She and Holak Ven now lived together in Ket Mhulhar's beautiful apartment. She no longer felt odd about being there, in fact she had come to love it. She felt that she had finally earned Ket Mhulhar's respect, and that Ket would appreciate the loving care with which Pasa treated her home and possessions. And Holak.

Even her family had finally come around. Her father contacted her every night, and even her sisters were now in constant touch. Perhaps they had an ulterior motive; Pasa Henz had achieved universal respect in the new Eberes, and her name had been publicly considered for high office. But Pasa had no plans to return to Eberes, not while life in Dalyi was nothing short of wonderful.

She loved being ambassador to Dalyi. Her reputation in Dalyi was that of a gallant soldier who had shown mercy in victory and who had then risked her life to save Holak Ven. She had risked being branded a traitor rather than do the dishonorable thing and follow orders. She had a big heart that was in the right place, a quality admired by Dalyinese, even among Ebereans. She was the most popular ambassador who had ever resided in Dalyi.

She was also in love; deeply, laugh-out-loud-for-no-apparent-reason, starry-eyed, not-unpleasant-insomnia-causing, no-appetite/huge-appetite in love. She and Holak Ven were together now, and it had just happened, as naturally as night turning into day. Nothing had been said or even whispered at. They had arrived from Taray together, and they had moved into Ket's apartment together. Although the embassy was in Sha'n Res, Pasa always returned to Kasma Dor at night. She would often conduct state business at the consulate in Kasma Dor instead, just to be closer to home. And it was home.

Once in awhile she would puzzle over the way things turned out—an Eberean general subletting a Dalyinese general's apartment while setting up housekeeping with another Dalyinese general—but she wouldn't linger too long over it.

For the first time ever, Pasa Henz could truly say that she loved her life.

Pasa Henz glowed. For the first time ever, she was a star, and she loved every moment of it. On the days she remained in Kasma Dor, she and Holak would walk most of the way to their respective offices together. People would smile at her glowing face and greet her, "good morning, Ambassador," and she would slip her arm through Holak's and greet them in return. That was the best thing of all.

One day, several weeks after her appointment as ambassador, she stopped in at the Space Administration building to surprise Holak and take him to lunch. She would needle him mercilessly about his promotion; Holak had long insisted that he never gave a damn whether he made general or not. But now that he had finally made it, she could tell that he was having difficulty trying to conceal his pride. She found this single instance of self-deception endearing, like just about everything else about him as well. Okay, this is getting a little nauseating, Pasa told herself. Then she felt herself glowing again.

The area was restricted, and Holak had to come out to meet her. His uniform tunic was off, and he looked exhausted.

"Lunch? Can't do it, hon. Swamped today."

Pasa was about to let it go when an evil foreboding crossed her brain. Her brilliantly lit world suddenly clouded.

She pulled Holak aside. "It's ready, isn't it?"

Holak started to lie, then saw that it would be useless. "Yeah, babe. It's ready."

Pasa fought back a rush of tears. "When do you leave?"

Holak could hardly face her. "Tomorrow."

Pasa felt as though she had been punched in the stomach. Was it just this morning that she had positively floated into work?

Holak took both of her hands. "Sweetie, this thing hauls serious ass. Look, it took Ket, what, two years to get to Earth.

Celin Kwa's ship? Nine months. You know what it'll take me?
Thirty-five days. Forty, with a headwind. That's a joke, Pasa—
you see, in space, you don't have any atmosphere so you don't
have . . ." He trailed off when he saw that she wasn't listening.
"Damn it, Pasa, I'll be gone what, three months! C'mon, it won't
be that bad."

Pasa looked at him coldly. "It won't be that bad? What'll I
do if you get killed, which is a damned good possiblity?"

"You'll go on living, Pasa. You'll continue being the best
damned ambassador who ever hit Embassy Row, then you'll
probably be elected premier of Eberes, and believe me, that nutty
country of yours needs a premier who doesn't have her head up
her a—"

"I don't care about that! You know what I want, Holak? I
want everything that I have *right now.* And I want your kids.
I'm fifty-eight years old, Holak. I've busted my ass all my life
and only now, at this moment, have I really gotten anything I've
worked for. I want kids. I want to be pregnant every year! I
want people to say 'hey, look, Ambassador Henz is having a
baby. *Again.* How many's she got now? Eight? Nine?' "

"I'll give you all that, love. As soon as I get back."

"Get back from what? A strange planet where you'll have to
fight Celin's assault team *and* the natives? You really think
you have a chance of getting back? And anyway, Ket'll be
there—"

Holak laughed and nodded his head. "So. That's what all this
is about. Ket. You're still jealous."

"I never said that."

"You didn't have to. Look, I love Ket. I've always loved Ket.
I always will love Ket. We've known each other forever, and
saved each other's asses more times than either of us could
count. We've made love hundreds of times. Sorry, but we have."

Pasa started to turn away. Holak grabbed her arm.

"*But.* I'm not the guy for her. If I were, it would have happened by now. Which also makes it safe to say, she's not the
girl for me. So where does that leave me? I've loved. But I've
never *been* loved. I mean, Ket loved me, but she didn't adore
me. No one ever has, not until you. You think I want to give
that up?"

"Then don't," Pasa urged him.

"I'm not. God's sake, Pasa, I'm just going to *Earth*. I've been there before, you know. Come on, I jam in, pick up Celin, jam out. What's the problem?"

"There is no problem. Because I'm going with you."

"What? I'm sorry. For a moment I thought you said, 'I'm going with you.' "

"Shut up, Holak. Of course I'm going with you. I'm not letting you die without me. And don't tell me I'm not qualified. You're bringing an assault team, not a research team, right?"

"Well, that's classified, but—"

"You know, my memory may be going, but didn't I command an assault team? Didn't I teach assault training at Tira Gen? In other words, Holak, is anyone more qualified than I?"

"Yeah, okay, fine, but aren't you forgetting something? Like, what's Eberes supposed to do for an ambassador while you're gone?"

"That's why *chargés* were born, Holak. Now I'm going with you. These men are renegade Ebereans, and as an official of the provisional government, I have a right to be there. Besides, it's only a few months, right?"

"And what if *you* get killed?"

"I'll go to heaven with a smile on my face. Holak, you want to save Ket. She's your dearest friend. Well, I love you. That makes her my friend, too. Friends help each other, the way you and Ket always have. Besides, do you really want to go another three months without . . ." She whispered in his ear, and Holak Ven, for the first time since cildhood, actually blushed.

Holak shook his head in defeat. "You're gonna be a serious pain in the ass to go through life with, if you don't get your way, aren't you?"

Pasa Henz's life turned bright again. "But it makes life so much more interesting, doesn't it?"

Earth
NOW

20

"Entering orbit in ten, sir," Captain Huul said.

"English *only*, damn you!" Celin Kwa snapped. "You've had more than enough time to learn it, Huul. And that goes for the rest of you."

"Oh, shit!" Huul exclaimed, thinking to himself, is that English enough for you, Kwa?

"What's wrong?" Kwa demanded.

"These people are a little more advanced than we thought, sir. They've got orbital tracking devices, and it looks like we've scored a hit."

"Damn it! Can you lose them?"

"Well, there'll be the usual comm-blackout when we enter their atmosphere. If I can hold the ship at fifteen degrees, there's a chance our signature won't be picked up again before we land."

"Good. Do it. This is supposed to be a stealth mission. I'd hate for us to land surrounded by a bunch of googly-eyed Terran busybodies."

•   •   •

Tom Courtland, fully costumed and exhausted from three hours in the makeup chair, sat dozing in his dressing room, barely cognizant of the television blaring away in front of him.

He awoke with a start.

". . . which NASA sources have emphatically denied, but strong rumors still persist that a UFO was spotted just outside the earth's orbit at 8:23 this morning."

"Ginny, is it possible that the UFO entered the earth's atmosphere and was lost in the comm-blackout we've experienced since the Mercury project, and which continues through shuttle missions today?"

"Uh, that is a possibilty, Jim. But NASA has declined any further comment. Back to you, Jim."

Tom Courtland jumped up so suddenly his chair fell backward. "Bobby!" he shouted. "Frank, Kathy!"

He ran onto the set, but Bobby, in Holak Ven costume, was on the phone already.

"Mom, Dad, get out! Get out now! Go according to the plan! Do it!"

"All right, son," Shirley's voice, a little louder than usual on the cell phone, was her only indication of fear. "Sy already called the airport—we can make the next flight to LA. Just let me put a few things together—"

"No, Mom! Now!"

"All right, son, all right. Calm down."

"Mom! You and Dad get in that goddamned 'vette and go!"

He rang off. "Kath!" He lowered his voice. "Have you got the MP5?"

"Bobby, relax. There'll be plenty of time to go crazy later. Now, dismiss the cast and crew. I'll take it from here."

"Okay," Bobby said, breathing heavily.

"Hey," Kathy said, kissing him. "It'll be all right. I love you."

Bobby laughed reluctantly. "What a time to get me all hot and bothered."

Kathy chuckled knowingly. "Wait till afterwards. Then you'll really be horny."

Hundreds of crew and extras had no idea what was happening and traded looks of puzzled amusement.

"Okay, gang," Bobby said into his megaphone, "that's it for the day. Same time tomorrow. Thank you."

There were confused murmurs among the cast and crew, but everyone began moving toward the exits. Gwen Hayes, who was not in this scene and therefore not in costume, came over to Bobby with a look of concern on her face. Bobby had earlier been relieved to find that he no longer ached over Gwen Hayes; she was a nice girl and a hell of an actress and a friend and that was all.

"Bobby, is something wrong? Are your parents okay?" She had always been fond of Sy and Shirley.

"Nothing serious," Bobby answered quickly. "Go home, Gwen. You've got an early call tomorrow."

Gwen looked at him dubiously. "Whatever you say, Mr. Director. Are you sure there's nothing I can do?"

"That's nice of you, Gwen, but go home." He kissed her cheek and turned away.

When the soundstage finally cleared, Bobby, Frank, and Tom—all still in their costumes and makeup, gathered before Ket. Ket tried to begin giving orders, but started to laugh instead.

"What's so funny?" Bobby asked.

"It's just that . . . I'm the Thradonian here, and I'm the only one who looks like a Terran!" The men gave halfhearted chuckles, and Ket realized it was time to get down to business.

"Did your parents get away safely?" Ket asked Bobby.

"As far as I know," he replied.

"Do better than that," Ket snapped. She softened immediately. "Bobby, you can't go into combat with anything else on your mind, clouding your judgment. Make sure they made their flight."

"What's our move, Kath?" Frank wanted to know.

"Check weapons and equipment. Then we do the only sensible thing. We find them first. Bobby, you drive me in your Porsche. Frank, Tom—which of you has the faster car?"

"My Ferrari," Tom said. "I can wax a Porsche any old day."

"Well, you're not going to. Stay behind us at all times. But we'll be going very fast."

"What about the cops?"

"Let me worry about the cops."

"I'm hotter than hell in this outfit and makeup," Tom complained. "Plus, we'll be in the desert? Christ!"

Ket put her arm around Tom. "I'd keep that costume on, Tom. It might be the best protection you've got."

As blinding as the speed of the Juma spacecraft's liftoff was, its landing was even faster. One moment the ship was in the upper atmosphere, and the next it was on the ground and already deploying its camouflage netting.

The ship had landed several miles from the first signature reading. The ship's detectors had easily homed in on Ket's escape pod, far beneath the earth though it was.

"The men are ready to go, General," the major reported.

"Tell the men to stand down. We're not going yet."

"But, sir—"

"Major, there are still seven hours of daylight left. On this planet, we are aliens. We are sure to attract attention. Can we afford that? Our mission is stealth."

"Yes. Sorry, sir."

"Have the men get some rest. They'll need it. And post a guard on the exterior-view screen."

"It'll be done, sir."

"One other thing. All pulse-guns set to nonlethal fire."

"Nonlethal? But, sir—"

"The people on this planet are not enemies of Eberes. Not yet, anyway. When they are, it will be because I wish it so, not because of a foolish and unnecessary killing."

"Yes, sir."

Celin Kwa was actually stalling for time. There was something about this atmosphere that gave him pause. His mission, which had been so clear, had now fogged in his mind. What was it? Find Ket Mhulhar and kill her? Find her and capture her, use her as a bargaining chip? He truly did not know anymore. All he did know was that he wanted to see her. Speak with her. Have a drink, one general to another. If he could just talk to her, he felt, then everything would take care of itself.

That shouldn't be too much to ask, should it?

• • • •

The two cars kept in constant cellular contact. The speedometer was pegged straight on one-fifteen. Bobby's eyes were wide and shining due to the long-awaited chance to finally open up the Porsche and the prospect of risking his life in combat.

Ket put her hand on his shoulder. He loved when she did that; it felt like a touch straight out of heaven. He chided himself for a chauvinistic thought; how could a general, someone who had proven herself in the crucible of battle many times over, have such a gentle touch?

"Ket," he began. That surprised her, because she knew he preferred calling her Kathy. "It's stupid to ask, maybe, but . . . are you scared?"

Ket shook her head. "It's never stupid to ask. I'm not scared . . . but I will be. That's what being a soldier is all about . . . being scared to death—of death—and then doing your job anyway. That's what makes us so proud of what we are."

"Well, I'm scared now," Bobby said. "I'm scared of losing you."

"I'm glad you said that," she replied, rubbing the back of his neck. "And now that you have, put that thought away. If you worry about me, then you'll be distracted—and that's when people get killed. So don't think about me. And do exactly as I say. I know that's hard for you—you've been a boss for so long. But this is different. Don't think, don't examine—just do what I say. Slow down!"

Bobby obligingly tapped his brakes and downshifted, as Ket called the warning back to Tom. Bobby zoomed past a lurking Highway Patrol car at just over the legal limit, slow enough to warrant a pass.

"See what I mean?" Ket said. "Just do as I say, and it'll all work out."

The drive from LA to the I-10's Washington Street exit in Palm Desert took just over an hour. They drove the few miles to Highway 111 at a more sedate pace, and Ket motioned for both cars to pull over on a vacant stretch of desert scrub.

Ket felt for them at once. The heat had to've been brutal.

Their Thradonian costumes drew attention like a magnet; cars slowed down and honked their horns in greeting.

"I don't think we could attract more attention if we were naked," Frank remarked.

"*I* would," Tom said.

"Okay," Ket said. "They probably landed about six miles to the east, that's just out of visual range from where I landed, and it's far enough off the main road that there shouldn't be any passersby around. They'll probably stay in the ship till night falls, so we're lucky. We have them bottled up."

"Wish I had some C-4," Frank observed. "That'd take care of the ship in a big hurry, blammo, end of problem."

"You'd never get close enough to do it," Ket said. "They'll have a full sweep around the ship on their viewscreen. Okay, Tom and Frank, follow us. We'll try and get in as close as we can."

"I don't know if our cars can get through the sand," Tom said.

"We should be all right," Frank said. "It's packed pretty hard. We can walk the rest of the way, we're tough."

"Okay," Ket said. "Let's do it."

"Wait, Kath," Frank said. "I picked this up especially for you during my . . . purchasing trip." He took a Kevlar vest out of Tom's trunk. "I don't know if this'll stop one of your pulse-guns, but it's worth a try."

Ket smiled and gave Frank a kiss on the cheek. "It might," she said. "Thanks for the thought." She donned the vest and Frank helped her with the velcro fittings. "Bobby, is there enough water in the car for everyone?"

"More than enough."

"Everybody drink a quart at least on the way there."

"But what if I have to go when—" Tom asked.

"I don't think that'll be a problem, once the balloon goes up," Frank remarked drily.

"Sir," Captain Huul said, "I'm getting a signature reading. Very weak, but it's there."

"It's not the escape pod?"

"No sir, it's beyond the escape pod. Five, maybe six clics out."

"Is it possible she might have found a place to live around here?"

"Yes, sir."

"Well, keep at it, Captain. Let me know if the signal increases."

This could work out quite well indeed. If Ket was only a few clics away, they could swoop in, pick her up and be gone, long before anyone knew it. Things didn't always have to go wrong, after all.

Now if he could just finish his reading without any further interruption. This Scrooge was surely the biggest fool he'd ever heard of. If Celin Kwa were in his place, his generosity would be the stuff of legend. Then he would enjoy much more than everyone's goodwill. He'd also be basking in the gratitude of the idiot nephew's charming wife and that of "dear, distant, unmovable Miss Flora," as well.

The sports cars were able to make another few miles before the sand made further headway impossible. Laden with weapons and equipment, the four made the rest of the way on foot.

Ket held up her hand to signal a halt.

The camouflage netting was just visible. But several hundred yards to their right, a four-wheel-drive SUV was hidden behind a Joshua tree.

"I'd better check that out," Ket said, slipping out of her flack vest and handing the MP5 and its extra magazines to Bobby. She unclipped her holster, slipped out the Glock and placed it near the small of her back.

"Shouldn't one of us go with you?" Bobby asked.

"The way you look? I'll take care of this. Stay here and keep down."

"But, Kath—"

"You're on active duty now, Colonel," she cut him off. "Those are my orders."

"Aye-aye, sir," Bobby replied.

Ket proceeded as quietly as she could, heading for the SUV

not directly, but in a great half-circle. When she got close enough, she saw two people standing outside the SUV. One was looking through binoculars in the direction of the ship, and the other seemed to be . . . making a sandwich?

"Oonah!" she cried. "Sy? What're you doing here? You were supposed to be in LA!"

"Kathy!" Shirley exclaimed, rushing over to hug her. "See?" she said to Sy. "I told you they'd be along eventually. We rented the four-by-four at the airport. We figured the Corvette would never make it in all this sand. But we were just about to call you, Kathy."

"Good thing you didn't. The ship would have picked up any signal this close." She turned and waved for Bobby, Frank, and Tom to come over. She could see them moving with difficulty; it was blazing hot, and over their costumes they wore various bandoliers, backpacks, and holstered weapons. "I'm very upset with you for not following the plan, Oonah."

"Well, I'm sorry, Kathy. But I went crazy enough when Bobby was off in the Gulf War—Sy's blood pressure went all the way up. We just weren't going to go through that again."

It struck Ket that all through her military career, it had never even occurred to her that her parents might have felt the same way. Had they been worried to distraction over her safety? She felt a brief flush of shame and then dismissed it. There was no time now.

Shirley muffled a shriek. "Kathy! Behind you!" Ket turned and drew her weapon in one smooth motion.

"Hey don't shoot, it's me, for God's sake!"

"Bobby? Why are you still in costume?"

"Mom, Pop, what the hell are you doing here? You were supposed to—"

"We're giving you covering fire and supporting your withdrawal," Sy spoke up for the first time. He still had not taken the binoculars from his eyes. "Don't worry, the old farts won't get in the way."

"If anything happens to you . . ."

"Nothing's going to happen," Shirley said. "Kathy's here, isn't she? What's the plan, General?"

Ket picked up a stick and began drawing in the sand. "The

ship is here. There's only one way in and one way out; you can't see the hatch from here, but it's facing us."

"Can't we attack?" Frank asked.

"Attack what?" Bobby replied. "We don't even know what the ship is made of. What if we blow off all our ammo and don't even make a dent?"

"That's true," Ket replied. "But it could work for us; the Dalyinese way is to attack, we never put anybody under siege. We like to go in with a massive force and end it as soon as possible."

"We can't do that here," Sy said.

"No, we can't. We'll have to wait for them to come to us."

"Where will they go?" Bobby asked.

"It won't matter," Ket replied, "as long as—" She put her hand to her mouth. "I can't believe I forgot that! Bobby, Frank, Tom, I need you here now! Frank, give me that knife."

"What for? You're not going to—"

"Just give it to me." Frank withdrew the huge trench knife from its scabbard on his belt. Kathy took the knife and without pause made an incision in the middle of her left hand, which was quickly covered in blood.

"Stand by with the medical aid kit," Ket ordered. "Okay the three of you, let's go."

"You want us to . . . cut . . . ourselves?" Tom was aghast.

"Tom, they'll be looking for a Thradonian signature . . . my signature. Come on!"

Bobby took the knife and cut into his hand, ignoring the pain as best he could. He held up his bloody hand, and with a loud clap, the two clenched grips. He squeezed with all his might, but was amazed at the power emanating from Ket's grip. He had felt her loving touch many times, but never her raw strength. She could have easily broken every bone in his hand.

"Well," he said, "I guess I know who's going to be in charge of the remote in *our* house."

Frank and Tom, reluctantly but quickly followed suit. "We're blood brothers now, Kath," Frank said during his turn. "I wouldn't have it any other way."

"I guess we're blood brothers, too," Tom said during his turn. "But can anyody tell me why we're doing this?"

"When they come out of the ship," Ket said, squeezing, "they'll have their detectors out, looking for a Thradonian signature. Well, now they'll have four of them. They won't know which way to go, or if the equipment is malfunctioning. Anyway, it's an advantage. You never know what might work."

"What about me, Kathy?" Shirley demanded. "Don't we get to be blood sisters?"

Ket hugged her. "You're already my Oonah," Ket said. "You can't get much closer than that."

"Okay, what happens now?" Bobby asked.

Ket considered. "By now, they're probably getting the hint that the area is virtually deserted. The leader'll send out a two-man reconnaissance patrol to take a look around, establish a security perimeter."

"Why only two men?" Frank asked.

"That's the book. The ship holds ten, you never want to be more than twenty percent under full strength. That way, if you have to get out fast, that's fewer troops to worry about picking up."

"How do you know they'll be coming this way?"

"They don't know we're here, and that's where the escape pod landed. My signature will be strongest in that direction. Which gives me an idea . . ."

"General Kwa," the major said, "the sun will be down in an hour."

Kwa looked up from the comm-viewscreen, annoyed at the interruption. He was scanning the local comm signals and had come up with something interesting. He had no idea what he was looking at, but it amused him no end. In what seemed to be a crudely painted picture that moved, a hunter with a sort of an ancient weapon was chasing an . . . animal of some sort. But the animal, who had very long ears and somehow spoke English, kept foiling the hunter. The animal kept referring to the hunter as a "maroon." Kwa hadn't the slightest idea what a maroon was, but he guessed it was unflattering. Anyway, it was damned funny.

"Well, if the sun will be down in an hour, it'll be down in hour. What am I supposed to do about it?"

"Should we send out a reconnaissance team?"

"Oh, very well," Kwa said, reluctantly switching off the viewscreen. "Two men only, and tell them to stray no farther than two clics from the ship. They are to remain in visual contact at all times."

"Yes, sir." He saluted and went back to help prepare the team.

"What a maroon," Kwa said.

Sy saw the hatch open through his binoculars. "We've got movement," he called.

"All right," Ket ordered, "you know the plan. Move forward, stay low, and hold your position. No shooting. Oonah, take the binoculars from Sy. Keep an eye on the hatch. Sy, take the Mini-14, the one with the scope. Keep it trained on the hatch. Anybody else comes out after the first two, you know what to do."

"I'm ready, Kath," he said. He checked the action to make sure a round was chambered.

Ket touched his shoulder affectionately. "I'm sorry you're . . . doing this again after all these years."

"A man has to fight for his family, Kathy."

"Or her family," Shirley added. Ket smiled and followed the other men, who were crawling forward to their positions.

"There aren't any snakes around here, are there?" Tom whispered to Bobby.

"You're in the desert, Tommy, what do you think?"

"I wish you hadn't told me that," Tom replied.

"Rattlers don't *want* to bite you," Frank said from behind them. "That's why they rattle. To warn you off."

"Yeah, well, if I crawl right on top of one, I won't have time to be warned off, will I?"

"That is a problem," Frank agreed. "Try reasoning with them."

Ket had started behind them but was crawling through the brush as easily as a gymnast shinnies up a rope. "Let's go, you guys, hurry it up!"

"First time I've ever seen a general down in the shit with the troops," Frank remarked.

Bobby grinned. "That's m'girl," he said.

21

Shirley took her eyes from the binoculars when the first Eberean jumped down from the open hatchway. "My god, he's huge!" Shirley exclaimed.

"Big son of a bitch, all right," Sy agreed, locking in on him with the laser-dot point in the center of the scope. "He must be seven feet tall."

"I thought they'd be wearing armor, like in *Star Wars*," Shirley said. "You know, those guys in the white at the beginning? These fellas are just wearing like grey . . . smocks, it looks like. And, is that a beret? Are they actually wearing *berets*?"

"Not really the time for a fashion report, Shirl," Sy remarked.

"Gee whiz, Sy, we're actually seeing aliens land on our planet! It'd be so exciting . . . under other circumstances."

The second Eberean placed his pulse-rifle between his knees as he adjusted his cap.

"Now that fellow's a dandy," Shirley observed. "Look at the way he fusses with his beret, making sure it's just right. I'm so glad vanity really is a universal trait, Sy."

The two Ebereans seemed rather casual about their task. Their weapons were held loosely in their slings, and the two ambled away from the ship as though out for a stroll instead of a patrol.

"Okay, Sy, get ready. If this goes wrong—"

"I know what to do," Sy replied. "Our son is out there, remember?"

Frank peeked from behind scrub brush. "About a hundred yards, Kath."

"Okay, everybody wait—nobody move until I do."

"They're coming," Shirley said. "No, wait, they're stopping . . . Sy! I think the dandy fellow is actually . . . stopping to pee! Oh, my God! They *are* big fellows, aren't they?"

"Shirl. Just keep an eye on the hatch, will you?"

The two Ebereans finished their ablution and once again proceeded forward. "Kath," Frank said from his lookout position, "This is an elite assault team? They're morons! They're not even covering each other! They might as well be holding hands!"

"Don't underestimate them," Ket warned.

The soldiers moved toward the defile where Ket and the others were waiting. Together, they walked up the defile and down the other side. For a moment, they were cut off from visual contact with the ship.

Ket knocked the first one unconscious with the haft of Frank's trench knife. Before the other soldier could react, Ket grabbed the first soldier's pulse-gun and turned it on him. She fired. The almost silent pulse dropped the second soldier in an instant. Ket checked the selector on the pulse-gun and saw that it was set to nonlethal.

"Gee, Honey," Bobby said, "I always said you were a knockout, yuk-yuk-yuk."

"Get their tunics on, and their caps. Hurry!" She gave her pulse-rifle to Bobby, as Frank picked up the other one.

"There's no safety like on your guns, so be careful."

"Safety, hell!" said Frank. "Where's the damn trigger?"

"Squeeze the grip once, then release and squeeze again. It'll fire until you let go." She stripped compact pulse-pistols off of each soldier, gave one to Tom, and held on to the other. Then she picked up their solar-grenade bandoliers.

Frank and Bobby put on the Eberean tunics and caps as quickly as they could. "Now stand up," Ket ordered. "Turn back to the ship and wave. All they're going to see are a couple of Thradonians."

"Yeah, Thradonians with running makeup," Tom cracked.

"They won't be able to tell that from here," Ket said.

"What happens now?"

"We wait for it to get dark. Bobby, Frank," she called.

"Yeah," Bobby said out of the side of his mouth while he smiled and waved at the ship, his heart pounding away at his chest.

"You and Frank start patrolling the perimeter. A half circle—don't get on the other side of the ship."

"What're you going to do?"

"A little reconnaissance of my own."

"What the hell was that?" Celin Kwa demanded. "Where'd they go?"

"Nothing, sir," replied Captain Huul. "Looks like they went over a defile. Yep, there they are. Sir, is the whole planet as boring as this? I mean, look at this, nothing but brush."

"It's a new world, Huul," Kwa replied. "How could it be boring?"

"How's it going over here?" she asked Sy and Shirley.

"We're okay, hon," Shirley said.

"Think you can hold out a little longer?"

"Don't worry about us. You just get on with your plan."

"Just keep behind this vehicle. Sy, if anything goes wrong, I want you and Shirley to get into this thing and take off. Don't look back. I mean it."

"Of course, Kathy," Shirley replied.

Ket nodded and crept away.

"We're not really going to run away, are we, Shirl?" Sy asked her.

"Run away to what?" Shirley answered.

• • •

Ket grabbed Tom and had him wait with her until Frank and
Bobby made their next pass. "Stop," she called out to them. "It's
going to be dark soon, so this happens now. Frank, Bobby, I
want you to give me two minutes. Then I want you to turn and
wave at the ship, call them out, as if you'd found something."

Frank looked at Bobby. "Okaaaay. Then what?"

"Make it really good. I want them to send out as many troops
as they can." She gave Tom a solar grenade. "Frank, Bobby, as
soon as they get about fifty feet from you, I want you to jump
for cover right into this defile. Tom, that's when you toss this
grenade. Just push this button in the center and throw it right in
the middle of them. Can you do that, Tom?"

Tom gulped. "Yes, ma'am."

"Good." She rolled another grenade out to Bobby and Frank.
"Don't pick it up yet. Wait a moment, look down at the ground,
pretend you're picking up a rock. Bobby, Frank, whichever of
you gets the grenade, toss that at the same time as Tom's. Take
cover, then when it goes off, blast them with the pulse-guns.
You too, Tom, they'll be close enough for the pistol. Has anyone got a problem with this? Any questions?"

"No, ma'am," Frank said.

"Okay. Two minutes. You have your orders." She bounded
away into the scrub brush.

Frank gave Bobby an arch glance. "Script girl, huh?"

"The best," Bobby replied.

"Okay, a minute forty-five," Frank said.

"Let's make this good, guys," Bobby said.

"And they say marines have all the fun," Frank said.

"Sir! The patrol is signalling! They've got something!"

"What is it?"

"I don't know, sir. But we'd better get some backup out there."

"Very well, Major. Take the rest of the men and get out there.
It's probably something that crawls or a picnicking couple, but
I suppose it's time to make our presence known. Find out what
it is and report back at once."

"Yes, sir! All right, let's move it on out!"

• • •

"That's one, two—damn, they're big—five, six," Frank reported. "Tom! You ready in there?"

"Ready, Frank."

"Don't screw this up."

"Why does everyone always think I'm going to screw up?"

"Just don't." Frank waved to the approaching Ebereans. "Over here, guys," he shouted. "Oh, shoot, English, they don't speak—too late now! Ready, Bobby let's go!"

With a final wave back at the patrol, Bobby and Frank leaped over the defile and into cover. Tom's grenade was a second earlier, but Frank's landed in the middle of the patrol. Both went off in a giant, gaseous hiss.

All six Ebereans fell, stunned.

Acting exactly according to plan, Bobby, Frank, and Tom leapt up and ran toward the Ebereans, firing at them where they lay. All six were struck with nonlethal fire before they could get up again. They stood over them, breathing heavily and trembling visibly.

"Well, that was interesting," Frank remarked.

"If our kids go military," Bobby said, "it'll definitely be from their mother's genes, not mine."

"Jeez, I really have to pee," Tom said.

Frank stared down at his costume trousers. "I sure don't," he said.

Shirley hardly realized she was weeping when she took the binoculars away from her eyes. "He's all right, Sy! Bobby's all right! So are Frank and Tom."

Sy was a little moist himself. "I feel like I just went through that myself," he said raggedly.

"I don't know what I would've done if anything had happened to Bobby," Shirley said, her voice cracking.

Sy hefted the rifle in his hands. "I do," he said.

• • •

In the confusion of the attack, Ket had worked her way around to the hatchway of the ship. She peeked in and saw two Ebereans staring at the pseudocarnage on the screen.

"I don't understand what happened, sir," one of them said. "Why would our own guys—"

"It obviously wasn't our own guys," an angry voice replied, and Ket swore the voice was familiar. Pistol in hand, she swung up the hatchway into the ship, firing as she went. The source of the first voice fell and slumped over the control panel. When she landed in the ship and recovered, she was holding the pistol on a very familiar face.

"Celin Kwa!" she shouted.

Kwa's face screwed up in confusion at the sight of this . . . this creature. "You know me?" he asked in bewilderment. In the heat of the moment, Ket at first couldn't understand why Kwa didn't recognize her.

"Kwa. It's me. Ket Mhulhar."

"Ket Mhulhar? But how can that be? You're a . . ."

"Terran. Yes. No. Well, I was surgically altered before Kasma Dor fell."

"Ket Mhulhar?" Kwa repeated.

"Celin, it's me. You were a division commander under me at Truska? I used to come to your parties at the Embassy? We used to hit that bar near the waterfront at the—"

"Ket? What have they done to you, beautiful Ket?"

"From what I've been told, Celin, I'm not bad by Earth standards. Anyway, Celin, I must know. What is happening at home?"

Bobby poked his head inside the ship. "Bitchen!" he exclaimed. "Say, uh, Kath—"

"Holak Ven!" Celin shouted. "How the hell—"

Ket began to laugh. "Celin. Celin! Calm down, it's not Holak—it isn't—I'll explain later, Celin. But it most definitely isn't Holak Ven."

"I'm hopelessly confused," Celin said miserably. "You're not, but you *are*, Ket Mhulhar. And he is, but isn't, Holak Ven. Ket, please. Anything you can say would be most helpful."

"Later, Celin. What do you need, Bobby?"

"These, uh, these guys out here? What do we do, hon? I

mean, what do we do with them? If they wake up, they're gonna be really pissed at us. I don't know if we can whip'em again."

"It's all right. The pulses were set to medium nonlethal. They'll be out for at least a few hours. Just lay them out near the ship."

"Anything for you, babe."

"Bobby?"

"Sweetie?"

"You were wonderful. You're a good soldier. And you kept your promise. I'm proud of you."

"Thanks, General." He saluted and blew a kiss.

"'Sweetie,'" Celin asked slyly, "have you fallen in love?"

"Hopelessly," she replied. "I never even saw it coming."

"With a Terran?"

"Well, I'm a Terran now, too, Celin."

"Yes, I suppose you are. Well, Ket, I imagine that congratulations are in order. When I left Kasma Dor, our garrison was about to surrender; the last to fall."

Emotion hit Ket like a truck. "Tell me," she wept. "Tell me everything."

"Tears, Ket?"

"I told you, I'm a Terran now," she replied, brushing her sleeve across her eyes. "Keep your hands where I can see them, Celin. I don't want to pulse you until I've heard everything."

"First," Celin said, "shouldn't we toast your great victory? A glass of Eberean Koba? I believe on Earth it's called . . . whiskey."

"I would love a shot of Koba right now."

"Then let us by all means do so. And then I shall reveal all."

And so he did, and Ket's tears didn't cease. Tears of joy, tears of loss (for really, there had truly been no need for her to leave Thradon, after all), and tears of realization that Earth was now her home for better or for worse. For Ket, an honest person—most brutally honest with herself—realized that in Dalyi, she was no longer needed. And that was the hardest truth of all.

"One other thing, Ket, and I hate to mention it, given your obviously delicate emotional state."

"Up yours, Celin. My emotional state is not delicate. Get on with it."

"It's about your dearest friend, Holak—no, he's all right. We had him, but he escaped. Someone on our side helped him. They're quite the item now, by the way. A love story leaving scorched tracks from Dalyi to Taray and back again. So you see, you're not the only one who's fallen."

Feeling guilty because Bobby, the man who had risked his life because he loved her, was standing guard just outside the hatch, Ket allowed herself to mourn the loss of Holak Ven as a once and future lover. But it was her own fault. She had put him off long enough; he was the man who most deserved to be loved, and loved well.

She regarded Kwa with a nod. "Pasa Henz," she said.

Kwa looked surprised. "How could you have known that?"

"An Eberean helped him to escape, you said. I can't think of any other Eberean who would risk everything for Holak. I'm happy for them. She'll love him as I never could."

"You always were the brightest spark, Ket."

"There's still one thing you haven't told me, Celin."

"And that is?"

"Why are you here? To capture me? To kill me? Why, if all is lost for you, anyway? Why not just flee to Taray, or somewhere like that? I'm sure you have money. Why do this?"

Kwa leaned back and sighed. "Oh, my beautiful Ket! That's why we Ebereans have always been such pitiful soldiers. Unclear objectives always mar our purpose. It's so much *easier* to be a revolutionary!"

"You haven't answered my question."

Kwa took another shot of Koba. "Ket, I . . . didn't know what to do. For the first time in my life, I had no purpose. I had no drive. I had no *mission*. All those years, the planning, the preparation, the dreams! To flip the coin that no one thought could be flipped! A poor weak nation, and we conquered a rich strong nation! Imagine that!

"And that was the high-water mark. I knew it the day we lowered your flag and raised our own. *Children* would have been smarter: 'Very well,' they'd've said, 'we took your flag, now you know we can, don't you feel silly?' We had our revenge.

But then what do you do with it? It's not enough to win—what do you do afterwards? Except, lose it back, because you've stayed too long? How can we rule people who hate us, who will soon decide they'd rather die than live one more day under our rule? You found that out. Why couldn't we learn from you?"

"You didn't think there *was* anything to learn from us."

"So, Ket, what do I do? I'm a hunted man in Dalyi. And how safe could Eberes be for me now? Or all of Thradon, for that matter? I need your help, Ket. Why do you think I had the troopers' pulse-guns set to nonlethal, if my intentions were anything else?"

Ket laughed sardonically. "Well, you can't stay here. This planet is far from ready for contact—although they think they are. It's not—"

"Kathy!" Bobby poked his head inside the hatchway. "Kath—you'd better get out of here . . . now."

"What is it, Bobby?"

"It's, uh . . . it's . . . another goddamned ship!"

"What? All right, you guys fall back to your parents' four-by-four and get ready to bug out! Move!"

"What about you? I'm not leaving you here—"

"Active duty, Colonel! Go!"

"Yes, General!" He turned to go, then turned back. "By the way, General—I love you." He ran off.

"Heartwarming," Celin Kwa remarked. "I may vomit, but the best to you both. What do you plan to do with me now . . . Kathy," he added with a smirk.

"I don't have time to think about that right now . . . Charlie," Ket said, adjusting the pulse-pistol to its lowest nonlethal setting. "Why don't you take a nap while I figure it out?" She shot him in the chest, and Celin crumpled immediately.

She got up and went into the arms locker, quickly grabbing a pulse-rifle and another grenade bandolier. On the viewscreen, she saw that the second ship, a hundred yards away, still hadn't opened its hatch yet. Good. That'd give her a little extra time to get into position. Who were these guys? Maybe Celin had been lying about the Dalyinese victory. Maybe this was an Eberean chaser squad looking for both of them. Well, one thing was sure—they wouldn't get her alive, and they wouldn't kill any of her friends. She'd sight in on the hatch and pick them off one-by-one. Then she'd storm the ship. If she had to, she'd turn the grenades up to full lethal and take everyone with her.

It's funny, she thought to herself, as a fleeting picture of Bobby's smile crossed her mind. All those years as a warrior, and she never once gave a hoot whether or not she lived or died. If she lived, there was the job well done and not a little glory; if she died, she would be entombed in the General's Crypt of the Valley of Honor for all time.

And now? All she could see was Bobby's face no longer smiling, just the numbed bewilderment of the shock of loss. And Sy and Shirley, who were really no less than her Earth parents, suffering the profound loss of a child.

It struck her yet again how selfish she had been all those years, not even stopping to think what the loss of their only child would have done to her parents. Only now did she understand the look of pain in her mother's eyes when she proudly showed off her battle scars. Only now did she get it, why her father grew suddenly quiet when she would blithely relate stories of enemies trying to kill their little girl.

She wiped her eyes again. This time it's different, she told herself. This time, I'm fighting for people I love.

But all those years, it dawned on her, I was so ready to die for everyone else. Yet, I was only living for me.

And so General Ket Mhulhar girded for battle, knowing that for the first time in her combat career, she desperately wanted to live.

22

The first thing Shirley thought when the second ship set down
was how right it seemed that the landing was achieved in almost total darkness. In all those flying saucer movies, the UFO
movies, the ship landed in a blaze of lights that could be seen
for miles, usually by people on their way to an outdoor privy.
How *stupid* was that? Wouldn't the crew of the flying saucer,
or spaceship, want to come down with no lights? So that fewer
National Enquirer readers could see them? It amazed her that
no one ever thought of that before, but it was true; why land
on alien soil, where you really don't know the mood of the natives, with enough lights for a Hollywood premiere? So, these
fellows, whether they were good guys or bad guys, at least they
had some sense.

"Stay down, Shirl," Sy warned her. "We don't know who
these guys are."

Frank, Bobby, and Tom appeared behind them. "Where's
Kathy?" Shirley asked.

"She just ordered me back here, told me to make sure you
guys book if it heats up. Jesus," Bobby added, "was it just this
morning that I was on a soundstage, and now I'm for all intents
and purposes back in the Gulf?"

"This is hotter than the Gulf ever was for us," Frank remarked.

"Hatch is opening," Sy warned. "Okay, there're two guys getting out. These aren't total loxes like from that other ship. These guys are . . . wait, one is a woman . . . I think . . . these guys are serious . . . look, they're covering each other, keeping low—"

"They're good guys!" Shirley exclaimed. "They must be Dalyinese! Their outfits are totally different . . . more like coveralls. They're with us!"

"What do you mean, *us*?"

Shirley went under her shirt and brought out the Dalyinese colonel's insignia Ket had given all of them. "Didn't you bring yours?"

They all shifted uncomfortably; none of them had. "Well," Shirley said, "we're Dalyinese Army too, you know."

To everyone's horror, Shirley raced out from cover, waving at the two aliens.

"Mom!" Bobby shouted.

Sy jumped in front of Bobby and blocked his way. "No, Bobby! You guys can't go out there! We don't know who they are! Tom looks Eberean, and you and Frank look Dalyinese! Now stay here!"

"But, Pop—"

"I'll go! Stay here! Frank! Tommy! Hold him!"

"Daddy! Mom!" But Sy was already closing in on Shirley. In the distance, the soldiers brought up their pulse-rifles.

Holak Ven saw the sudden movement on the viewscreen. "Tell them to hold their fire," he shouted at Pasa.

"Steeg! Gor! Hold your fire! You are not—repeat, NOT— cleared to fire! Stand down your weapons!"

The two troopers obeyed instantly. "Orders, General," Steeg said.

"They have weapons," Ven said, noticing the holsters on Sy and Shirley's hips, "but they're not in hand. You are to affect a nonthreatening stance and parley."

"Sir," Gor said, "sir, the smaller one . . . I think she's a woman . . . has something around her neck that looks—" Gor squinted as Shirley grew nearer. "General Ven? You're not gonna believe this, sir. What the hell?"

"Don't keep me in suspense, Gor."

"Sir, I don't know what to make of this but . . . sir, she's wearing a damn *colonel's* necklace!"

"What do you mean, a colonel's necklace?" Pasa Henz jumped in.

"Ambassador, she's right," Steeg affirmed. "It's a goddamned colonel's badge. It's the badge of colonel in the Dalyinese Army," he said in wonder.

"I'm coming down," Holak said.

"Hi!" Shirley waved as she approached the two Dalyinese assault troopers.

The two glanced at each other and slowly returned her wave. "*Hi,*" Gor replied experimentally.

"Dalyinese?" Shirley asked. She leaned forward, exaggeratedly moving her lips. "Dalyinese, right? Dal-yin-ese?" She waved her colonel's badge.

Gor shrugged at Steeg. "Dalyinese," she replied. Then she snapped to attention. "Colonel. Ma'am." She nudged Steeg, who also came to attention.

Holak Ven appeared in the hatchway, Pasa Henz right behind him.

"Sy!" Shirley said as he came up behind her. "Look! In the doorway! It's him! It's the cutie-pie from the tape!"

"The 'cutie-pie?' " Pasa whispered to Holak. She had assimilated English on the voyage, but *cutie-pie* wasn't in the vocabulary databanks.

"She thinks I'm handsome," Holak whispered back.

"So now I have to worry about you in space?" Pasa nudged him, and they both descended through the hatchway.

"You're Holak Ven!" Shirley exclaimed. "We got your tape! My goodness, you're so big in person!" Shirley peeked around Holak at Pasa Henz. "I know you, too! Victoria St. Louis is—well, you obviously wouldn't know Victoria St. Louis, but she's playing—anyway, you're that Pasa Henz Eberean girl! It's so wonderful to meet you! I'm Shirley Albertson. This is my husband, Sy."

Shirley pumped their hands enthusiastically. "We were the ones who found Kathy—Ket—when she landed! She's wonderful! Don't worry, we've taken good care of her!"

"You were—she's all right?"

"She's fine! She's here, somewhere."

Holak Ven enveloped Shirley and Sy in his arms. "Thank you! Thank you for—"

"Sir!" shouted Steeg. "Movement! It's . . ." He waggled his head as if to clear it. "Sir, have I gone crazy? It's . . . it's you! And, what the . . . Nev Hederes? And . . . Celin Kwa?"

Sy pressed Steeg's rifle downward. "It's all right. It's like . . . theatre. It's not really who you think it is."

"What is going on here?" Pasa demanded.

"It's a long, long story," Shirley said. "That's my son Bobby, and his friends Frank and Tom."

"Movement to your right, Sir!" Gor warned. "Wait! A Terran. Armed with a pulse but not in firing mode."

"A Terran?" Holak asked, squinting into the darkness. "Is that—"

Her long, loose blonde hair was visible first, fluttering in the slight breeze. But the walk was still the same, the ramrod-straight carriage that had always intensified her beauty by making her bearing regal. Even in her Terran form, Holak knew her right away.

"Ket! Ket!"

They ran to each other in the darkness.

Bobby drew Pasa Henz aside. Pasa knew that she shouldn't have felt a stab of jealousy when Holak had run to Ket, but there it was. Looking at this pseudo-Holak didn't exactly lift her spirits right now.

"You're Pasa Henz," Bobby said. "My name is Bobby. Those are my parents."

"Bobby," she replied, polite but distracted.

"I'm, uh . . . I'm sort of, well, no, I am, with Ket."

She perked up. "You're *with* Ket?" She looked at Bobby with a critical eye. Tall for a Terran. And somehow, not *entirely* unattractive. She suddenly realized that she was acting like a complete imbecile and chuckled aloud. She put an arm across Bobby's shoulders. "You're the man who finally won Ket Mhulhar?" She amended that quickly. Maybe it was just a brief affair; God knows Ket was once famous for them. "I mean, you're . . . what's the English word? *Dating* her?"

Bobby laughed. "No, it's pretty serious. We did the Five-Point Kiss and everything."

Pasa's flower bloomed again. "Oh, that is wonderful news!" She took his arm. "So tell me all about it . . ."

Ket and Holak returned misty-eyed and holding hands.

Ket went over to Pasa Henz and wordlessly gave her the Embrace of Thanks. Then she looked into Pasa's eyes.

"You've brought honor to every one of us, Pasa, as I always knew you would."

Pasa's mouth trembled as she fought to hold back a sob. This might not have looked like Ket Mhulhar, no longer possessing the large, imposing, Thradonian presence, but it was all still there. The one woman in the world whose respect she genuinely craved.

Ket hugged her again, this time, a Terran gesture of affection. "He deserves you, Pasa. And I know you'll make him happy."

A sob finally did escape from Pasa. "Thank you, General."

"Ket. Call me Ket, Pasa. As my closest friends do."

"Thank you, Ket," she smiled through tears. "You can call me . . . Ambassador." The two looked at each other and dissolved into teary laughter.

Tom nudged Frank. "This is probably the wrong time to bring it up," he whispered, "but shouldn't I remind everybody that we have an early call tomorrow?"

"I think you should let them all enjoy the moment," Frank replied. "I mean, face it, Tommy. How often are we ever gonna see something like this actually happen?"

"Yeah, well, don't look now." He nodded his head toward the Eberean ship, from which Celin Kwa was making a somewhat shaky exit.

"Uh, Mr. Ven?" Tom said. "Over there?"

"Holak! Pasa!" Celin Kwa called as he drew closer. "Oh, Thank *God* you're here!"

"Oh, I'll bet you're just thrilled, Celin," Holak replied.

"Now, Holak, be reasonable. I only—" He stopped abruptly

and looked behind him. "What the—" he stammered as he saw his virtual twin aping his every gesture.

"What the—Holak, be reasonable," Tom said, sounding exactly like Celin Kwa.

Ket, tried not to laugh and then gave in to it. "You've already got the part, Tommy."

"Part?" Celin Kwa demanded. "What part?"

Ket squeezed his cheek. "You, sweetie."

"Too bad you won't be around to see it happen," Holak said. "Because you're back on that ship and under guard to face the tribunal back in Dalyi."

"Oh, come on!" Celin demanded. "What have I done that was so terrible? I didn't murder any civilians. I governed an occupied city, that's all."

"He's right, Holak," Pasa said. "Although I hate to admit it. He always said Eberes was going to lose, and he purposely avoided doing anything—"

"That's right!" Celin said.

"Oh, yeah? What about torturing me?"

"All right," Celin admitted. "You do have me there. But who do you think made your escape possible?"

"Pasa," Holak replied promptly.

"Really. And why do you suppose she wasn't followed? Why do you suppose I didn't comb the city for her after she destroyed her locator? Do you honestly think we couldn't have captured you both in Taray?"

"Maybe," Holak said.

"Holak, it's finished. What else do you want?" He turned to look back at Tom. "Stop that!"

Frank nodded to Holak and said, "Why don't you just play a little catch-up? See if that makes you feel better."

Celin began backing up. "Now, just a moment, Holak . . ."

Holak Ven's powerful hand snaked outward and caught Celin Kwa just left of the center of his jaw. The Eberean literally flew backward for almost fifty yards, coming to rest with a thunk against the other spacecraft.

"Still have that right hook," Ket said affectionately.

Holak nodded. "You were right," Holak said to Frank. "And it does make me feel better."

Epilogue

Jiggs Larsen, the lead electrician for the film _Bobby's Girl_, sat in a corner at the film's wrap party, wolfing down a fat hero sandwich while slurping a tall beer. He had to admit, this film, and he'd done a lot of them, was the most fun he'd ever had in seventeen years in the biz.

First of all, the last movie he'd done that had a megahit— we're talkin' _Titanic/Jurassic Park_—buzz this early on was five years ago, and that had been a pure pain in the ass from start to finish, with a too-young, pencil-necked creep of a director who ran his set like freakin' Stalin. Bobby Albertson, although he had moving-up-to-the-A-list pressure, had kept a loose, fun set.

Second of all, _everybody_ on this nutty set was in love! Bobby and his producer, that majorly hot blonde, Kathy Miller. At first he thought she was an ice queen, but then he realized that she just knew exactly what the hell she was doing, and he respected that.

Tom Courtland and Victoria St. Louis, somehow, no one saw _that_ one coming, just left work together one evening and that was that. It seemed to be okay for the both of them. Tom was less of a mirror-lover than before, and Miss St. Louis, off that stupid diet and away from that muscle-brain Chuck Hansen and looking much better with some extra pounds, had started acting more like a human being toward everybody.

Even the extras who were so chummy with Bobby and Kathy, those two tall ones who were *always* in costume—he'd never seen them in street clothes or even without makeup, not once— even *they* acted like a couple of high school sophomores.

Jiggs had seen plenty of soundstage romances before, but not like this. Usually it was summer camp, and after it wrapped, everybody went their own way and the love stuff became a memory. Not this time, he thought.

Yeah, he'd miss this picture, all right, he thought, slugging down the rest of his beer. He hoped he could get more work with Bobby, who he knew would be hotter than freakin' Nogales in July after this show opened. But Bobby had already said to the press that he was gonna take a long trip after it opened, research or something like that—didn't say where, just that he'd be gone a year or two, maybe more.

Oh, well, Jiggs thought, cracking another beer. After this movie, he'd be hot, too. That was Hollywood; even the techies got touched with the success brush when a movie hit. Just like they got hit with the failure brush when it flopped. Oh, he thought, there's that other really tall dress extra who's always in costume, too. He didn't have a girl, though. Wonder what his deal is?

"I love this," Celin Kwa said to Ket.

"It *is* catching," Ket said. "That's why they call it the show biz bug."

Celin took a long drink of the last of his own Koba and sighed beatifically. "Do you really think I can be a star?" he asked.

Bobby came up behind Ket and slid his arms around her. "Well, we'll get you started, Celin. We'll set up theatres, get you guys going on filmcraft and manufacturing the equipment. I'll direct your first picture. But hey, the public still has to like you."

"Of course they'll like me," Kwa said. "Why wouldn't they?"

"I would hope," Pasa Henz said, "that maybe Dalyi doesn't

have to own the franchise on making movies. Eberes needs a new industry, and that just might be it."

"That's the ambassador talking," Holak Ven said affectionately. "But I think it's a good idea."

Bobby kissed Ket on the neck. "I'm so glad Sy and Shirley are coming with us," Ket said. "And Frank and Tom and even Victoria. It wouldn't be the same without them."

"Are you kidding? Would Dad miss a chance to play golf on another planet? Not on your life. And that's another industry for Eberes, too, Pasa."

"Why, thank you, Bobby. Golf and movies; Eberes as a leader in . . . leisure? Well, it's a thought. But tell me, Bobby, when my second half begins in about ten years, do you think I ought to give show business a try?"

"I'd cast you, Ambassador. You definitely have presence."

Celin Kwa raised his glass. "To second halves," he toasted. "Mine will be the most fun of all. I spent my first half as a villain; now I fully expect to reap the glory of being a hero. Or . . . on the *screen*, anyway."